Cover art by Stephen Cooney

James Ward Kirk
PUBLISHING

Copyright James Ward Kirk Publishing 2014
Internet: jwkfiction.com
Twitter: @jameswardkirk
Facebook: James-Ward-Kirk-Fiction

ISBN-13: 978-0615987941 (James Ward Kirk Publishing)

ISBN-10: 061598794X

Cover Art Copyright Stephen Cooney 2014
Cover design by Mike Jansen 2014
Edited by Krista Clark Grabowski

PROLOGUE

IN ancient Hawaiian mythology, sharks are heroic and revered as the great guardians of the Hawaiian people. In these stories the shark gods have roamed the waters changing back and forth between human and shark. The gods have used their mystical powers to watch over the Hawaiian people, and at times have even rescued shipwrecked people and taken them safely back to shore.

Ancient mythology prominently declares sharks are the guardians of the seas.

Who will protect us when our guardians become the hunters?

A devastating new species has arisen from beneath the Earth's surface, conjuring up fear within the small town of Bodega Bay. A series of attacks pits the town's sheriff, a Hawaiian marine biologist, a world-renown shark expert, and an ex-sheriff with something left to prove against a trio of ancient killing machines.

This summer the ocean turns red.

Michelle- Thank you so much for the support with my writing AND with CARA- you deserve all the happiness in the world AND I wish you the very best. Enjoy the book - it's QUITE the thrill-ride with some great characters and Read it on land and give yourself a few weeks before heading into the water- it's a good thing you don't swim anymore- Sharks are Fast - Keep Reading - BuilD your Gehlert library

All the Best -

CARA Pg. 7

San Andreas Fault Observatory at Depth
Parkfield, California
35°53'59."N, 120°25'.58"W
Tuesday July 1, 2006
1:55 pm (PT)

They were minutes away from defeating one of Earth's most notorious killers.

"Are these calculations correct?" Maverick Brown addressed his group. "This town's the fucking epicenter of the entire San Andreas Fault. We are so close." He shuffled the papers about on the table. "We've spent years researching this."

"Doctor Brown, we are ready."

Maverick Brown had been the country's leading seismologist for the last fifty decades. His lengthy essays were published across the world. His vision was to create a warning system for those affected by the inevitable devastation of earthquakes. But, now on the dime of the SAFOD and using Parkfield, California as the epicenter for his research, Maverick liked his chances. The barren town, now populated by only a handful of ranchers and farmers, offered a clear shot to the nerve center of the San Andreas Fault line. Parkfield offered many tremors, and slight to moderate activity, making research an easy task.

Maverick brushed aside his long grey hair, and glared at the computer screen. "How's the drilling?" He had never tapped the artery of a major active earthquake site.

"We are almost to our pre-determined coordinates," Yvonne, the young Cal-Tech intern said. A slight push of her index finger adjusted her glasses.

"The Japanese and Taiwanese have done this very experiment." Maverick addressed his team. He motioned with his hands. "The cool thing is we are using technology we borrowed from the petroleum industry. We're able to drill deep into Andreas' cavity and watch her wince in pain." He took a breath in and slapped his hands together. "And, unlike them, we are about to gather information from the heart of an active earthquake zone."

"Sir, we've delivered a borehole seven inches wide, and two feet deep," Yvonne added.

"Punch it and drop the instruments," ordered Maverick. His faded green T-Shirt was soaked with sweat. "We're ready to tame this bitch." He watched the computer as it engineered the drills from the research tower just north of the epicenter. Maverick and his team used cutting-edge technology to administer these practices, eliminating the margin of human error. Maverick also believed in keeping his team safe and away from the perils of the actual drilling. Once everything was declared safe and zoned off for proper security measures, the team would gather samples from the drilling and conduct analysis back at the research facilities.

"Sir, something's wrong," Yvonne said. A blood red sphere pulsed on the glowing computer screen.

Maverick raced to the screen. "This can't be. She's slipping." His hand slammed the table, jostling a half-filled coffee cup. As soon as that wave of coffee diminished another ripple tore through the liquid.

Yvonne noticed the ripple in her coffee cup. ""Sir, that wasn't from you."

"The fault, it's slipping." Maverick threw up his hands in frustration. "The extra punch with the drill probably agitated the fault line." His eyes fixated on the ripples.

His team scrambled for answers and cover from the impending earthquake. A thunderous jolt from beneath the surface jerked the tower to the right. The grinding metal screeched throughout the facility. A taut snap of the girder released the tower from its foundation.

Maverick lost his balance and skidded across the floor. *This can't be happening. We were so careful.* Unable to withstand the inevitable, the foundation released itself from the intense tremor, hurtling the tower to the ground.

Beneath the surface, a small crack in the ocean floor erupted, spewing forth rubble and rock. The earthquake tore apart the ocean floor, separating a series of trenches along the California coastline. One trench in particular exploded apart, unleashing a trio of predators into the ocean's depths.

One by one the monstrous creatures rose from the fractured earth, their long bodies twisting and turning from the earth's womb, spiraling about until they were completely free from their prison. Their blackened eyes rolled backward, and then returned again to visually steer their migration north to Bodega Bay. One after another their dorsal fins broke the surface, their strength no match for the visceral jolt of the earthquake.

Maverick smashed the side of his head against the desk. Dazed, he took one last look at the jittery computer screen. He tumbled diagonally across the tiled floor, keeping watch on the red dot as it rippled out farther than expected. The numbers continued climbing on the Richter scale. His anger rose. He felt blood seep from his temple.

The sun filled the inside of the falling tower as the number finally rested on 7.1. Maverick scrambled from the rubble and heard screams from all around. It was complete chaos. His battered body bled through his green shirt. His elbows and knees were torn and scratched open. *This fucker's running up the entire coastline and right for San Francisco.* He crumbled to his knees in another wave of pain and watched the ocean roll from the pulverizing blow. *"I have to chase this."* He was known as The Earthquake Hunter. His peers compared him to tornado and hurricane chasers. It was this extreme danger and never-ending quest to defeat nature's serial killer that had kept him motivated.

One more time he rose to his feet and limped his way to the idle motorboat tied to the dock. The research tower was just miles away from the ocean and Maverick's team always had a twenty-foot motorboat ready to explore the ocean after an earthquake hit. This time Maverick would use it to chase the fault line as it cracked its way up the coastline.

"Hey, Boss, you need some company?" Yvonne asked.

Maverick pivoted and returned his attention to the voice and the demolished town. "Yvonne, are you okay?

She gave him a slight nod. Her light blue blouse was ripped, exposing a small piece of her powder blue bra on her left shoulder. Her tan khaki shorts were soiled and dirtied from the debris, while her ivory white Converse sneakers were splattered with blood and rock. A superficial gash twisted its way down her petite calf muscles, pushing a trickle of blood to the surface.

"Get in." He helped her into the boat as they entered the ocean. A squeal of sirens filtered throughout the area as rescue teams swarmed over the demolished area. Maverick kept his watch on the ripples in the ocean. His temple continued bleeding as he wiped off the blood and flicked it into the ocean. Yvonne's own droplets fell into the water after she boarded the boat.

The sound was a quiet hum, yet it had drawn their attention. The smaller of the pack broke away and headed for the sound. A fresh scent of blood in the water captured its attention, igniting its long dormant hunger for flesh and meat. Its black eyes rolled over before the monster gained speed and closed in on its prey.

Yvonne noticed the dorsal fin break through the water first. "Maverick." she tugged at his scraped up elbow.

"What?" He turned and saw what she was talking about. "Shit, he's gaining on us fast."

"Isn't it unusual for a shark to chase a boat?"

"It's odd there are sharks out here at all in the aftermath of a quake. They usually scatter and wait for the tremors to cease before they emerge again. The electrical fields get jammed after a quake, and the sharks act confused for a while."

"That's probably a myth," she said with a frightened laugh. But she knew Maverick's interest in sharks was serious after she accompanied him one time on a shark hunt in the Pacific.

"Well, there's only one, so don't worry. We'll follow the quake up the coast and record everything first-hand."

"Yeah, I don't believe we're going to have to worry about that. "

"Why?"

"That's why." She tapped him on the shoulder.

Maverick turned to his left to see another fin slice through. "Fuck me." His hands took the wheel and tried to divert the path from the shark, when a third fin emerged off the bow.

"Do we have anything on board we can use to fight them off?" she asked.

"Check under the seat, maybe there's a flare gun." Maverick was contemplating his next move when the trio picked up the pace.

"Which one do I shoot?" she asked. Her fingers nervously loaded the flare gun.

"Are you kidding me?" Maverick had no answer to her question. They were sitting ducks with no way out. "Pick one."

The smaller shark emerged first off the stern. Its pristine, ivory teeth stretched out for the kill.

Yvonne squeezed off a shot at the shark, sending the monster howling back to the ocean's depths. A spiral of smoke dissipated in the misty air. "I have another flare." She fumbled the flare in her clammy hands and failed to reload the weapon.

"It's ironic, you know?" Maverick shook his head and burst out with laughter.

"What is?" She continued scanning the ocean for the others.

"We've come this close to defeating nature's most persistent and decisive killer. The earthquake has obliterated the population for thousands of years." He paused to watch the fins approach the boat with daring speed. "And in the process we are about become the victims of nature's fiercest and smartest killer of them all." Maverick let go of the wheel and let the boat spurt forward. "Those aren't great white fins, Yvonne. They're something else." His eyes tracked the sunshine over the water. "Take a good look at the light because in a few minutes, it will all go black---," his words were interrupted by a fierce wave on the left side of the boat.

Maverick raised his hands in a meager defense as one of the larger sharks vaulted from the ocean and clamped down hard on Maverick with its jaws.

Yvonne, in another adrenaline rush, clicked the flare gun shut and prepared to fire at the shark as she toppled to the stern of the boat. Maverick's blood sprayed across her face as his body snapped in half like a toothpick. She pulled the trigger releasing a flare at the menacing shark, but the beast submerged before impact. The ocean embraced the boat's debris as it sprayed everywhere from the visceral hit, sending Yvonne toppling into the ocean.

A blanket of red splashed against her and Maverick's severed head emerged from the water with part of his fractured spinal cord still intact and his grey hair trailing behind. Yvonne let off a curdling scream as she bounced in the water and waited for her own death.

Her wait would be over fairly quick.

A short pop from below severed her lower torso while she beat on the nose of the smaller shark in a futile attempt to defend herself. A spray of bright red blood erupted from her mouth as her body was dragged below, caught inside the jaws of the shark.

A final gargling of water soon ended her nightmare.

The tremble rocked the beach. A line of sandcastles crumbled in the chaos of scrambling parents. Christina trudged through the hot sand searching for her daughter. "Caitlin! Caitlin!" Her voice echoed through the beach and was lost in the crowd.

A child poured beige sand from her flowery bucket. Her small hands patted it against the sandcastle strengthening the still intact structure. The two year old whistled a simple children's tune to pass the time, her attention never faltering among the scampering people.

Christina tore through a series of demolished castles with her powerful legs as she kicked up sand on her way to the little girl. "Caitlin!" Her arms opened, she skidded to her knees and waited to embrace her daughter.

"Mommy!" Caitlin beamed. "Where's Cara?"

Christina searched for her brother and niece. They were supposed to meet up at the beach during his visit to the west coast. The sunlight burned her eyes and blurred her vision. "Maybe they went for a swim." Her hands brushed away her long hair as she focused on the rolling ocean. The quake ignited a furious uproar of waves that swallowed a bunch of swimmers.

"Cara! Cara!"

A young girl with Downs Syndrome walked over to Christina.

"Hey Bro, you made it," Christina welcomed him. "I bet New York doesn't have this much chaos."

"In the subways for sure," he said with a laugh. "Cara, you sure love the beach!" He took his daughter's hand.

"Are you okay? That was some quake."

Cara's brown eyes wandered off to the water and she released her father's hand. She walked slowly to the edge of the water, balancing on her new orthopedic braces. A series of laughs ensued from the little girl after the waves retreated from the beach. She threw her hands up in the air and down again mimicking the action in the ocean.

"Cara, what are you doing?" Her father knelt down beside her.

She returned the gesture with a quick peck on his cheek and then she brought her hands together in sign language.

Her father read the series of signs. "Open. Close. Swim. Open.

Close. Swim."

"What's she doing?" Christina asked.

"She's telling me something." He stared at her hands.

"What is she trying to say?"

"I don't know." He tried to understand her. "Open. Close. Swim."

A series of screams from the ocean reached the beach.

"She's not saying swim, is she?" Christina was scared.

"Cara's telling me something else. It could mean fish," he said. He moved his hand from side to side mimicking a swimming motion.

Cara continued signing for another minute then turned her to the ocean, eyes wide and curious. Her father and aunt took notice of what Cara found interesting.

"Jesus," Christina said, swallowing her words until it hurt.

A tall, dominant dorsal fin emerged in the ocean before gliding below with a swimmer caught in its jaws.

Farrallon Islands
Marine Research Center
Northern California Coastline
37°41'53.88"N, 123°0'5.76"W
Tuesday July 1, 2006
1:58 pm (PT)

With her social life in complete ruins, the country's premier marine biologist began unraveling stitch by stitch. With no man to rest her weary head upon, a deaf mutt called Warthog would be her salvation.

Her holiday weekend was already shot to hell. A supervisor with a warped sense of humanity, (and a vacation in the Caribbean), had left her stranded babysitting elephant seals for three agonizing days. In less than seventy-two hours, the Fourth of July would kick off the whirlwind weekend on the shores and beaches of Northern California. Her deepest fears concerned the waning elephant seal population that had called the Farrallon Islands home for decades. Their once promising numbers spiraled further down after each devastating attack at the jaws of the growing great white population. The sharks had established the islands as their home as well, even straying along the northern coastline of California, reaching Bodega Bay, a small town just north of the islands. They satisfied their seemingly insatiable appetites by devouring the elephant seals or performing random human attacks within the bay.

Ashleigh Wilkinson, a spirited woman of Hawaiian descent, was arguably caught within a mini mid-life crisis upon reaching her mid-twenties. She worked full-time at the Marine Research Facility, a division of the United States Fish and Wildlife Service, and occasionally part-time for world-renowned video journalist and shark aficionado Darrin Nesmith-Coyle. Coyle welcomed her talents as an expert marine biologist. Her dark blond hair, straight and fine, had become a tangled, frayed, knotted rat's nest, indicative of her lengthy hours at the facility. Her smooth skin kept its dark tan, but rings had started forming beneath her weary eyes. She attempted a weak smile through her cracked crimson lipstick, but deprived of a natural sleep cycle over the past month, she had started to slide into a self-serving depression, where every detail picked away at her thinning patience.

The seals started groaning about, instigated by movement from beneath the watery surface. Ashleigh started making her rounds across the rocky island, monitoring the ocean's surface for any sign of dorsal fins lurking about. Her feet ached from the jagged rocks jutting into her thin beach sneakers; blood collected in their soles. The blinding sun provided constant warmth to the meandering seals. Ashleigh offered their afternoon snack---fish. And plenty of it.

She carried the chum-stained white bucket she had borrowed from a local fisherman across the island. Her white capris pants shifted about between her legs as she snaked her way across the twisting terrain. Her dark blue short-sleeved shirt sported the name of the facility in white cracked letters across the front, and had a picture of the islands encased in a circle directly in the middle.

She called out to the gathering seals: "Lunchtime, boys and girls!" Some had already jumped into the cool waters, while others lay sprawled out across the rocks, resting in the lazy summer sun.

A faint rumble, distant at first, caught the seals' wandering attention. Their creaking barks alerted Ashleigh to immediate danger. Her eyes quickly darted out across the shimmering ocean, waiting for the dorsal fin to emerge. *They have to be here somewhere.* No immediate sign of any shark.

She meekly blew out a whistle of relief, but the barking did not cease. Another treacherous rumble from beneath the island startled the seals, and became intense enough to stop Ashleigh in her tracks. The patient ocean turned choppy and rolled in a series of violent waves.

Ashleigh knew what was causing the disturbance. Her position within the seal colony prevented her from making it back to the facility in time. She kept moving. Another violent shake jolted her about, causing the bucket of fish to dislodge from her right hand and spill out across the rocks. The cracked bucket rolled about, eventually finding refuge between several rocks.

The tremor threw her to the ground with disturbing force. The ocean was alive and sent one powerful wave after another crashing into the island. Her lips quivered with the fateful word: Earthquake.

W orking his oily, cheesy fingers through the half-eaten platter of bacon and cheese covered waffle fries, former Sonoma County Sheriff and pro surfer Rick Chatham swirled the last remnants of honey whiskey around in the Golden Gate Bridge shot glass. His lips parched, he took one last mental trip around memory block. He ran his tongue over his cracked lips, moistening them for the final shot of Jack Daniels whiskey. Rick's slouch indicated his current mid-life crisis was more serious than he had originally thought. Only a few years removed from being the heroic Sheriff of Sonoma County, his once proud legacy was receding like his hairline. A tough, respectful cop, Rick had begun questioning his own ethical code, and the elasticity of his moral fiber. A rapid acceleration toward forty-five rendered him susceptible to certain health issues like encroaching love handles, consistent aches and pains, and the frequent reminder of his ineligibility in the dating game. He would forever embrace the loneliness bachelorhood offered. At least he operated on his own clock and on his own terms and had nobody to answer to. He snapped a few stray fries and gorged them down his throat with a devilish smile.

Rick had always possessed a sixth sense. His bones always knew when something bad was about to happen. He had the feeling the last time he surfed. He felt the rumblings before they happened, probably a result of living in the Bay Area for so many years.

Now, as he consumed his Jack Daniels and fries, tremors shook the small pub. Glasses careened off their high perch over the bartender's dodging head, shattering everywhere. Rick firmly grabbed the bar's golden rail for balance. The tables rattled, scattering patrons, plates and silverware off the wooden anchor tables and onto the brown-planked floor. Several patrons headed for the door, others crouched underneath the bar as instructed.

Rick just sat there with a patient look sprawled across his face. A product of the culture, he had become used to the quakes with uncanny comfort. They would come and go, just letting off some steam. He had a different feeling about this one. Like a boxer's punch to the pit of his stomach, Rick felt something wasn't right about this earthquake. His mouth swelled with the whiskey for one final swallow before the quake finished off the coastline.

Ashleigh's temple purged itself of fresh crimson blood, minimizing her ability to traverse across the island. She cautiously attempted a crawl across the craggy surface trying to gain a better sense of what was happening. As she peered out across the fierce ocean, her wandering eyes picked up a disturbance a few feet from the seal's restless colony. A series of dorsal fins sliced through the active water. Her fall had blurred her vision and kept her from clearly distinguishing the fins. A throbbing headache left her dizzy and whirling about attempting to regain her balance. One more time she tried to locate the dorsal fins, but was unsuccessful.

A few yards off to Ashleigh's blind-side, three shadows glided underneath the chaotic surface of the Pacific Ocean at a breakneck pace, methodically raising their elongated dorsal fins through the choppy waters. Schools of frightened fish scattered upon sensing the oncoming pack of predators, while the elephant seals had carefully ducked in and out of their tumultuous path. Thin columns of seaweed swayed back and forth underneath the monsters' furious wake.

The trio then disappeared into the surrounding blackness.

"**I** don't think this is safe, Cody." Hammer Hawk warned his friend. Eyeballing the horizon, Hawk witnessed the thunderous wave approaching. Hawk was a few years younger than Cody, and mostly followed Cody's reckless lead. Hawk had a terrible knot in the bowels of his stomach, a feeling that certainly didn't subside with the earthquake's powerful attacks. He wanted to appear fearless in the face of Cody's daring jaunt into the sea. He continuously pulled at the dangling reeds of black hair that kept sweeping across the front of his pocked and freckled face. Cody always talked about surfing the quake, but Hawk didn't think Cody would actually attempt such a ridiculous stunt.

Cody Kincade, the most prolific surfer on the western seaboard didn't care. He was about to catch the wave of a lifetime. The Hammer was just being a crybaby.

"Relax," Cody said. He brushed blond hair from his eyes. "I've waited all my life to catch this fucker." He stared down his surfing buddy and best friend since grade school. "You need to grow a set of balls," Cody said, with a quick slap on Hawk's sunburned shoulder. "You see that wave on the horizon? We're riding that bitch until she breaks and bleeds."

"What makes that one so damn special?"

"When I was a kid, my dad caught this very same wave. Do you remember the nineteen eighty-eight earthquakes that rocked Oakland?"

"Yeah, I was headed to the World Series with my old man." Hawk remembered the fateful day.

"My dad always told me of this super wave that rises from the ocean after a quake," Cody said. He wrapped his fingers around his black and red longboard. His specialized surfboard had intimidating skulls and skeletal drips of blood scattered throughout. The dark, harrowing urban tale according to Cody's followers was that it was *his* blood on the board after he wiped out one year in the Tornado Tournament. He mesmerized his younger fan base with the stories of how he painted his own board in his blood to remind him of his failure and to power his return to glory. Ever since that wipe out, he'd never lost another competition. His last match was the most perilous of them all, when he took out his main competitor, snaking his way toward the wave that would lead him to victory. The fiery twenty-six-year-old had always lived on the edge of sanity. Cody's esteemed pedigree was rich in surfing, dating back to his great-grandfather, Alexander Kincade. Cody's body perfectly suited the intense sport's rigorous demands. He was slim, yet harnessed surprising strength and agility. Cody's unique sense for the waves also proved powerful when it came to competition.

Today he tempted the fates once again.

"Got your longboard ready, Hawk?" Cody turned around and finished undressing down to his white and blue swimming trunks. He then stepped into a tight black skull wetsuit, watching as Hawk began the same process.

"Yeah, but," Hawk said, wanting more time. His jittery fingers jammed the wetsuit's zipper on his blond chest hair. He nervously muttered abrasive words under his breath. He had hoped to delay Cody long enough to miss the quake's rolling wave that started to form a few miles from the rocky inlet of Bodega Bay.

"Good, then suit up." Cody grabbed his longboard and gunned it for the water's cool edge. His fingers fastened the cord tightly around his left ankle before he performed the initial duck dive, diving head first into the water, quickly vanishing underneath the surface.

"Shit." Hawk finished off his transformation and gripped his own longboard, a smooth yellow and orange portrait of a comet blasting through the sky. Hawk's own signature move was called Comet, where he would enter into the tunnel of a wave with a slowly and methodically before shooting out of the edge like a Comet entering the Earth's atmosphere, moments before the wave's mighty jaws wrapped around his body. Hawk's dancing toes captured the filtering sand as he performed his own jittery duck dive into the surging wave.

"Hey, Hawk!" Cody resurfaced a few feet away from his nervous counterpart. "Did you get those brass balls yet?" He cupped both of his hands around his mouth and shouted. Cody sat idling in the turbulent water, waiting for Hawk to join him in paddling for the monster wave approaching the twosome.

Hawk caught the tail end of Cody's sly remark, his face easily breaking through the water's rough surface. "Balls! They're the size of fucking dimes!" He reached down and felt his shrinking testicles. "And they're probably a pair of wrinkled prunes!" He called back to Cody. He dabbled his legs over the sides of his board, waiting for Cody to give the signal.

"Here we go!" Cody lay down on the board and began paddling toward the surging wave. Hawk followed suit, lazy and weary of Cody's harebrained idea.

Cody roared toward the monstrous wave, taking a deep breath in. Hawk, mere feet behind his friend, felt a rush of adrenaline pumping through his veins.

Its finely tuned senses had picked up on the intermittent splashing, urging the predator to gain speed on its prey.

Hawk broke the surface first, ready to engage the rolling wave.

The monster roared open, clamping down upon its slowing prey, its jagged teeth scissoring through the wood and plastic, sending shards everywhere.

Hawk felt the sharp pull, instantly thinking it was the wave's aggressive undertow. His body was sucked underneath, caught in the monster's steel trap. The jaws cut through his skin with jigsaw precision.

Cody was late breaking through the choppy surface, his head turned left, then right, trying to locate Hawk. His eyes had caught something lurking underneath the surface. His first thought was that of a great white shark. Their presence was common amongst the surfers.

He screamed for his friend. "Hawk!" Hawk's body lurched through the water. "Hawk!" Cody shouted for him. It was too late.

"Cody! Sh–!" Hawk was pulled back underneath before he could finish his warning.

Cody knew what had his friend in its deadly grasp. Seconds slowly ticked by before he witnessed a large geyser of his friend's blood spurting through the water, sending fragments of the Hammer everywhere. The ocean turned red from the brutal attack. Cody saw Hawk's severed board floating aimlessly in the dancing waves.

"Shit," Cody said. He saw the mammoth dorsal fin break the surface, swimming right for him. Cody's innate feel for the ocean had gained him the advantage over the surging shark.

He watched his wave approach him with a thunderous roar. He knew if he could surf that wave, he'd gain enough power to get free of the shark.

Cody looked back one final time at the approaching dorsal fin. "See ya later bitch," he said, returning his stare to the monstrous wave.

The dark shadow crashed through the fierce wave with unmatched velocity.

Its mouth stretched open, teeth ready for the kill.

The monster slammed into Cody, knocking him from his board, shattering several of his ribs, and taking the surfer for a deadly ride underneath the water. His torso was caught inside the killer's mouth. For a brief moment, he watched as those sinister black eyes stared him down, waiting to finish him off. This was no great white, at least not a modern day species. Cody had seen the resident great whites up close and personal before, but this menace was different. *This shark had to be twenty feet longer than the residential great whites.*

Cody slammed his fists against the shark's ash grey face, using his nails to dig away at the predator's blackened eyes. His act of heroism had bought him a second or two to try to wriggle free from the shark's vise-like grip.

He managed to break free and had started his ascent for the surface when the shark regrouped and attacked its prey once more, dragging Cody farther into the ocean's depths. Cody's teary eyes blinked away the dimming sunlight moments before his left leg became twisted in a right angle inside the shark's mouth. His leg snapped right below the knee, sending a heavy mist of red swarming around his flailing body.

Cody's wave crashed over the bay with a fury, blanketing his screams. A littered patch of the berry-colored fluid swerved about, leaving its twisting trail floating in the salty water.

Fisherman's Wharf teemed with greedy tourists, wallets open, fingers ready to part with their hard earned cash. The highly popular destination rapidly escalated into one of the hottest spots on the West Coast. The wharf had become the definitive destination for a chance to ferry a ride to the historic prison, Alcatraz.

Captain Winston Arkham piloted the small ferry across the bay every day, three hundred and sixty four days a year. (He took Christmas Day off). The boat's capacity was about two dozen people. The elderly captain was pushing eighty-six years old but barely showed his age. Arkham was a solid man, built to last through decades of erosion. A fearsome pilot during the Second World War, he had engineered many heroic missions. Arkham's claim to notoriety came from his consistent pounding of the overbearing Japanese on Iwo Jima. As the war faded from memory, Arkham found his way to San Francisco, earning keep as a street entertainer, offering black and white sketches of passing tourists for ten bucks each. Shortly thereafter a now deceased friend had offered Arkham the desirable position of Captain on the ferry, giving the vivid storyteller a chance to relive the Iwo Jima mission each day. Winston Arkham took the job for two hundred bucks a week back in 1973 and had not missed a day of work since.

As the rigid columns of people crammed aboard the hearty boat Winston made his usual rounds, introducing himself to the crowd.

"Is it safe?" a woman asked, referring to the tremors that had rocked the Bay Area minutes prior.

"Yeah, sure is." Arkham definitively answered the woman's question. "Just a tremor, that's all."

A snickering teenager cracked wise from the rear of the crowd. "Aren't you kind of old to be piloting a ferry? I bet he can't hear, old people are deaf and dumb." The teenager looked to his friend for support, and shared a disturbing laugh with him.

Winston, at least thirty feet away from the wisecracking teens, abruptly stopped and turned on a dime. He clenched his fists so tightly his fingers turned purple, and marched to the rear of the ferry. Winston's transformation over the last ten years allowed for minimal stupidity on the part of anyone, let alone a bunch of raucous teenagers. He ran a tight ship, just like he did when he flew his planes during the war.

"Excuse me?" Winston coolly sliced through the crowd toward the mid-ship of the ferry.

"I don't think you have the facilities to function, never mind pilot a ferry."

"How old are you, punk?" Winston growled. His hands were still tight fisted, and ready to unload if necessary.

"Seventeen. And you? One-hundred?" He snorted.

"I was already enlisted in the military and engaged by the time I turned seventeen."

"Good for you. I want to see the prison sometime this century."

Winston shot back, keeping pace with the teenager. "Eager to see family?"

"Anyone can pilot this scrapheap," he replied.

"I'll make a deal with you." Winston's hands retreated back to open palms, allowing blood to flow once more to his long wrinkled fingers.

"Go ahead."

The crowd began bristling from the delay. The earthquake had subsided, leaving the tourists antsy to depart for the prison. They sat on the benches running along each side of the ferry.

"If you beat me at a match of arm wrestling, then I walk off the ship and you can pilot this scrapheap to see your family. If I beat you, then you apologize to everyone here for your lewdness and then you get off MY ship."

"You really expect me to arm wrestle with you? I'm afraid I'll break your arms." The teen looked over Winston's slim frame.

"Pussy."

"Where?"

"Right here." Winston headed over to the only table aboard the boat, sat down, and placed his elbow upon the rickety table.

The teenager complied and did the same. "It'll be over before you're done blinking."

Winston's tanned, wrinkled hand wrapped around the pale white teenager's hand.

"Go!" Winston barked the order.

The teenager attempted to rush to victory, but found himself at a standstill with the wiry Captain.

"Come on, you're not even trying," Winston growled.

"I'm toying with you, old man." The teenager's pupils dilated with adrenaline.

Winston pinned his elbow tightly to the table, then flexed his fingers to gain the upper hand on the unsuspecting teenager. Winston's strength eventually overpowered the cocky youngster, sending the teenager's hand crashing to the table. "I won. Now apologize and get off my ship."

The stunned teenager grabbed his throbbing hand and rose from the table. "I'm sorry." His voice echoed through the cheering crowd. "The prison's stupid anyway." He muscled his way to the ferry's exit, followed by his friend.

A child, nary a day shy of his eighth birthday said to Winston, "That was incredible."

"It was nothing." Winston turned around. "Say, are your parents here?"

"Yeah, right there." The boy pointed to his father.

"Bring your dad over here please," Winston said.

"Am I in trouble?" The child's eyes welled with uncertainty.

"No, I have a surprise for you."

The boy returned moments later with his dad.

"Sir, I'd like your permission to have the boy help pilot my ferry today." Winston extended the invitation. "I'd like him to be my First Mate."

"Wow, yeah sure," the father responded with eagerness. "Jack, are you up for that?"

"Yeah." Jack followed Winston toward the bridge. "Dad, did you see him beat that kid arm wrestling. The Captain is so cool."

Winston overheard the boy telling his father about how he had beaten the teenager at arm wrestling moments earlier.

Winston grabbed the microphone and greeted the restless crowd.

"Ladies, gentlemen, boys, and girls, welcome aboard. I'm sorry for the delay. I had to rectify a certain situation. But I have a special guest here today to help me pilot the ferry." Winston slowly bent down and held the microphone in front of the boy's face. "What's your name son?"

The boy spoke into the small microphone. "Jack."

"Jack will be my First Mate for today's voyage." Winston always picked a kid to help him with the piloting duties. He had held this special ceremony since he had taken the job.

The crowd erupted with appreciation.

Winston continued with the introduction. "We are going to ferry over to Alcatraz, or The Rock as it's known by millions of tourists. The Rock sits alone within the bay, waiting for a new wave of people to roam its hollow hallways and corridors. This infamous prison has housed many sinister prisoners including Mr. Al Capone himself. It even spawned several movies. My favorite one starred Sean Connery and Nicholas Cage," Winston churned story after story to the crowd.

"Are there sharks in the water?" Jack asked Winston. "My daddy says there are."

"Well, he's right," Winston confirmed Jack's question. Winston noticed a sleek, thinly veiled blanket of fog approaching the ferry. Holding up his hand he cautioned the passengers. "San Francisco's well known for her foggy landscape. I don't even think I've seen the Golden Gate Bridge on a clear day yet. So, once the fog passes, we will be able to spot the prison."

They swam a few feet underneath the water's surface. Their fins kept underwater in an attempt to spring their own surprise attack. The trio expertly drifted through the water, ready to display their own version of teamwork. The aggressive leader would start the attack, then the other two would follow suit and swallow up their prey.

Winston squinted through the dreary fog, catching a smooth black shadow darting underneath the bay's surface. "Hey gang!" He whistled over the crowd's mindless chattering. "If you look over to your right, or starboard side, you'll be able to catch a glimpse of one of our resident great whites," Winston called out, then looked over at Jack. "Would you like to see a shark?"

Jack looked about for his father who mingled inside the interior of the crowd. "Sure," Jack replied, his words were minced with a slight lisp. Jack's front tooth was missing, causing the youngster to slur some of his words.

Winston flicked the ferry into autopilot and brought Jack over to the starboard side of the ferry. "Hang onto the railing tight son. The ferry's a bit topsy-turvy in the waves."

Jack obliged, clamped his fingers around the metal railing and peered over into the foggy water. "I don't see it."

"Wait for it." Winston took his eyes of the boy for a split second to gain another look for the shark. "Here it comes," Winston responded. *It's coming way too fast.* Winston felt something was wrong with the shark. The residential great whites had never attempted this before. He slowly, yet methodically, grabbed Jack's elbow. Winston spun his head around and caught another shark barreling down on the port side, the left side of the ferry. The mid-ship, or center portion of the ferry's floor was clear Plexiglas and was a tailor-made design for Winston's ferry. The remaining half was wood. "This isn't good," he murmured. He attempted to clear his throat and warn the passengers, but the sight of the third shark gliding underneath the Plexiglas floor diverted the Captain's attention.

With the impact of a torpedo, each of the sharks slammed into their respective sides of the ferry, jolting the boat from side to side like a spin top, jostling the passengers from their cushioned benches. Passengers cried, screamed, and screeched for Winston to do something. Anything. A small handful of passengers were hurtled overboard into the eerie bay below.

"Daddy!" Jack screamed for his father. Jack watched his father's shirt being thrown overboard. "My daddy!" Jack pulled free from Winston's protective grip.

Winston was losing control as the ferry rocked back and forth. He made a gallant run for the boy's father, hoping it wasn't too late. *They won't attack them. They will just go away. Quietly.* Winston tried to quell any fears he had of sharks.

Jack skidded across the watery floor and slammed into the steel railing. The ferry was beginning to swamp with water. "Daddy!" He yelled overboard into the rolling fog. Jack saw his father lurch through the water, splashing a wave against the side of the rocking ferry.

The first shark zoned in on the splashing and screaming. With a giant yawn of its mouth, the leader of the pack chomped down on its unsuspecting prey and clasped it tightly between its four-inch teeth. A swath of fresh blood spilled into the bay.

A small, petite woman flailed about in the water in a lackluster charge for the ferry. Her arms and legs splashed about wildly, kicking up a wall of water behind her. The second shark, slightly smaller than its leader, catapulted its dorsal fin through the water. The shark bore down upon the woman then zoomed underneath the surface, feet away from her. She felt something cut into her abdomen, a sharp piercing. She lost feeling below her waist. Her head went into a dizzy spin of fear. Her dismembered body limply bobbed like a cork, until the shark came back for seconds and finished off its kill.

Another man splashed about, inciting the monster's fury. Carelessly swimming back to the ferry, the swimmer's feet dangled about behind him, wildly kicking about. He felt the sharp instruments graze past his toes and took in a deep breath of relief. The third shark had missed him by several inches.

The swimmer, a male in his early forties, and seemingly allergic to swimming, dunked his head into the water and caught the shark's disturbing glare rushing toward him. Before he could raise his head, the shark cleanly devoured his face, severing it from his body. A gush of warm blood escaped into the bay, urging the other two sharks to detour to finish off the dead swimmer.

Winston stared through the fog and witnessed the shark's methodical killing spree. He called out for the boy as he noticed the dwindling number of passengers. The smattering of passengers left onboard vigorously fought for their lives.

Jack's father swam for the rear of the boat, but was soon pulled under by the smaller, quicker third shark. A series of bubbles rose to the surface and faded into the rollicking waves.

The other two sharks took a brief respite from their kills and slammed onto the ferry once more with all their weight. Their snouts crashed through the wooden sides, sparking several leaks. Winston watched water flow onto his ferry and slowly envelope the floor.

Winston turned on a dime and lurched for Jack. He watched as the remainder of the people scattered into the water from the shark's violent rocking. *It was like ringing the dinner bell for Christ's Sake.*

"Jack!" His father's voice screamed for his son. He slammed into the rear of the boat. He felt the propeller churning against his skin, ripping away the fabric of his wet shirt and knew at any moment the shark would come for him once more. He desperately gripped the rim of the sinking ferry, his nails clawing into the wooden floor.

"Daddy!" Jack tugged at Winston's grip. "Let me go!"

"It's not safe, son." Winston refused to let go of the squirming boy.

Jack's father called out to his son. "I love you! It's too late for me. Winston, there's three—" his words were cut short by the powerful lurch from below. The shark had Jack's father between its mighty jaws, ready to clamp down for the final kill. He was pulled under, leaving his nails still embedded in the wooden floor above. Jack's father caught sight of the shark's face in the blade of the propeller, moments before the beast rammed him into the churning blades, spraying blood all over the shark's skin. The monster rolled its eyes backward to protect them from the prey's debris, leaving the shark vulnerable for a brief moment. The beast felt the propeller's mammoth pull suck him in. The shark, momentarily stunned and unable to escape, became twisted within the screwing propeller. It sliced the right side of the predator's face. After several jarring maneuvers, the monster retreated from the propeller scarred and bloodied from the whirling blades.

Winston felt the ferry come to an abrupt stop. The rear of the boat sank deeper into the bloody water. He could still hear the waning screams in the bay as his men, women and children met their watery graves.

"The propeller's dead. The damn shark must've hit it and jammed the blades." Winston's feet slipped on the watery surface, unable to make back into the cockpit to radio for assistance. "Jack, what are you doing?" Winston was unable to deter the boy from breaking free. Jack's small size enabled him to scurry up the descending ferry, making it to the Captain's cockpit. "Jack, we are sitting ducks out here." Winston turned to the boy. "Come help me," Jack sanctioned Winston's assistance.

Winston's right foot managed to find solid footing, enabling the wily veteran to eventually make his way up to Jack. The ferry's entire rear was submerged, leaving the top half of the boat still above water. Not much time for Winston and Jack to radio for help.

Winston closed the door behind him. The bridge was small, but had enough room for at least three decently sized people. The rectangular box had windows on every side, a sprawling control panel, and the captain's wheel directly in the center of the room.

"Jack, turn on that switch. Hurry." Winston gripped the black CB radio. "Flip it, flip it now!"

Jack did as he was told and the radio whispered to life.

"Dirk, do you copy," Winston said into the CB microphone. "This is Winston and we are several miles off the shoreline of Alcatraz. It's foggy out here, and my ferry's sinking." Sweat poured down his face, soaking and blurring his eyes.

A male voice responded—it was Dirk. "Winston, what happened out there in the Bay?"

"Multiple shark attacks."

"Any survivors?"

The descending bridge had now reached sea level. Winston and Jack were trapped.

"Only me and the boy." Winston gave the boy the flare gun. "Ever fire one before?"

Jack shook his head. "No."

"Here." Winston pulled open the gun and slid the flare in. He clicked it back and handed it over to Jack. "Now fire it up into the sky as far as you can."

"Two?" Dirk questioned Winston's answer. "Two out of twenty-four?"

"Yeah. We don't have much time. We're trapped in the cockpit and sinking fast."

Jack aimed the gun toward the front windows and pulled the trigger. The flare burst through the glass and whizzed into the foggy sky.

"Winston? Winston?" Dirk's voice continued over the radio.

Winston let the CB fall from his wrinkled fingers. He reached high for the harpoon stick hanging from the wall and wrapped his left hand around it. With his right, he grabbed Jack close to his chest.

His eyes followed the ascending dorsal fin breaking through the water. He could see the murky shadows of the shark approaching the submerged bridge. Water began pouring in from the shattered window above, swamping the room.

Their eyes met each other's for one final time. Winston's squinted hard, his mouth turned into a fierce mechanization of courage and grit. His hand steadied the harpoon gun. The monster's eyes were pitch black and soulless.

"I'm sorry kid, but you are about to see a shark up close and personal." Winston braced for the attack, his finger rested on the trigger as the shark's snout crashed through the window of the bridge, its mouth agape, ready to devour.

He wasn't one for the celebrity spotlight, but nagging thoughts had wormed their way into Darrin's better judgment. He could still hear his agent's voice echoing inside his head, chattering with persistent measure. *You have to promote your work, your new book, your brand new National Geographic special. Push, push, push. Sell, sell, sell.*

He only agreed to do the interview as a personal favor to his agent.

At thirty-five and battling through a bitter divorce, Darrin Nesmith-Coyle had reached the top of his profession, albeit at the cost of his personal life. All the blood, sweat and proverbial tears researching great whites had finally culminated in Darrin's prized trophy: a series of powerful documentaries about the great white and their hunting patterns across the globe.

Matt Lauer worked his journalistic magic, introducing the hot new commodity to the American public.

"Just relax, this is going to be a simple interview, no frills, except the entire show's live," Matt encouraged Darrin to remain focused and calm. "I recently signed on to do some extra several primetime specials. Tonight's show will be my first and I am personally psyched for this one. No pressure though," Matt responded with his charismatic smile.

"Yeah, no pressure," Darrin agreed, rubbing his clammy palms together with enough friction to start a forest fire.

"Today, we have world-renowned shark researcher Darrin Nesmith-Coyle. On tonight's primetime special, we are going to explore the world of Mr. Coyle and his obsession with nature's natural predator, the great white shark," Matt drummed up the necessary drama.

The camera turned, zooming in on Darrin's sweaty face.

"Hi," Darrin fumbled for the right word.

"Camera shy?" Matt asked.

"I'm used to the open waters, I guess." Darrin recovered in time and nervously rubbed his face. He had a clean-cut look, freshly shaven, and dressed casually in a dark-blue Hawaiian shirt with blue and yellow flowers and Old Navy carpenter jeans. He never shied away when it came to his wardrobe. A comfortable wardrobe had always suited him, and he wasn't about to get all dressed up for an interview. Deep down, Darrin was a geeky older version of his childhood brilliant but socially inept.

"Going for the casual look I see," Matt referenced Darrin's look.

"I dress like this all the time," Darrin affirmed. He lazily ran his fingers through his dark brown shoulder length hair, ruffling the half-ass comb job he did back at the hotel. "I prefer the casual look to the suit and tie combination." Darrin gazed over Matt's impeccable wardrobe. "Uh, no offense."

"Yeah, that's cool. I'd rather not wear the suit either, but don't tell my producers." Matt pretended to keep the secret between the two of them then reclined in the chair, crossed his left leg across his right knee and prepped the guest for his next question.

Darrin bounced in the chair, restless to get back into the field and start filming his follow-up to the Red Triangle.

"Let's talk about your new special, airing tonight on the National Geographic Channel," Matt professionally set up Darrin's lead. So, you're a shark guy?"

"Ever since I was a kid, yeah, I love sharks." Darrin's tall frame, a healthy six-foot-two, was ill equipped for the small leather chair the studio had provided him for the interview. "I even have a necklace that holds one of the very first mementos from my encounter with a great white shark off the coast of Australia." He held up the cream colored, faded three-inch serrated shark tooth, proudly displaying it for the camera.

"How did that happen?" Matt capitalized on the human side of the story he knew the American public had a soft spot for.

"I was about nine or ten. I went on this crazy ass shark expedition with my uncle Derek, who was a professional photographer for National Geographic's magazine." Darrin thoroughly enjoyed the limelight when it came to telling stories about sharks.

"What happened?"

"Our charter boat encountered a fifteen-foot great white." Darrin spun the tooth around, showing the other side. It had faint streaks of red stretching diagonally across the surface. "And, well, the guys had the ingenious idea of leaning over the boat with the camera, which had just taken a dip in the chum bucket."

"Chum bucket?"

"Yeah, the bucket that holds all the good stuff to feed the shark. Our intern had sweaty hands, and dropped the camera into the water after we dropped in the chum." Darrin shrugged it off.

"That doesn't help when shark fishing." Matt blew a whistle of drama through his dried lips and reached for his bottled water.

"So," Darrin coolly set up the drama for Matt, "the camera's dripping blood and grinded up guts into the water, and these whites out there, man, they shoot up like a rocket if given the chance." Darrin smacked his hands together around the tooth like thunder.

Matt definitely was enjoying the course the interview was taking. It was white-hot, unpredictable, and sure to become a smash-hit during the holiday sweeps period.

"The white crashed through the water, snapping the camera inside his jaws, and slammed back into the water. It busted off a tooth right into the cameraman's skin by his knuckle. The cameraman took a quick piss in his wetsuit, and then scraped out the tooth with his fingernails and gave it to me."

"I saw the blood on the backside of the tooth," Matt referred to the red streaks. "That is blood, isn't it?"

"Yeah, but whether it was Steve the cameraman's or the white's, I couldn't tell you. But it makes for one hell of a story," Darrin finished off the story with a pleasant grin.

"That it does," Matt paused for a moment and turned to the large LCD teleprompter to read the next segment from the screen. "When we return from this short break, we will continue with Darrin Nesmith-Coyle and his love for great whites, and how he's rapidly changing the landscape of documentary television." The music faded into the commercial break.

"Man, *that* was a great story," Matt applauded Darrin. "Great timing."

"What are we talking about after the commercial break?" Darrin fidgeted in the chair.

"Hold on a minute," Matt interrupted Darrin's question. "I'm getting late-breaking news from our sister station in San Francisco."

"San Francisco? What's going on there?" Darrin asked, trying to take a peek at one of the monitors ahead of him.

Darrin eventually found the story breaking on the television screen. "Ashleigh," he muttered.

"Darrin, we are going to have to delay the rest of the interview," Matt apologized.

"Why?"

"The San Francisco area was just rocked by a series of devastating earthquakes," Matt brought Darrin up to speed. "Sources indicate they registered just shy of a 7.5."

"I understand." Darrin wrestled into his pocket to retrieve his newly purchased Apple I-phone. His fingers traced their way over the smooth surface, bringing up the instant newsfeed on NBC's sister station in San Francisco. His eyes scanned over the thermal map, noticing the hot spot was the San Andreas Fault line. "This is not good."

Matt came back from break and addressed the American public with a serious tone as he introduced the late-breaking news.

"San Francisco is under siege," Matt began the tag line to his primetime story. "The mayor has issued a state of emergency, ordering the evacuation of several homes and buildings in the Bay Area."

"This will definitely affect the patterns of the great whites," Darrin interjected without even thinking about overstepping Matt's dialogue.

"Sharks?" Matt whipped his head around. "Thousands of people are being misplaced, and your main concern is the great white shark population?" Matt was unable to make the connection.

"Because it will impact people's lives," Darrin said, determined to get his message across.

"How so?"

"There will be a spike in the great white population, elephant seals will continue to decline, and the waters will flood with activity."

"How does that affect people's lives?"

"I'm sure people will be trying to transport across the Bay Area with personal boats, jet skis, and other forms of transportation. And that could make for a feeding frenzy."

"I'm trying to clarify the details." Matt urged Darrin to make his point quick at best.

"In addition to the widespread panic, minimal shifts in the earth's electrical fields will no doubt short circuit the shark population." Darrin rose from his seat.

"Where are you going?"

"I'm catching a flight to San Francisco."

"It's too late, the earthquake has already hit," Matt said, rising from his own chair.

Abruptly turning around, Darrin stared down Matt with narrow eyes. "It's only beginning," Darrin snapped back. His face wrapped up like a condensed rubber band ball. Pulsating veins surfaced from underneath his tanned skin. "This earthquake may have faded into the history books, but I warn you, it was like ringing the dinner bell for these whites, and if anyone can help, it's Ashleigh Wilkinson."

Rick gazed up at the rocking television set, catching the tail end of the Today Show's primetime special on 'the premier shark guy' Darrin Nesmith-Coyle. The static swallowed up the rest of the picture, freezing the DirecTV satellite signal on Darrin's face as he held up the bloodied shark tooth. Rick's attention snapped. He wiped off the residual whiskey across his faded grey gym sweats. His attempts at the gym were declining, leaving the retired sheriff to wonder if he should retire his tank top collection. He always enjoyed the channel's groundbreaking programs and was a sucker for anything with National Geographic stamped across it. However, in this particular case, his personal distaste for the shark population had drawn him to the fuzzed out Today special. One of the bottles teetered above the bartender's mirror, eventually crashing down upon the bar, splashing him with Captain Morgan rum. His light blue tee-shirt, now had his least favorite alcohol streaked across the chipped Pink Floyd graphic in the center of the shirt. "Is everyone okay?" Rick bristled, turning around as he continued to rub off the wet alcohol from his shirt.

"Yeah." The bartender's word was jittery. His teeth clapped together in a fearful rhythm.

"You scared, kid?" Rick turned back to the bartender.

"I'll be fine." He rose and brushed off the specks of glass from the obliterated Captain Morgan.

"Where're you from?" Rick noticed the bartender's fish out of water stare stretched across the kid's face.

"Boston, Massachusetts."

"It shows."

"What does?"

"The fact is you have never experienced a real earthquake before, or quite possibly a natural disaster." Rick scooted off his chair and attempted to lend a hand to the other disjointed patrons.

"It's that obvious?"

"Yeah," Rick answered. "Come on, get up, everything's okay." He calmly instructed the shaken patrons. They showered the former sheriff with a well-deserved thank you and even a God Bless.

"It's a summer gig while I visit my aunt and uncle." The bartender took notice of Rick's fluid motions. "My name's

Ethan."

"I really don't care." Rick brushed the kid's story off out of habit not callousness. "I'm sure you have your reasons, Ethan."

"Is anyone hurt?" he asked Rick.

Rick offered up some free advice. "No, but call the medics anyway."

"Okay, I'll do that." The spirited teen jumped on the task. He noticed Rick returning to the bar. "Is everything okay?"

"I need a drink," Rick looked over the disheveled collection of ransacked alcohol. "I'm nursing a mid-life crisis."

Ethan said, "Vodka, rum, or perhaps some more Jack Daniels whiskey?" Ethan ran his lanky fingers over each bottle, attempting to straighten out the titled liquor demons.

"Ah, kid, you know my weakness." Rick tapped the bar. He did a quick turn of his head, catching the tail end of the customers groggily exiting the pub on their own accord. "JD please, I'll take the JD whiskey," he motioned for Ethan to give him the full bottle. "And, don't forget to make that call for the paramedics. We still have some shaken citizens of Bodega Bay strewn about the pub."

"Here you go." Ethan handed over the bottle. "Would you kindly do me a favor and don't drive, okay?"

"It's the beach, who the fuck drives on the beach?" Rick tilted his head and shrugged his shoulders, mocking confusion.

"A good point, I guess." Ethan walked over to the end of the bar and picked up the telephone that had fallen during the earthquake. He placed the phone firmly on the counter, working the numbers with a furious impatient pounding of his fingers. He put his hand over the receiver, watching as Rick left the pub. "Where are you going?"

"A walk on the beach," Rick said. He waved goodbye, with the bottle of whiskey and started his trek toward the Bodega Bay coastline.

A mist thinly veiled as a rainstorm swept over the boroughs of New York City, instantly negating the local forecast of clear skies and lows in the upper sixties. The small, pocket-sized digital thermometer attached to the cabbie's dashboard flashed the information.

Darrin's irritating cab ride had left him just enough time to catch the six forty-five out of Gate C 35. Sprinting, he reached the customer service desk with his palm already open, a worn American Express Blue credit card wedged between his left index and middle finger. "I need to book a seat on the six forty-five to San Francisco." He took a needed breath in, his legs burned from the lengthy run down the airport. His face turned an embarrassing shade of cranberry red, he had the definitive look of desperation. His darkened Hawaiian shirt managed to squeeze off a button in the process, leaving a portion of his chest exposed to the curious woman standing behind the counter.

She appeared sweet and was, Darrin noticed, on the short side, probably five-foot two or a five-foot three, with long blond hair dangling above her shoulders. Darrin took a passing glance at her chest, noticing the small breasts attempting to peek through a very tight silver blouse she wore with a black skirt that wrapped around her knees. His eyes were left staring at the dangling gold New York Yankees necklace hanging from her smooth neckline. Darrin's impromptu guess was that she was at best twenty-one. Her purple tinted contacts looked over the disheveled documentary star. Then, underneath her fresh manicure, was Darrin's newest book about the Red Triangle.

"Oh, my." Her words were quiet and squeaky. "You're the shark guy."

Fuck me. I just want to get on the damn plane. "Yeah, that's my book." He attempted to brush aside the small talk in exchange for a ticket.

"Can you sign it for me?" Her ocean-blue eyes welled with excitement.

Darrin's eyes followed the board behind the girl. He had precisely fifteen minutes to find a way to San Francisco. "Do you have a ticket for me?" He again asked her the question. *All tits, no brains.*

"I can see what I can do." She let off a friendly smile and tapped the computer screen with her bright pink nails. Darrin caught the girl's name on the silver-plated name badge on the right side of her blouse.

"I'd appreciate it, Casey." Darrin urged her to speed things up.

"So are you headed to the Bay Area for another awesome special?" Casey tried to keep the awkward conversation going.

"I'm heading out to see an old friend." Darrin's introversion surfaced. He wasn't one for socializing, and did a fine job of sidestepping that landmine when he could. His interviews in the past were curt, short and vague. His best work came through both visually and verbally within his documentaries. Darrin had no problem flexing his geek hood when it came to talking about sharks and the oceans, but couldn't find the right words to string together a sentence when it came to strangers, especially the ladies. He had lucked out with his ex-wife, for she was just as shy as he was.

"No bags or carry-on?"

"I travel light." Darrin felt around in his shirt pocket for his identification.

"Driver's license ought to do it." Casey smiled and continued flirting with Darrin.

Unaware of her advances, Darrin retrieved his license and slid it across the white marbled counter. Darrin watched as she scooped it up with her French manicured fingers with fake diamond studs in the tips. He continued looking around, gazing at the rapidly changing landscape of arrivals and departures. His eyes zoomed in on the six forty-five to San Francisco. The flight digitally displayed it was nearing full occupancy.

"Am I in?" Darrin quizzed Casey after noticing the flight had filled up.

Casey said, "If you want to be, sweetie." She handed back his driver's license. "You are the last seat on the flight."

"Thank you."

"You know, I definitely like the shorter hair in the picture," Casey said with a longing stare. "But," she took in a deep whistle between her teeth, "I love the longer hair, and it suits your roguish nature."

"Roguish?" Darrin repeated, again giving no signs of interest in the bubbly ticket agent.

"I've watched some of your work, and well, you definitely *are* the Indiana Jones of the ocean." Casey attempted to pique Darrin's interest with the compliment.

"Do I have a window seat?" Darrin leapfrogged over her aimless rambling.

"I believe it's an aisle seat." She referred back to the lime green computer screen.

"I prefer the window."

"Is that so you can look out over the ocean for sharks?"

There's no ocean in the center of the United States. Is she totally fucking brain dead? Darrin leaned over the counter, taking in a whiff of her Chanel No.5.

"Can I have my ticket please?"

"Yeah, hang on a sec." She attempted to print up the ticket. "I have a window seat, but you are close to the exit door. Seat 17, Row F. Are you over eighteen? Because if you're not you can't sit by the exit door."

Does she ever shut up? My God, she's gonna wear her tongue out. "Thank you." Darrin finally ended the conversation, which had lasted nearly five minutes, but felt like an eternity. Darrin noticed the odd flight number of the airline: Delta 1313.

He hurried down the corridor, tapping his ticket against the palm of his right hand where a five-inch scar lay embedded in his skin, a nasty parting gift from a ten-foot blue fin shark. His thoughts drifted as he passed numerous newspaper and coffee stands. Darrin picked up his pace; afraid he was going to miss his departing flight. His thoughts were drifting into the Red Triangle and her dangerous allure for the great white shark population. It was only a matter of months since his last visit to the triangle where he tagged several whites for educational and preservation purposes.

Using his Apple I-Phone, Darrin dialed up his team while he bustled through the crowded airport. He traced his finger across the smooth screen and brought up the first member of the team, Gavin Bannister. He hit the send key and within a few short moments, a groggy Gavin answered the call.

"Gavin, we need to get the team together. I am flying into California as we speak," Darrin began the conversation, unaware it was Gavin's voice mail and not Gavin himself on the other end of the call. Darrin quickly went over all the details, including his expected arrival at San Francisco International Airport.

His next phone call yielded the same results, another voice mail courtesy of Daniel Locke. Locke was Darrin's second team member, usually the cameraman and technical geek.

Gavin was more of Darrin's understudy, leaving Ashleigh as the fourth and final member of the foursome. The gifted marine biologist helped keep the boys on an even keel. Together they would have to find out exactly what was happening along the

California coastline.

Darrin thought back to what Casey had mentioned concerning his shark hunting persona. *Indiana Jones of the ocean? I can totally see that. Instead of running from boulders and Nazi soldiers, I'm thwarting the evil attempts of the great white. Harrison Ford, eat your heart out.*

Rick shuffled his feet across the sandy beach, oblivious to its emptiness. His left index finger was planted into the top of the half-empty whiskey bottle as he swung it back and forth in a slow, methodical pattern.

Gazing out across the wild ocean, he saw several powerful waves forming, ready to exercise their might against the shoreline. Easing the bottle up to his lips, he cautiously sauntered over to the approaching water. Rick stood quietly, squinting through his blue Ray-Ban sunglasses, watching the mighty waves. His head began spun crazily on its axis, leaving the former sheriff stuck in a hazy state of awareness. The intense aftereffects sent the remnants crashing over Rick's black Crocs, showering them with strings of greenish seaweed, before the wave retreated back into the bay. He walked further into the ocean, submerging his lower torso underwater. The coolness felt great against his sweaty skin.

Sober, Rick would never dream of re-entering the water. His memory still sizzled with what had happened the last time he had entered the ocean's deadly realm. Another wave picked up steam behind the previous one but Rick, distracted, kicked away the seaweed that had started to make its way between his toes.

Out about one hundred and fifty feet, a dorsal fin broke through the surface, sliding fluidly through the agitated water.

Rick, unable to detect anything at all, regained his shaky composure and valiantly downed another shot of hard whiskey. He then let the near emptied bottle sway by his side while he peered through his darkened glasses, briefly catching the oddly shaped triangle slicing the water's surface. His cloudy determination was that he was about thirty feet from shore, minus a foot or two for margin of error. Rick's processing was slowed considerably as the alcohol jammed his rather acute senses. Twirling around, he stumbled through the sucking waves, unable to gain any traction. His slow trek toward the shore had left his ankles scraped up from the jagged rocks, broken branches and other assorted debris scattered about the ocean floor.

The shark's senses picked up on the microscopic droplets of fresh blood in the water and aborted its current course, redirecting its growing hunger toward the new scent. The monster's methodical hunt began, its forty-foot frame powered ahead with the kinetic energy of a freight train.

Rick bounced in the water, trying to shake the seaweed from his feet. The motion sent thin streams of blood into the water.

The shark closed in on its prey. The predator was aware of the shallow waters and had to act fast to avoid drowning. Opening its mouth, several rows of imperfect, saw-like teeth jawed, anxious for the kill.

Wincing, Rick twisted his body around and shuffled his wrecked body to a drier location.

The shark snapped down on the passing elephant seal, crunching down upon its prey, and then swallowed it whole. The killer satisfied with its kill, rolled over in a furious wake, driving a series of abrupt bubbles to the surface.

Rick sat down with his wrinkled knees curled up to his chest. A cool, sudden swath of ocean splashed against his legs and buttocks, giving him a brief smile. The salty water rinsed out his scraped up ankles. Inspecting the fresh wounds, he noticed some shards of skin peeled back, but no major damage.

"Shit, this is just peachy fucking keen," he managed to spurt out as he lowered his head from the sun's glare.

A few yards away the rolling wave had brought something else in from the ocean and laid it out across the beach.

Rick, tired of massaging his wounds, looked around for something else to occupy his wandering mind. Using his hands, he urged himself to stand back up. He caught an eerily shaped carcass a few short yards away. *What the hell is that*? His mind churned with endless possibilities. Walking with ginger steps, he approached the object with caution. He was lifting the whiskey bottle to his lips when he spotted the half-eaten carcass on the beach.

Rick's face went pale as a ghost. His anxious fingers dropped the bottle to the sand.

"It can't be." He fumbled for words. His body trembled with fear, lungs filling with air; he prepared to hold back the ascending vomit. The burning puke roared through his lips, spewing a mist of alcohol and cheese covered french fry lunch across the beach.

Rick fought to gather himself and returned to inspecting the half-eaten carcass inches from where he stood. As a seasoned sheriff, Rick started to investigate the scene, noticing the corpse was none other than resident Pro Surfer Cody Kincade.

"What the fuck happened here?" Rick questioned the bizarre incident. "Cody," he said, while shaking his head in an effort to alleviate the pressurized migraine beginning to overwhelm him.

Cody's upper torso was still intact, barely. Streaks of blood stretched from his ears down to his chin. His skin was torn and fragmented, the kind of incisions made by a saw, or another type of serrated teeth. "Is that a rib sticking out of his side?" Rick knelt down for a better angle at Cody's mangled body. His throat again swelled with surging vomit. Cody's rib cage seemed to have encountered some sort of brute force, leaving the tip of a rib exposed through his skin. The surrounding area was a deep shade of purple, a possible sign of heavy bruising from some sort of impact.

Rick scanned Cody's lower torso, staring at the surfer's mutilated left leg. The limb was severed directly below the kneecap, bone and all, leaving only dangling strings of skin behind. Cody's right leg was severed as well, immediately below the pelvic bone. Staring down at Cody's cloudy eyes, Rick's stomach churned once more, sending another wave of vomit barreling up his throat.

Farrallon Islands
Marine Research Facility
3:01 p.m.

Ashleigh limped back to the facility, pushing the door open with a hard press of her left hand. The old wooden door creaked open, revealing the cramped quarters inside. There, whimpering underneath her chair, her deaf mutt laid, legs crossed over his head. His eyes followed his loving master as she grazed the top of his head with her wet fingers.

"Hey, boy," she called out to him. "How's my Warthog?"

The mutt rose gingerly, a daily fight with arthritic joints had limited Warthog's mobility.

"Time for dinner already?" Ashleigh looked at the clock on the cracked wall. "It's only three o'clock."

The islands were home to only one building, a run-down shack that had been transformed into a year-round monitoring facility. Ashleigh courageously occupied the shack for part of the summer, switching off in shifts with another marine biologist after July fifteenth.

She used her wily nature to construct her mobile home, amplified with the best gear on the market, and courtesy of the United States Fish and Wildlife Reserve. Usually when Darrin arrived for his routine monitoring of his great whites, he pulled out a cot and kept Ashleigh company for the duration of his stay.

She had grown close to Darrin and the boys over the last year, especially during the Red Triangle shoot. Her experience in the field, as well as her knowledge of the area, had helped Darrin produce, direct, and star in one of the most successful great white shark documentaries on National Geographic in the last twenty-five years.

Warthog quietly lapped away at the water in his charcoal water dish, oblivious to everything else.

Ashleigh's black LG Chocolate phone vibrated across the wooden table, skipping about the scarred surface. She was too busy washing up in the small bathroom to notice. The bathroom barely fit two people, with a small porcelain sink that had given way to thin cracks and rust over the recent decades, and a cramped shower with minimal water pressure. She patted her face with the aqua blue washcloth before stepping into the even smaller shower. The showerhead barely affixed itself to the wall, dangling from its rusty confines inches from Ashleigh's wet hair. She began scrubbing away the dirt and blood from her fall. The water pressure weakened with every thrust, giving her just enough water to rinse off the thin veil of soap.

"This sucks," she muttered, sticking her hand out of the grimy shower door, reaching for the white towel.

Ashleigh began drying her hair with the towel, as she looked for another one to wrap her body in. Her stomach growled with hunger as she moved into the kitchen in search of an afternoon snack. Her luck drying up, she continued drying her hair with a thorough ruffling of her hair as she casually approached the table in the center of the room, searching out the granny smith apples. She quickly noticed her phone had moved several inches from where she had left it before leaving for the elephant seals.

The blue digital reading displayed three missed calls, all from the same phone number. Before she could react and dial the missed calls, the phone vibrated again, displaying the caller ID: 1-518-555-5403.

It was Darrin.

Still buzzing from her fall, she wondered what Darrin wanted. It had been a few months since he had wrapped up filming on the Red Triangle. *Was this simply a courtesy call? A how are ya doin' Ashleigh?*

Pressing the slim phone against her right ear, she waited for the introduction.

"Ashleigh?"

"Yeah, what's up? My God, it's been a few months."

"Not much. I can't stay on for long."

"Why? What's up?" Ashleigh paced about the small room barefoot, still wrapped in her wet towel.

"I'm pre-boarding on a plane headed for 'Frisco." His voice crackled over the deteriorating reception.

"You're coming here?"

"Yes."

"Reasons?" Her head raced with possible reasons. Ashleigh had fancied Darrin as an older brother during their recent assignments together.

"I'm curious about the 'quakes out there earlier today," Darrin replied.

"Earlier today, oh, you must be in New York? Boston?" Ashleigh was a scatterbrain when it came to area codes and locations.

"Yeah, I'm at JFK. I'm catching the last flight out to San Francisco."

"Want me to pick you up?"

"Yeah, that would be so cool."

He's such a dork. "What's got its fingers wrapped around your mind?" She knew Darrin's mind was embroiled with something of importance.

"I fear the whites will spark an abnormal pattern of violence." Darrin's response was right to the point.

"Are you concerned the earthquake will shift their patterns?"

"Something along those lines. I want to make sure our boys and girls are leaving the locals alone."

"I was just feeding the elephant seals when the earthquake hit."

"Are you okay?"

"My ankles and knees are scraped up, but I'll manage."

"That's good news. I only have a few more minutes before the pilot requests that the cells are turned off."

"What else did you want to know?" She led him directly to the question. "Kermit? Miss Piggy? Gonzo?"

"Yeah, how are they doing? Are they staying out of trouble?"

"Somewhat. They are definitely leaving the seals alone for now." Ashleigh was referring to Darrin's tagged great whites. Kermit was the lead great white at sixteen feet and four hundred and fifty-five pounds. The current Alpha male, Kermit had started mating with Miss Piggy, the area's only female great white. Miss Piggy weighed in at four hundred pounds and eighteen feet long. Gonzo was the beguiled of the trio, a rogue great white who'd rather play and attack the local seal population. He was shorter than his friends at thirteen feet but was just shy of four hundred pounds. His shorter frame allowed him the luxury of swimming up and down the California coastline quickly and with ease. The trio was tagged over a year ago when Darrin first came to the area to film the mysterious aura the Red Triangle possessed. Darrin asked Ashleigh to keep tabs on the frequency of the returning whites, and found out his three visited the area the most, causing some unrest amongst the local surfing population.

"I'm glad. They should be making a return trip for the summer any day now."

"I saw their dorsal fins the other day." She confirmed his guess.

"Well then, it's imperative I return back to the coast and check in on them."

"I'll freshen up and swing by the airport." Ashleigh attempted to find dry clothes in the small bedroom. She finally found a change of decent clothes: a maroon San Francisco sweatshirt with the Golden Gate Bridge in the background, faded blue denim jeans, and her own favorite pink Crocs.

"Ash, I'll probably be at the airport a bit after three in the morning."

"I'll worry about it when I get there. I'll double check the arrival times." She finished pulling the faded Levi jeans up over her slender hips, and stuffed her size six feet into the Crocs, all while still balancing her cell phone in the crook of her neck.

"Until then, Ash."

"See ya." She finished off the pleasant conversation and wedged the phone into her front pocket then finished up in the bathroom. She grabbed the first aid kit from underneath the cabinet and sat on the edge of the toilet. She took a few minutes to inspect the fresh wounds, added a few dabs of Neosporin, and a Band-Aid to her scraped up ankles.

"Jesus." Rick said, attempting to keep the surreal in some kind of contained logic. His hands frantically brushed off the wet sand and blood his jeans had collected when he kneeled next to Cody's dead body.

He had to get hold of Sheriff Davenport and report the grisly incident. Along the way, Rick passed by Skippy and Bunny's beachfront house. "I can try there." He started to formulate a plan for reporting Cody's dead body. A burst of clarity erased part of his previous Jack Daniels buzz. "Hey!" Rick shouted out to the sauntering elderly couple.

Skippy shuffled about his rickety front porch, nursing his recent knee operations. His aged fingers clenched the cane, still unable to master the skill of a walking aid. Skippy's stubbornness had proved to be a constant obstacle in his daily routine. Bunny's attitude wasn't much better. Her shrewd stubbornness mad her unwilling to ask for assistance, always willing to do everything on her own accord, right or wrong.

Skippy and Bunny Manning were lifelong residents and avid seal watchers since their retirement era had brought them to the Bay Area several years ago. Both of them were pushing seventy, their bodies already breaking down from the harsh years of working and daily life. Bunny's condition crippled her muscles leaving her with the inability to walk on a consistent basis, always searching for a cane, walker, or a wheelchair. During the last year however, Bunny's body simply gave up the struggle, confining her permanently to a wheelchair. She continued her habit of reading a book every day, a lasting effect from her librarian days in the school district.

Her loyal husband, Skip, carried his wife on his shoulders for the duration of their marriage. But as time slithered through the hourglass, so did his physicality. The first sign of erosion was when he took a nasty spill down the stairs, breaking his hip. A lengthy recovery period ensued, as did a significant demand on his knees. Skip's knees eventually buckled from the wear and tear, and he was forced to have both knees replaced. The couple was now looking for someone to live in their house and aid each of them in their daily routines. Bunny and Skip had a deep relationship with the former sheriff and had always welcomed him to their home, personal or business related.

"Rick!" Bunny called out to the frantic ex-sheriff as he approached their front porch.

Skippy continued grumbling about, trying to rebuild the strength in his knees. He eventually turned around and greeted his old friend. "Hey Rick," he said, taking notice of Rick's profuse sweating. "Are you taking up exercising again?"

"I found a dead body on the beach, and need to use your phone to call Sheriff Davenport." Rick huffed out the sentence, his body doubled over in cramps from the lengthy run down the shoreline.

"Oh my," Bunny said from behind her husband. "Anything you need, Rick."

"I haven't seen you run that fast since they closed down the last Pacific Pastry last year," Skippy snipped back.

"Very funny." Rick hopped up the stairs and gave Skippy a good slap on the shoulder. "It's always good to see your sense of humor's still intact."

"I've got some great jokes for you then." Skippy attempted to present Rick with his comedic insight.

"Is it more wife jokes?" Rick asked. "Hi ya Bunny," he greeted Skip's wife and gave her a quick peck on her cheek.

"Hey there," she returned the greeting. She turned her wheelchair around and followed Rick into the dimly lit yellow kitchen. "Want some green herbal tea or some coffee?"

"Hell yeah." Rick replied with an enthusiastic pep in his voice. "I have to shake this headache before Reed stops by and starts asking me all those questions about the dead body." He looked around for the telephone.

"Telephone's over there, on the wall," Skippy said.

Rick quickly dialed the sheriff's office, placing the phone in the crook of his neck.

"How do you like your coffee?" Bunny asked, as she prepared the coffee for the threesome.

"Black and bitter," Rick said as he was waited for Davenport to pick up.

"This is the Sonoma County Sheriff's Department. My name's Deputy Jonas Marsh. How may I be of assistance?"

Rick searched for the right words. "Jonas, get me Reed." Rick decided being curt and efficient would yield quicker results.

"What for, Rick?"

"Don't mettle with me. I need Sheriff Davenport."

"He's very busy at the moment."

"Doing what?" Rick bristled.

"Police business."

"Police business?" Rick crudely mimicked Jonas. "Could you be any vaguer?" Rick's distaste for Jonas had become part of the public conscience ever since Jonas and Rick became embroiled in a bitter feud encompassing the awkward politics of Rick's duties as Sheriff of Sonoma County.

"Yeah, that's what I said."

"Are you being a dick on purpose?"

"Listen, your job as sheriff is now a part of our past. We now have an efficient leader, one who will not tolerate the annoying rumblings of a drunk who has nothing better to do than call the Sheriff's Department."

"Well then, hotshot, I guess you are not interested in Cody Kincade's half-eaten corpse that washed upon your shores." Rick went to hang up the phone.

"Wait, hold on, Rick."

"Oh, we're changing our tone now, aren't we, junior?" Rick took a deep inhale of Bunny's fresh coffee brewing. "Cody's dead, and I'm personally requesting Davenport. And Slim Bennings, the coroner too," Rick urged.

"Reed's helping the San Francisco Police Department and Coast Guard search for survivors in the Bay."

"What happened?"

"A distress call was dialed in right before Winston's ferry sank in the Bay."

"What happened to the other people on board? Winston's ferry is the only ride in town over to The Rock." Rick looked around the kitchen, watching the wooden mallard clock over the sink turn another quarter inch closer to three fifteen. "Did he say what caused the accident?"

"The old man talked about sharks," Jonas responded, casting a net of doubt on Winston's wild story.

"Sharks?" Rick mused. "I know the great whites like to roam the bay, but to cause a ferry accident? I think Winston could've been sipping too much from the ol' spirits."

"Nevertheless, Reed's tied up right now. I can offer you my assistance," Jonas said. "Where are you?"

"I'm at the Manning's."

"I should've figured. Are you still friends with that old coot?"

"Yeah. We're building my boat, and it's almost finished." Rick began to grow tired of the conversation with Marsh. "I have some hot coffee waiting for me, and a blitzing headache, so I'll have to accept your offer. I certainly can't process the scene without some sort of police presence. And, well, a deputy is pretty close to being a sheriff." Rick managed to add some salt into their old wound.

"Do you always have to get the last word?" Jonas was well aware of Rick's decade old game.

"Absolutely," Rick defiantly stated and promptly hung up, preventing Jonas from getting another word in.

"So Cody's dead?" Bunny scooted over in her wheelchair and handed Rick his mug of coffee.

"Yeah, but from what, I honestly can't say," Rick said. He sipped some coffee.

"I overheard you say something about a shark?" Skip inserted himself into the dialogue. He was well known for blatantly inserting his advice into any conversation.

"Yeah, Deputy Dog's attributing the ferry accident to Winston's grumbling about a shark attack."

"That's insane," Skip said. "Sharks don't sink boats." He paused to dangle the tea bag in the mug's hot water. "Especially not a fifty-foot ferry."

"I agree, but something out there put one hell of a dent into Cody's body." Rick finished off his beverage.

"Only time will tell," Skip responded. "I doubt our resident great whites are responsible for Winston's accident. They are usually hermits and only attack the occasional elephant seal or surfer from time to time. I don't think they would demolish a ferry." Skip took a breath and sipped his tea. "This isn't the movies, you know."

"I should head back down to the beach and meet Jonas," Rick said. He gave his thanks for Skip and Bunny's charming hospitality.

Jonas Marsh, a semi-veteran of the Sonoma Police Department, hurried down the newly cracked steps, (a residual effect of the earthquake), and clasped the door handle to his 2008 army green Jeep Wrangler Sahara Unlimited. Jonas's tenure was longer than Sheriff Davenport's, earning Jonas the exclusive right of longevity and respect of Sonoma County's residents (Or, at least that was *his* perception).

Jonas was Sheriff Rick Chatham's deputy during the last two turbulent years of Rick's administration. Jonas held a grudge because Rick had promised him the position of sheriff once he decided to vacate the post after his near-fatal accident, but the voters turned and elected former San Francisco Sheriff Reed Davenport to the County Sheriff post. Jonas, at the age of thirty-three, became mired in his own life crisis, destined to step out of the sheriff's shadow, and onto his own stage.

Bodega Bay was a shallow, rocky inlet, straddling the county lines of Sonoma and Marin Counties. Jonas had to memorize where and when his jurisdiction ran out. Rick's location was inside Marsh's realm of power, and a good thing it was, because Deputy Jonas Marsh loathed the idea of sharing.

"Rick, you crafty ol' bastard," Jonas grumbled, grinding his jaw as he approached Chatham who wearily jogged along the shoreline. "Hey, you need a ride?" Jonas called out as the Jeep closed distance between the two men.

Hunched over in pain, Rick had no other option. "Yeah," Rick answered as he grabbed hold of the silver handle and stepped on the charcoal runner. "The body's another twenty or thirty feet south," Rick said pointing in the generalized direction.

"You look like shit," Jonas said. "Retirement's a bitch, ain't it?"

"It's definitely more than I bargained for," Rick held on tight as Jonas picked up speed, kicking up sand in the process.

"Still working on your boat?"

"Yeah, me and Skippy are slowly gluing it together."

Jonas applied the brakes on the Jeep. "I see something straight ahead," Jonas said, grabbing the Walkie-Talkie that was velcroed to the dashboard. Jonas was wearing brown khaki shorts, sneakers, and a blue Polo shirt, with his Deputy badge pinned on the right side of his muscular chest. He definitely was a gym type of guy, hitting the beach gyms twice a day.

"Oh, shit." Jonas stopped in his tracks. He saw first-hand what Rick was chatting about earlier: Cody's half-eaten body, completely visible and disfigured. "What the fuck did this?" Jonas reached for his radio.

"I don't know," Rick said. "Perhaps a shark."

"Our resident sharks aren't that violent. This boy suffered an ass kicking." Jonas dialed Sheriff Davenport's frequency.

"I don't know where to begin." Rick's tired body was ready to collapse.

"Did you touch the body?" Jonas quizzed him.

"Like fondle it?"

"No wiseass, did you disturb the scene?"

"The scene is disturbing enough without groping the dead." Rick continued toying with his former Deputy.

"Stop fucking with me Rick," Jonas warned.

"For Christ's sake, Jonas. We're not dealing with the fucking Boston Strangler here," Rick angrily shot back. "We're dealing with either a shark, or a whale."

Hard static crackled over Jonas's radio. The voice was rough, edgy, and hard to distinguish, but Rick knew the person on the other end of the radio.

"Reed, we have another situation here at the beach," Jonas chirped into the radio.

"Situation?" Davenport's voice could be heard on the radio.

"Situation, that's what I said. We have a dead body."

"Dead body? Who?"

"Cody Kincade," Rick interceded.

"Stay out of my business Rick," Jonas again warned him.

"Is that Rick?" Davenport's voice demanded of Jonas.

"Yeah, it's him," a dejected Jonas replied.

"Jonas, put Rick on, now." The sheriff's respect for Rick was obviously higher than it was for his own Deputy.

"I hate you," Jonas muttered into Rick's left ear as he slammed the radio into Rick's chest.

"Reed, what's going on?" Rick asked.

"Still chasing those heroic ghosts of yours?"

"Sheriff, I've stumbled upon Cody's body." Rick rubbed the back of his neck, trying to stop the hot sun from leaving nasty sunburn.

"Say again?" The sheriff's voice echoed the request.

"I think Cody was the victim of a shark attack." Rick looked around, taking in Bodega Bay's rocky inlet and the quieting waters. "Are you busy?"

"Busy as a bumblebee in a honeycomb," Reed quipped back. "Listen, I want you and Jonas to secure the area until I return."

"How long will that be?"

"Sun's starting to set, but we've made some positive headway out here," Reed continued. "I've found fragments of the ferry, and it's not pretty."

"Any survivors? Walter?" Rick asked.

"No sign of any survivors," Reed replied. "Oh, shit." His voice lurched. "Rick, I gotta go. We've found survivors!"

"Okay, I'll see you when I get back on shore," Rick ended the transmission, handing the radio back to Jonas.

"So?" Jonas gripped the radio and began marching across the sand, digging in his heels.

"So?" Rick echoed Jonas, as he tried to keep up with the quick, younger Deputy.

"Yeah, what are we supposed to do?" Jonas questioned as he made his way back to his Jeep.

"Aren't you the Deputy?"

"I take orders, I don't give them," Jonas snapped back.

"Could've fooled me."

"Anyway, what did Reed yap about?" Jonas stopped short, taking in a deep breath. His chest sent a surge of crippling pain through his torso.

"He wanted us to secure the scene until he returned from the bay." Rick walked up behind the startled Deputy, peering over Marsh's right shoulder. "Are you okay?" Rick asked, noticing Marsh's reddening face and contorted facial expressions.

"Yeah, don't worry about me," Jonas snapped back. "Get my camera."

"What's the magic word?" Rick opened the door and began his search for the camera.

"Pretty please." Jonas caught his breath.

"Seriously, are you going to be okay?" Rick exited the rear driver's side of the Jeep Wrangler, camera securely tucked in his palm. He then handed it over to Jonas.

"Yeah, thanks for the concern." Jonas took the camera and headed back toward Cody's corpse.

"My old man died young. His bum ticker did him in." Rick dragged his tired feet back across the beach.

"I know, I was your Deputy when your father died. I'll be fine. I'm on medication for my fluctuating blood pressure slash cholesterol." Jonas looked around. "We're losing daylight. What can you tell me about this whole thing?" Jonas raised the camera and took multiple pictures of the body, snapping off several more shots, all at varying different angles, low shots, high shots, eerie close-ups of the severed limbs and Cody's ripped torso.

"I was at Whitebeard's when the earthquake hit," Rick began his story.

"No surprise there. No doubt you were drowning your retirement in liquor?"

"Only days that end in the letter Y," Rick quipped back.

"After the quake, what happened in your neck of the woods?"

"I gathered myself, helped the patrons regain their composure, scooped up a full bottle of whiskey, and headed out for a stroll."

"A suicide stroll?" Jonas asked, knowing full well Rick's recent decline.

"Perhaps, I don't know. I needed some fresh air, and figured a walk on the beach would help me cleanse the fog in my head."

"I understand. I don't mean to pick away at you, it's my nature." Jonas turned around and gave Rick a firm slap on the shoulder. "This town still needs you," he chirped.

"Really?" Rick felt accomplishment swell within him.

"No. What the hell would we want with a washed up ex-sheriff who can't find his way out of a whiskey bottle?" Jonas jarred Rick's psyche.

"I called you to come out here for Cody's body." Rick churned inside. "And you have the balls to personally attack me?"

"Oh, calm down," Jonas said while he scribbled notes down in his black Mead notepad.

"Calm down?"

"You really have gotten temperamental in your old age." Jonas squinted at the body to enhance the details of his written deposition.

"I went for a swim." Rick coolly sidestepped the perfectly positioned verbal landmine Jonas had wanted him to step on. "When I felt refreshed, I came back to shore and sat down for a breather."

"Where was the body in relation to you?"

"I was over there," Rick said pointing to his previous position. "Then I walked over, stopped dead in my tracks, puked a few times, gathered my wits and headed straight to Skippy's place to call Davenport, but I got you instead."

Both men heard the approaching boat. Rick instantly knew it was the sheriff's Boston Whaler, a sleek thirteen-foot boat, virtually indestructible. Rick preferred it for his personal fishing expeditions, using it on his days off from the office. Rick walked away from Jonas to catch a breath and explore his options.

"Jonas, do you copy?" Reed's voice broke through the radio.

"Yeah, I'm right here Boss," Jonas confirmed.

"Is Rick there too?"

"Yeah, he is. He's bringing me up to date about how he found the body."

"Was he drinking?"

Jonas turned and spotted Rick walking along the shore, kicking away emptied clams.

"Not that I can tell. He did say he had a drink or two at Whitebeard's before he came out to the beach for a walk." Jonas covered for Rick even though he hated the thought of it.

"I'm heading right for you as we speak." Reed waved to his Deputy.

"Yup. I see you, Sheriff." Jonas waved back.

The Boston Whaler smoothly approached the beach, kicking up the sand. Reed pulled up the heavy outboard motors, preventing the boat from re-entering the water.

The Body

"Jonas." Reed greeted his Deputy. He adjusted his sunglasses, sliding them across each ear, preventing further slippage down his large nose. He then reached into his pocket, and pulled out a crumpled pack of Marlboro cigarettes. Sheriff Davenport slipped the cigarette between his lips, letting it dance around while he took in the scene. "Where's the body?" he asked while he ignited the slender cigarette inside his cupped hands. His blue butane lighter brought the cigarette to vibrant life. Reed slid his favorite lighter back into his right shirt pocket, right above the golden Sonoma County Sheriff's badge.

Sheriff Reed Tavis Davenport came to the Sonoma County post on the laurels of his heroic stand against the mayor of San Francisco. The newspapers had neatly woven the national story of how Davenport threw his body in front of the mayor during a botched assassination attempt on the steps of City Hall.

The year was 1989 and Davenport was merely a five-year veteran when a routine news conference on the Oakland-San Francisco earthquakes turned deadly. Davenport, then a brisk twenty-six years of age, dove in front of the mayor, taking three bullets in his chest while firing off several of his own shots at the gunman. As luck would have it, his expert shots killed the gunman and his own notepad stopped the blow of the assailant's shots. Davenport became a staple of the San Francisco Police Department for the next nineteen years before changing jobs and coming back home to Sonoma County. At forty-four years old, Davenport sported premature grey hair and several scars from his years on the job, but still managed to maintain an upbeat attitude. One particular scar, right above his left eyebrow, came from a nasty street fight after a suspect had defiantly resisted arrest.

Jonas's jealously of his boss's exemplary track record certainly didn't soothe the fact that Sonoma's very own Rick Chatham also had his own celebrated achievements. Jonas felt these two men consistently overshadowed him, and that brought a lot of angst to the Deputy's life.

"It's over here, Sheriff," Jonas encouraged Davenport to follow his lead.

"How's everything going with you and Rick?" Davenport knew of the shaky foundation between the two men.

"We're like two lions attacking the same piece of meat."

After taking another long drag on his Marlboro, Davenport efficiently studied the grisly scene. Turning to his right, Davenport caught Rick sauntering along the shoreline. "Jonas," he addressed his Deputy.

"Yeah, what is it Boss?" Jonas replied with a bitter tone.

"What have you learned from the scene?" Davenport turned back around, facing Jonas.

"Well, that has-been over there--" Jonas waved his hand, motioning Davenport to again look in Rick's direction.

"Rick, his name is Rick." Davenport had no time for bullshit. "Jonas, exactly what did he tell you?" Davenport whittled down his cigarette right down the nub, before flicking it into the sand and crushing it with his foot. He then picked it back up and stuffed it into the Marlboro box.

"I was ready to charge you a fifty-dollar fine for littering on the beach." Jonas joked with his boss.

"Yeah, good luck with that," Davenport cracked wise with the Marx Brothers. "So, what did he tell you Groucho?"

"That I found the body," Rick interrupted. He made his way back from his walk along the shore, and tapped the sheriff upon his shoulder.

"Rick, how have you been, my friend?" Davenport asked.

"I've been better. I just stumbled on Cody's body. What a fucking shame." Rick's emotions began rising to the surface. "It felt like it was only yesterday when he ended my professional surfing career. Nobody, especially Cody Kincade deserves an ending like this." Rick pointed down at the corpse.

"You got beat by a younger, faster version of yourself, Dick." Jonas attempted to ruffle Chatham's feathers. "It happens to the best of us."

"Jonas, read between the lines," Rick's gruff voice responded as he held up his left pointer, middle, and ring fingers, then slowly retracted fingers until only the middle one was left.

"I hear you, loud and clear Rick," Davenport noted as he walked around the body. His fingers reached into his pocket and retrieved a small silver cell phone. "Boys, can we stop pissing at each other? I'm starting to get wet over here."

"You don't have to tell me twice," Rick obliged.

Jonas shot off a gruff response, before he reached across his chest and clutched his left shoulder.

"Jesus, are you okay?" Rick asked one more time. "We really need to get the kid to a medic."

"He'll be fine. He probably ate at Senor Trejo's again. The chili bean dip always runs through him like a waterfall over a cliff." Davenport tapped in the coroner's number.

"Are you calling Slim?" Rick asked.

"Yeah, he's the one on duty for the 4th of July weekend," Davenport added.

"Ah, good old Slim. Always thirsting for the O.T." Rick gazed across the bay, catching a glimpse of a dorsal fin in the water. "Jonas, hand me your binoculars please," Rick insisted.

"What for?" Jonas worked the strap over his neck and tossed them over to Rick.

"I see a nude sunbather on the deck of a sailboat," Rick quipped back.

"Really?" Jonas changed tone and eagerly scooted over to Rick.

"Relax," Rick said. "Put that surfboard back into your shorts. I thought I saw one of our resident sharks out there." He raised the binoculars and peered across the bay, attempting to locate the dorsal fin again.

"Can you see it?" Jonas stared off in the same direction.

"Nah, it must've been the sunlight grazing across the water," Rick replied as he handed the binoculars back to Jonas. "Nothing. Nothing at all."

"Hoping for a lucky break?" Jonas asked.

"Yeah." Rick seemed demoralized over the situation. "Hoping."

"We'll catch whatever, or whoever did this to Cody," Jonas assured him. "You have my word on that."

"You know, that's the first intelligent thing you've said all afternoon." Rick slapped Jonas across the shoulder blades. "There might be some hope for you after all."

Rick walked in on the sheriff's conversation with the Sonoma County coroner.

"Slim, we have a dead body out here on the bay," Davenport chatted up a storm with the coroner. "I need you out here ASAP, and bring anything, and everything you need in order to secure the scene." He considered his next sentence as he paced about the sand, sinking his feet into the soft brown particles. "Fuck, it's a grisly one out here, Slim. A damn sight to behold if you ask me." He reached into his pocket for another Marlboro cigarette. The conversation continued for a few more minutes, as Davenport did most of the talking. "Dinner? Slim, just pick up a sandwich at the deli and get your ass down here." He shut the cell phone, and struck up a flame, again igniting the cigarette ablaze with flavor.

"Slim's still up to his delay tactics?" Rick asked the sheriff.

"I don't get it." Davenport's face briefly became engulfed in a thick veil of smoke, before he blew it away. "Our coroner not only has been on the job since President Eisenhower was in office, but also freaks at the sight and smell of blood. It usually takes him about five minutes to actually touch the sticky stuff."

"That's our Slim," Rick added. "At least he's down from ten minutes. Regardless, he was always very thorough for me when I was on the job."

"Oh, and he still is. That old bastard can run circles around anyone half his age," Davenport responded. "Good old Slim still has his wonderful annoying idiosyncrasies though." Davenport snuck another smoke, earning him the rightful designation of chimney smoker.

The three men turned around to see Slim's battered pale blue 1977 Ford Pinto stumbling across the beach. The black tires came to a full stop, their rims spotted with years of salt erosion. Looking into the grimy rear view mirror, the man pushed the last of his hot pastrami sandwich into his mouth, and then wiped the residual crumbs away from his jeans. The driver's side door creaked open, thirsty for WD-40. Johnny Cash blared 'The Rebel Johnny Yuma" through the ancient 8-track. A pair of black and white Converse sneakers pressed deeply into the shifting sand, as the man turned his weight toward the rear of the Pinto. The wiry man used all of his strength to open the dirty, slime-covered rear hatch. His lips still whistled the song while he moved around the red, white, and blue America patchwork quilt that lay upon all of his belongings. His wrinkled fingers traced over the well-worn ivory white tackle box and lifted up the half-broken handle, raising the box close to his chest. With his other hand, the man closed the hatch and walked in a slow, methodical pace toward the three men and the grisly scene.

"Slim," Davenport greeted his coroner, noticing Slim's new black suspenders with golden latches that held up a pair of blue jeans with their golden latches.

"Slim." Rick added his own greeting. Rick always wanted to know if Slim had an entire closet of red and black long sleeve flannel shirts. "That's a really nice shirt Slim," Rick said with a small nod of his head.

"Yep," was Slim's only response, and a gruff one at that. He was nearing his eightieth birthday, and was a curmudgeon if there ever was one. Slim had been through a dozen sheriffs, and a fair share of mayors, and yet there he was, still grinding it out. Slim was balding, with only isolated islands of hair along the perimeter of each ear. His taste for flannel baffled many of his co-workers. Who wore flannel during the summer months?

Jonas jumped into the conversation. "The body is over here."

"I have eyes, I can see." Slim brushed past the Deputy and stood some feet away from Cody's half-eaten corpse.

"Sheriff?" Slim looked over at Davenport who stood on the opposite side of Cody's body with Jonas and Rick.

"Yeah, what's up, Slim?" Davenport asked.

"Do we know what happened here?"

"We think a shark, perhaps?" Jonas offered the question up for debate.

"The boy's a bright one." Slim stared over the body. "There's blood here." He feebly fought back the urge to vomit his deli sandwich.

"Yeah, there usually is with dead bodies Slim," Davenport countered.

"I need a minute to process the scene," Slim said as he lowered the tackle box to the sand.

"By that he means--" Slim interrupted Rick with his vomiting at the other end of the body.

"Okay, I'm good." Slim regrouped and wiped off his face.

"Jesus, can't we find someone else to do this?" Jonas asked. He had no patience for the wisecracking coroner.

"He's the best we've got kid," Davenport stated.

"That's pretty sad." Jonas looked over Slim as he viewed the body. "Sometime today, old man."

"Remind me how this jackass is a law officer?" Slim opened up the tackle box and took out a pair of white gloves. Slim was a filthy collector of many things. His Pinto had become a traveling collector of junk. McDonald bags on the floor, old San Francisco Chronicle newspaper's strewn about the back seat, (his wife Mary had found a newspaper dating back to the Kennedy Administration in his backseat) and several used soda bottles bounced out of the ripped garbage bags inside the trunk space. But Slim had always kept his tackle box in mint order. Inside the box, all content was itemized, categorized, P-touched, and kept rigorously clean.

"Jonas's father is currently Deputy Mayor Timothy Marsh," Rick brought Slim up to speed.

"Oh yeah, that's right. Man, my mind's going the way of the birds," Slim snapped on the gloves. "I must've missed the memo on exactly when nepotism became part of the quota system."

"You see? He's certainly not the right man to examine the

body," Jonas questioned Slim's credentials. "He even put the gloves on the wrong hand."

"Oh relax, junior," Slim cracked a grin that stretched across his well-worn face. He adjusted each glove. "I'm just messing with you, just like I always do."

"I miss Slim." Rick smiled.

"So, what's up Ricky?" Slim asked his former friend and sheriff.

"A little bit of this, a little bit of that."

"Well, I definitely want to study Cody's body back at the lab," Slim said, continuing to process the scene. "He's been dead for roughly three hours, give or take a few minutes."

"Impressive," Jonas meekly responded. "What else can you tell us?"

"He put up one hell of a fight." Slim extracted a fractured tooth from Cody's rib cage. "Sheriff, if you would be so kind," Slim ushered Davenport over to assist with securing the tooth. Davenport opened up a clear Ziploc bag for Slim to drop the tooth into. "Do you have anyone for this?" Slim asked.

"There's a woman over on the islands," Davenport responded, snapping his fingers. "Oh, wooden nickels, what the hell is her name?"

"Ashleigh," Rick interjected. "Ashleigh Wilkinson."

"Have you met her?" Slim asked.

"A few times, briefly."

Davenport joined in. "Where abouts?"

"I attended one of her Marine Biology seminars when I was going through my shark phase." Rick really did want to talk about what had happened, and positioned to change the conversation.

"Oh yeah, I remember when you attended her seminar." Jonas didn't want to be left out of the group, so he decided to offer his own two-cents worth.

"I did learn a lot, and actually met her after the seminar ended." Rick flexed his fingers in front of him. "Pretty eyes, killer legs."

"I like legs, too," Slim's ears sprouted up like a curious puppy upon hearing Rick's admiration for a woman's legs.

"Anyway, maybe I can reach her and ask her to take a peek." Rick started to get caught up in the police business, even though his retirement was permanent.

"Cool." Sheriff Davenport gazed out across the bay, eager to wrap up the day. "Slim, are you done?"

"Yep. I could use some help loading the body into the Pinto."

"What are you smoking old man?" Jonas asked. "I'm curious to where exactly you are going to fit a dead body in your Pinto machine."

"I'll move some stuff around," Slim offered.

"I'll help you load it into my Jeep, and I'll lead the way back to the station." Jonas walked over and helped Slim prepare the body for transport.

"Will you put the lights on?"

"Are you serious?" Jonas looked at him, noticing his pupils widening.

"You bet."

"Okay, I'll bite. What color would you like? I have red and blue."

"Blue," Slim responded. His fingers zipped up the body bag while Jonas gripped the opposite end with his hands. "On three, okay?"

"If you hurry up old man, and if we go on one, I'll buy us a nice six-pack of Coronas," Jonas offered.

"On one it is." Slim lifted his end. "I like the way you think, Jonas Marsh. Or, should I say, Deputy Jonas Marsh?"

"Yeah, you have some charm as well old man." Jonas huffed and puffed his way back to the Jeep.

"I drink like a sieve." Slim replied with his patented wrinkled grin.

"Don't we all?" Jonas closed the rear of the Jeep. "Follow me."

Slim gave a nod of his head and returned back to his Ford Pinto. His hands turned the ignition, bringing her back to life.

"Ah, isn't it nice to see the kids playing nice?" Davenport poked Rick in the side with his elbow. The two men had become close in the years since Reed had taken over as sheriff, occasionally leaning on Rick for friendship. Reed also was one of Rick's biggest surfing fans, and widely rumored to have several of Rick's famous posters in his possession.

"Yeah, it brings a tear to my eye, the boys playing nice." Rick snickered back. "But they definitely have the right idea."

"Yeah, what's that?" Davenport watched as Jonas pulled away and shot a wave of his left hand at the two men, his blue light flashing on the dashboard. Slugging behind the Jeep Wrangler, Slim's Pinto chugged to the remaining lyrics of "The Rebel of Johnny Yuma."

"They're setting aside their differences, and enjoying an ice cold beer."

"You and I ought to catch up back at the station." Davenport said as he began to walk across the beach to his police boat. He suddenly felt like a kid again and attempted to initiate an old childhood game. "Last one to the boat's a rotten egg." Davenport's walk turned into a sprint as he felt a sudden burst of youthfulness.

"Hey, wait! I ride shotgun!" Rick's competitive edge remained intact as he raced his friend back to the boat.

Delta Flight 1313
Late Afternoon

arin Nesmith-Coyle couldn't get comfortable. His seat was wedged up against the window, and a relatively large person occupied the aisle seat, making it virtually impossible for him to maneuver in his own seat. The flight soon became a rather unpleasant experience, starting with a delay of thirty-four minutes due to mechanical problems. The non-stop flight was nearing its end barely in time. Darrin had suffered through the shitty Antonio Sabato Jr. flick *"Shark Hunter"* and the honey roasted peanuts that falsely claimed to have been salted.

He tried to stare out of the window and lose his growing impatience in the curves of the landscapes below, but the window was only a fraction bigger than a ceramic tile and limited his flight-time sightseeing. He pressed his legs tightly together in a meager effort to stop himself from urinating. His eyes searched for the lavatory.

"Attention passengers, this is your captain speaking." His voice boomed over the loudspeaker. "We will be landing at San Francisco International Airport in about an hour. The local time of our arrival will be close to one o'clock in the morning. The flight attendant will allow those with connecting flights to depart first," the captain's voice faded. Darrin had flown many times before, and the announcement had become ad nauseam for him.

Darrin's luck changed for the better when the large passenger seated next to him, decided to swap seats out with another passenger. Darrin quickly bent over and dug out a copy of the latest issue of National Geographic, the one with his cover story about the Red Triangle.

"Oh, cool," the soft voice said.

Darrin turned his head to see an eight-year-old girl staring him down. "Can I help you?" he asked with a polite tone. Her small, beautiful brown eyes stymied Darrin with their desire for knowledge. Her soft giggle beckoned Darrin to continue conversation, and when another brown set of eyes peeked out from the third seat next to the aisle, Darrin was at a loss for words. "Twins?"

"Yeah," the closest girl said. "I'm Karalyn, and this is my sister Gracelyn."

"Did you travel alone?"

"No. Our dad's in the next row. He noticed who you were,"

Karalyn kept the conversation flowing.

"Oh. Really?" Darrin folded the magazine, covering the shark's open jaws.

"Our daddy really likes your work," Gracelyn chimed in.

"He's familiar with my field of study?"

"Yeah, you study sharks." Gracelyn looked over the folded magazine. "Is it that your magazine?"

"Well, yeah," Darrin tapped it against the chair ahead of him, prompting the girl's father to extend his head around the corner of the seat.

"Hi there," his voice was deep and professional.

"Hi." Darrin returned the awkward greeting. He was used to being mugged for interviews at television stations, or aquariums, or even at local charities, but he had never been the object of anyone's curiosity on a flight.

"My name's J.S. Brady, and these are my twin daughters, Karalyn and Gracelyn."

"The horror author?" Darrin's attention perked up.

"Some say that," J.S. answered back with a modest shrug.

"I have some of your work. The werewolf stuff, and zombie book, man, that was really well-written stuff."

"Thanks," J.S. responded. "I'm working on a horror book as we speak, pretty much out of the box for me."

"It's a shark book," Gracelyn snorted with a giggle.

"Shark book?" Darrin asked with great interest.

"Well, yeah, of some sort. It's still in the pre-production phase. You know, flow maps, character sketches, and plot devices."

"I'm eagerly awaiting the chance to read it." Darrin again tapped the magazine nervously. "So, how can I help you out today?"

"My daughters have been on a shark kick ever since they learned I've been working on this shark book of mine, and, well, after I noticed you during the boarding process back in New York, I had to introduce them to you."

"Gracelyn, Karalyn this is Darrin Coyle, he's very, very famous," J.S. introduced the trio.

"I'm flattered, really I am," Darrin attempted to step aside from the conversation in a polite manner. "I'm a very busy man," he said to the girls.

"What kind of shark do you like?" Gracelyn asked.

"Yeah, do you like the great white, or tiger shark?" Karalyn asked.

"The tiger shark's pretty fast," Gracelyn answered her older sister, pretending Darrin wasn't even in the same aisle.

"True, but I read in class that the mako shark actually is the fastest. He can swim as fast as Daddy," Karalyn added. She brushed her short blond hair out of her eyes. Her fingers fiddled with a bright orange ponytail holder.

"As fast as Daddy?" Darrin asked, curious on how the girl's had such an acute repository of shark information.

"Yeah," Karalyn replied as he tied her hair into symmetrical pigtails. Her attention to detail had always quietly impressed her parents. Gracelyn had her own way of orchestrating her meticulous daily routine, from breakfast, schoolwork, and her love for arts and crafts. "He drives fast sometimes."

"Well, the mako shark, especially the long fin mako, swims up to over sixty miles per hour," Darrin said, interested in their knowledge of sharks.

"That's pretty fast." Gracelyn shook her head, whipping around her newly shorn hair that bounced just below her ears.

"I am intrigued to learn how you girls know about sharks?"

"We just finished learning about mammals, fish, reptiles, and amphibians in school. We spent a day on sharks and whales," Karalyn replied with a smile. "They're awesome."

"Daddy's favorite movie is '*Jaws*'." Gracelyn tied her own hair into pigtails using two identical yellow ponytail holders.

"Do you know what a great white shark's scientific name is?" Darrin asked his captive crowd.

"Like its first and last name?" Karalyn asked.

"Yeah, exactly like that." Darrin pointed the rolled up National Geographic in her direction.

"I bet it's Bobby." Gracelyn chortled.

"Or Jacob. Maybe it's something like Marty. Or Joey." Karalyn followed her sister's silly nonsense.

Darrin chuckled at the girls' infectious cuteness. "No," he held back another wave of laughter. "No, it's not that simple. A great white shark has a very long name."

"Oh," the girl's both responded. "Is it hard to spell?"

"I can't really spell it, and I study sharks for a living."

"Really? You can't spell the shark's name?" Gracelyn asked.

"Sometimes," Darrin answered. "Would you like to know their name?"

"Yeah, sure Buddy." Gracelyn snapped her fingers and pointed to Darrin.

"Okay, the name is," Darrin began, "*Carcharodon carcharias*."

"Charcoal what?" Gracelyn had a puzzled expression.

"Wow, I bet they'd be happier with a name like Joey," Karalyn said with a grin. "And it'd be easier to spell when the teacher asks you to write down your name."

"Oh, absolutely," Darrin agreed. "So, do you know anything else about sharks?"

"Some are big, some are small," Gracelyn added to the conversation.

"I like the hammer shark, they have a funny head," Karalyn brought up one of her favorite sharks.

"They're cool," Darrin responded.

"Which one's your favorite?"

"The great white," Darrin said with a sheepish grin. "I love their agility, speed, and predatory knack for executing the perfect kill."

"Attention passengers of Delta Flight 1313, we will be touching down in San Francisco shortly. Local time is one o'clock in the morning. After leaving the craft, you can expect frequent rain, and moderate thunderstorms," the captain announced. "Those of you with connecting flights, the flight attendants will allow you to exit the craft upon our final taxi into the terminal."

"Are you going to see family?" Karalyn prodded Darrin.

"Somewhat," Darrin said while he checked his buckle. "You girls should double-check and make sure your seat belts are locked."

"This is the captain once again. Please observe the no smoking signs and fasten seat belts signs that are now turned on indicating our descent into rainy San Francisco."

"What do you mean, somewhat?" Karalyn again pushed Darrin for an answer. Her fingers worked over the belt, snapping it securely in place.

"I'm visiting some close friends, who in an odd way, are like family to me." Darrin gazed out the window noticing the top of the Golden Gate Bridge as the plane passed over it.

"Well, I hope you have a good time with your friends," Gracelyn said with her girlish grin. "Friends are important."

"I will, and the two of you have a great time with your parents," Darrin returned the favor, and prepared for the final descent into San Francisco.

H is foot slammed hard on the brakes, bringing the Ford Focus to an abrupt halt in the center of the bridge. Overhead, he heard the loud grinding of an airplane heading into the nearby airport. The young man craned his neck toward the windshield, catching the tail end of the airplane's descent. His sweaty fingers grabbed the keys, ready to snag them from the ignition. His daredevil routine had started to cause minor traffic jams, forcing cars to swerve around him. Some of the passing motorists yelled out to see if he had broken down, and needed any assistance.

Trey Darwin was beyond help. He had plotted out the perfect plan over the last few hours. He would drive the car across the bridge during light traffic, ditch the car on the bridge, walk across to the nearest red railing, and then just like that, jump to the water below. He took in a sharp, deep breath. He processed the previous four hours, which had culminated in the firing of the twenty-eight-year-old from his employment at Cisco Enterprises. One of his friends had found Trey's fiancée of nearly three years in bed with not another man, but several men during a routine business trip of her own. (She chalked it up to curiosity before her impending marriage). Trey had decided that with no job, fiancée, and an addiction to painkillers, it was time to end everything.

The slick conditions were not making Trey's plan run any smoother. A rolling coastal storm stampeded through the Bay Area, discharging large volumes of rain and foggy residue in its turbulent wake.

On the local radio station, Dave Matthews Band's popular suicide song, *Big Eyed Fish* poured over the airwaves. Trey sat back in the driver's seat, randomly checking his rear view mirror, noticing a definitive traffic pattern emerging in the early Wednesday morning hours. Now was the time for Trey to execute his plan. There were no cars coming across the bridge, there was a clear path to the other side of the bridge.

Hesitating, Trey's fingers toyed with the small green Yoda keychain his fiancée had bought for him during one her business trips to the Star Wars Convention. His fingers clasped the keychain, ready to disengage when his cell phone roared to life.

He stared down at the grey screen. The battery was nearing the end of its charged life. Nevertheless, there was the number: 555-4030. It was his fiancée, Renee. Hesitating, he counted to three, hoping the call would abruptly end. After three ridiculously loud rings the call died out, turning the screen black and leaving him all alone on the bridge in the rain to ponder his inevitable future. He blew a sigh of relief and withdrew the keys. The phone rang again and the same number scrolled across the LCD panel. Trey's instincts told him to answer the call. He raised the phone to his ear and hit the green send button, bringing the call to life.

"Yeah, I'm pissed," he angrily responded to the caller. "What do you think?" He looked around the darkness, searching for answers. Renee's voice resonated in his head, comforting and loving, urging his prompt return to her.

"I don't know," Trey responded. He wasn't in the mood for reconciliation. It wouldn't do any good. She'd turn right back into her addictive self, turning tricks with anyone, anywhere. Renee couldn't be trusted. "Do you feel you deserve another chance? I'm on the fucking bridge ready to jump after that shit you pulled on me. And, to top it off, I lost my job today when one of my partners blackballed me. My boss had to bring the hammer down on someone," he paused to take a moment to breathe. "I was *that* someone."

His ear tilted to catch her response. The battery was dying. Her voice crackled in and out with the approaching storm.

"Can you hear me?" Trey yelled into the phone. Renee begged him to come back to their home, their life, and their unborn child. She informed Trey of her newfound pregnancy, and that his friend had misinformed Trey of her tryst with the other men. She claimed sexual harassment and if Trey's friend (who worked for the same company as Renee) had stuck around, he would've seen her send a few hard knees into the testicles of each of the men, leaving them red-faced and crying for mercy. "Renee! Fuck," Trey growled as he palmed the phone. He decided to give his suicide plan another day to marinate. His fingers turned the keys and brought the Focus back to life. He quickly checked his rearview mirror and found nothing but pitch black. He began to pull forward, the front of his car still sitting across the middle lane into oncoming traffic. He was so jacked up on adrenaline he didn't bother to check in front of him.

A set of headlights crashed into the hood of the Ford, spinning the car around right into the oncoming grill of a speeding tractor-trailer. The impact of the incoming air bag caught Trey by surprise and slowed his reaction time. The barreling monstrous truck obliterated Trey's car, sending it spiraling through the air, and into the bridge's side guardrails of the bridge. The impact sent it through the guardrails leaving behind uneven random streaks of red paint stretched across each side of the Focus, digging into the car's newly painted body. The car was left teetering on the perilous edge of the Golden Gate.

Trey's wounds were severe. Blood flooded down the left side of his face. Out of the corner of his eye, he could see some fat guy running toward the car wreck. Trey reached for his face, tracing over the shards of glass embedded into his ripped skin.

The man waved a small, bright flashlight, attempting to get a good look inside the car. The light penetrated the spider web crack in the window on the driver's side and scattered into several directions. "Hey man, are you okay?"

Trey's ears picked up mumbling. He strained to catch sight of the source of the light. He scrambled to unlock the seat belt, and frantically pushed down the deflating air bag.

"Can you get to the back seat?"

The Ford's wheels began losing traction on the slick bridge, forcing Trey to act impulsively and attempt to reach the rear of the car.

The man called out, "I'm calling 911 and the cops," while he waved his cell phone about in some crazy pattern.

Trey managed to escape to the back seat, and curled up with his back pressed up against the front seats. Another sudden jolt sent the car hurtling forwards, moments after Trey managed to crack the heels of his feet against the rear window attempting to break free.

Trey took in what could be his final gasp of air watching as the man with the disturbing cell phone antics rapidly became a small speck as the Ford Focus careened toward the bay below.

The sudden force roiled the quiet water, diverting their attention toward the intriguing sound. Their black eyes rolled around as the threesome sped through the dark water, heading underneath the Golden Gate Bridge. The forty-foot mammoth shark, broke the surface first, agitating the water with his dorsal fin. Next the smaller hunter exposed its own dorsal fin. Finally, the thirty-five-foot shark, the middleman in the hunting group, sliced his way into the glowing moonlight, and then dipped back under the water, ready to attack.

Trey's car plummeted through the dark depths of the bay, and water itched to pour through the small cracks in the rear window. Trey scooted ahead and wound up his legs for one more fierce attack at the window.

They swarmed around the weird object sinking in the water. Their snouts banged into the metal object, jarring it violently as it continued tearing through the water's barrier.

Trey's body jolted about from the intense impact. His brain mustered one last shot of adrenaline as he turned his head, catching a glimpse of the mother of all great whites rearing up for another shot at the driver's side of the car. "What the fuck is that?" He returned back to the rear window but found another shark fiercely approaching. His wounds seeped blood into the water, encouraging the shark's insatiable appetite for the kill.

One by one the sharks circled around the waterlogged, descending object, curious about the weird new prey. The car's engine chortled and coughed then spit itself dead after thirty seconds. The radio still powered by the battery, pumped out the classic Guns and Roses tune, 'Welcome to the Jungle.'

The pulsing sound of the song's drums appeal to the pack's acute senses and geared them up for another violent push toward their descending prey. The leader of the vicious pack slammed its hungry jaws into the object, pounding in the door. The second shark, powered by brute force, crashed into the passenger side of the object, twisting the metal under its weight. The smaller, faster shark drove its face through the rear window sending a rush of water into the car. The leader again charged the car, this time shattering the window and catching its prey by surprise.

Trey punched the leader of the pack in the face, attempting to escape the onslaught. He repeatedly pounded his cut fists into the shark's open jaw, tearing away the skin on his hands. The smaller, scarred shark had half of its head in the rear of the car and snapped its jaws wildly in a desperate attempt to reach its startled prey. The shark sliced through the rear seats with deathly precision sending stuffing and debris of the seats flying about the sinking car.

The leader retreated with a fresh taste of blood, and prepared for the final charge. Trey was jolted again after another brutal attack from the passenger side of the car, pushing him into the driver's side, and toward the waiting, charging maw of the monstrous shark.

He felt the teeth grind down on his arm, severing it right above the elbow, spraying a sea of red across the shark's face. His left hand dangled by his side, attempting to reach for something, anything to defend himself with. His mouth went dry from screaming, his eyes refused to look at the shark's handiwork. The shark released its grip, swallowing the arm with one fluid motion.

Trey's fingers clasped the black knob of the cigarette lighter. He pushed it in just as the second shark shattered the other side of the car, poking its head into the car and snapping its jaws inches from Trey's lanky fingers. He fiercely yanked the burner from the socket and crammed the small, heated lighter into the opening jaws of the second shark. Startled, the shark swam away, leaving a small hole in the side of the window for Trey to escape.

Trey scooted through the bloody water as the leader of the pack again crammed its hungry snout into the driver's side of the car, becoming wedged inside. Trey lost momentum and any sense of clarity as he lost more and more blood. Almost to the surface, out of pure gut instinct, he sharply turned his head, catching the rising shark from below. The second shark sped upwards with its mouth agape ready for the kill. Trey felt the shark's mouth swallow his lower torso, and ended the blitzing attack with a furious snap of its jaws.

The shark swallowed Trey whole, as blood spiraled in the dark, murky water. Trey's blood and last breath filled the quiet surface of the water.

"**J**esus, would you look at the fucking time!" Slim cursed at the rest of the weary group.

"Why, what's up?" Jonas asked as he polished off the last of his beer.

"I have to get up early tomorrow to analyze that poor guy on the beach," Slim said while he swirled the last of his third iced tea.

"Ever since you passed beer number five, you went right for the iced tea." Jonas placed his finished glass upon the littered counter. "Man, we kept old Whitebeard in business tonight, eh boys?"

"Yeah," Rick was sloshed, yet hungered for more.

"We definitely need to put the brakes on ourselves tonight," Sheriff Davenport instructed his party. "I have a town to run tomorrow." Reed clanged his emptied Heineken beer bottle onto the counter.

"Yeah, I guess so." Jonas concurred.

Slim rose from his barstool, still lingering from his own parade of beers. "Fuck, I'm wasted off my ass."

Jonas asked the stymied group, "Now what?"

"I'm headed back to my boat for the night." Rick rose and walking unsteadily toward the exit.

"Yeah, that sounds like a plan. I say all of us head back to Rick's house for some shut-eye," Jonas urged.

"I'll walk it off," Slim said with a wrinkled grin. "But thanks for the offer."

"I don't think I'll be able to keep my puke down if I sleep in Rick's bouncing house on the wharf," Reed added.

"I plan to be ready to go at seven in the morning," Slim said to the sluggish party.

"Seven in the morning!" Jonas seemed surprised. "I won't even reach sobriety by then."

"What kind of a man are you?" Slim jaunted with the Deputy once more.

"What are you chattering about?"

"I served in two wars, and still managed to operate a highly active lifestyle." Slim bristled at the Deputy's lack of drive.

"Was it the Revolutionary and Civil War?"

"Yeah, keep running those slick jaws of yours," Slim tightened his fist. "Pretty soon I'll break it for ya."

"Oh, calm down Rambo," Jonas encouraged Slim to back off his tall horse. "We're all hammered pretty good tonight, so let's just take this up in the morning once we're all sobered up." Jonas walked over to Slim and grabbed him by the elbow. "Come on, Grizzly Adams, I'll walk out with you."

"Yeah, okay. But watch that jaw of yours," Slim warned.

"So I'll see you in the morning at the office?" Davenport asked his old friend.

"If I can wake up in time," Rick said, wiping the remainder of liquor from his chin.

"Please try to. I personally would like you to assist me on this matter." Davenport approached the door with Rick.

"I don't know," Rick fumbled for an answer.

"Well, sleep on it. I know you are searching for something to keep yourself occupied during your so-called retirement." He slapped him on the shoulder.

"Once a cop, always a cop," Rick said as reached down and searched for his keys inside his pockets.

"Yeah, it's something like that." Davenport gazed toward the full moon. "Man, what a view tonight."

"No promises. I found the body for you, I think that's where I stop." Rick stepped out of the moon's glow and disappeared into the thick, choking darkness of Bodega Bay before his friend could answer.

Davenport lit up another cigarette as he looked out across the water, sucking in a tight circle of smoke. "Oh, I bet you'll change your mind."

Off in the distance, three dorsal fins broke the surface, and glided underneath the white glow of the moon before descending once more into the heart of Bodega Bay.

Rick Chatham's fingers fumbled around for his golden house keys that lay buried somewhere inside his shorts' deep pocket. The houseboat rolled around on the water, bouncing off the dock, as Rick entered the foyer of the boat. He skidded his keys across the white marbled counter top, withdrew his sweaty shirt, and tossed it over the spiral staircase.

He begrudgingly made his way over to the sofa and retreated for the night. His body used up the last millimeter of energy as he collapsed on the couch. He turned on the television and started channel surfing, eventually zoning in on the fright flick of the night. The Sci-Fi Channel's premiere of Luther Castle: Zombie Slayer, starring Colby Sheridan and Gorem Edgar, two premier B-movie actors, and Mari Gold the loudest of all the scream queens.

Rick's eyelids began to close, then re-opened as he tried to get through the cheesy opening sequence that included a zombie, a lawnmower, and a reckless law officer with a paint ball gun.

Within moments, Rick's hand had let the remote control slide from his grasp and fall to the floor. His eyes were now firmly shut sending the tormented ex-sheriff into a highly active R.E.M. state.

The sun cut through the passing clouds, burning the backs of the waiting surfers. The Ninth Tornado Alley Surfing Competition was now officially ready to begin. New entries stood awestruck at their competition. The reigning champion, Rick "Hurricane" Chatham would be up against Cody "Lightning" Kincade in a battle that had rapidly worked the entire surfing community into a frenzied state. Each man had a stake at this tournament. Rick, the aging ex-sheriff, and powerful reigning champion of the previous five tournaments, would test his mettle against the rogue Kincade, a surfer steeped in rich tradition.

Lars Stevenson, himself a relic of the nineteen seventies, and a medal winning surfer, emceed the tournament, pairing himself with another superstar athlete from the circuit, Tony Dearth. Lars scooped up the microphone as he jostled about in his seat. He sent a friendly elbow into Tony's side, urging him to mike up and be ready in five seconds.

Clearing his throat, the masculine, booming voice of Lars Stevenson shredded the ears of the crowd with his patented introduction, "Good Afternoon Ladieeeees and Gentlemen, we have a sensational day of surfing today, don't we Tony," Lars introduced his broadcasting partner.

"Oh man, my bones are telling me to suit up and get back on the board!" Tony exclaimed to the roaring crowd.

"For our new viewers, my man Dearth has some explosive history at the tournament. He had our champion Rick "Hurricane" Chatham beaten in several of the tournaments. These guys fed off each other's adrenaline, and quickly became fierce competitors. Off the surf they enjoyed a respectable relationship that dissolved into theatrical hatred once their boards hit the water."

Lars enjoyed the sensationalism of the story. His producers enjoyed the ratings boost it brought. "Tell the listening audience what happened, Tony," Lars prompted. Lars quickly, coolly, sipped fresh lemonade as it danced around irregular ice cubes inside the glass.

"A few years ago, when Rick was taken out of the tournament with a lower back strain, I was the clear favorite to capture the Tornado Trophy," Tony relived the ordeal in its entirety.

"What went wrong?" Lars finished off the lemonade and reached for his chewing tobacco. His fingers reached across the red and blue Skoal canister, and released the pressure, taking in the seductive aroma of tobacco.

"As you know, great whites patrol this area, which has become known as the 'Red Triangle', and on that day, they were out in full force." Tony squinted his eyes in the glaring sunlight. His hands worked over the top of his full head of black hair, as he lowered his crystal blue Ray-Ban sunglasses from the top of his head. Once he slid them over his eyes, he cracked his tanned knuckles, picked up his beverage, and continued the story. "After I had taken the lead from Darby Bollinger, I felt something knock me from my board."

"And you knew it was a shark?" Lars looked over at his producer. He had roughly ten seconds to wrap up the conversation with Tony. "Okay, condense it down to a short story, my producer's ready to begin the introduction for the Tornado Tournament."

"Short version," Tony stumbled for words. "I was taken under by the shark, wrapped up inside his jaws like a crying newborn in a blanket. I don't know how I survived. The attack was abrupt and fierce and the shark's teeth severed my lower spinal cord, putting me in a wheelchair for the rest of my life. I can never surf again."

"What do you do now?"

"Besides broadcasting? I run a charity event every year to bring awareness to the increasing shark population, and to offer medical assistance to those innocent souls who have been attacked by great whites."

"Excellent work Tony," Lars stuffed a wad of black tobacco into the side of his mouth. "The surfers are ready, and will begin at the crack of the gun."

The crowd stared over the blistering sunshine and calm ocean, eager to witness the tournament's action.

"One, two, three," Lars called, and fired the pistol.

All thirteen of the surfers ran for the ocean, ready to spearhead their own triumphant story.

"Weather's calling for some swells, which will fit perfectly into our viewing agenda today." Tony looked around the departing participants with a pair of binoculars. "Cody Kincade has taken the lead, swimming with a passion ahead of the others. He's ready to take the incoming wave. Rick Chatham's directly behind him, snapping at Cody's heels."

"Here we go," Lars chewed through the broadcast. "Cody's the first out of the wave, sliding across the water like lightning in a bottle."

"And Hurricane Chatham, a split second behind Kincade," Tony added with a keen look of the binoculars.

"Cody's balance is off, and Rick Chatham takes the lead coming off the wave, darting ahead of the rogue surfer."

Tony's eyes fixated on a small silver triangle breaking through the surface behind Cody's board. "Lars, take a look at Cody."

"Is that what I think it is?" Lars asked, nearly swallowing his tobacco. "Cody has turned around and spotted the dorsal fin."

"This is about to get intense man, real intense," Tony played up the dramatic moment.

"Cody Kincade has gained speed on the Hurricane," Lars chatted up the drama. "Wait, what's he doing?" Lars noticed Cody give Rick a hard brush, passing him and getting ready for the final wave.

"He's acting like a punk, I tell ya," Tony said angrily.

The shark diverted its attention to the splashing sound in the water.

"Rick Chatham is down, and possibly out of the tournament," Lars announced. "Cody Kincade has a clear shot at the Tornado

Trophy."

Cody finished his wave, winning the tournament, not understanding what had happened to Rick.

"Wait, something's wrong out there," Tony felt it in the pit of his stomach. "Where's the shark?" He heard the crowd gasp as he soon found the chilling answer to his question.

The announcers watched in horror as the shark emerged from the surface, jaws agape as it clamped down on Rick Chatham's upper torso, pulling the startled surfer underneath the water. "Oh my God! Jesus Christ!" Lars choked on his new wad of tobacco. He puked it on the papers in front of him. He and Tony watched the nearby lifeguard dart for the water.

"Rick's being dragged under water! He needs help!" Lars screamed as he and Tony bolted from the press box and sprinted across the beach to the shoreline.

A few hours had passed when Rick's phone rattled on the coffee table. Lazily, he wiped the eye crud from the corners of his eyes. He had fallen asleep on the couch watching a series of bad science fiction movies. He had a pattern forming during his retirement. It involved consistent, addictive drinking and then blacking out somewhere inside his expensive boathouse.

His fingers wrapped around his cell, and clumsily Rick slid open the screen. He glanced down at the caller identification that flashed across the LCD screen: REED DAVENPORT.

"Yeah," Rick's voice was gruff and still groggy from the Captain Morgan rum. He began unbuttoning his shirt and headed across the living room. His eyes shuddered at the crisp sunlight coming through his glass doors. "Shit, is it that late already?" He brought up his hand, shielding his face from the burning morning sun. "I'll be right down," Rick's voice ended the short conversation as he entered the bathroom and placed the cell phone down on the wooden counter. Turning, he placed his hands on the shower's golden knobs and twisted them until he comfortably found the desired temperature. After he finished undressing, Rick stepped into the shower's steamy confines and let the water cascade down his scarred torso.

Neptune's Surf and Turf Diner
San Francisco
6:23 a.m.

Gavin Bannister closed the phone and tapped the table, looking directly at his friend, and fellow colleague, Daniel Locke.

"Ashleigh and Darrin are coming as we speak," Gavin said, holding up two fingers indicating to the approaching waitress that he was expecting two more guests. Taking a long sip from his pearl white mug of decaffeinated coffee, he stared off into the distance. His eyes seemed fixated on the young waitress cavorting with her loser of choice behind the busy counter. Gavin was the youngest of the four. His pedigree stirred the drink of the posh Harvard crowd, drawing him instant access to anything he wanted. His family tree had strong, deep roots in the Harvard political scene that earned him privileges. He had a degree in law, as well as marine biology. Darrin had brought him aboard, under Daniel's firm, steady guidance. Darrin always had a knack for bringing together unique talents, and Gavin's wealth of knowledge in law would prove useful, as Darrin's various contracts would need Gavin's fine-tooth comb.

Gavin was a reckless, impatient daredevil at times, usually going against the grain, and a maverick of the ocean. Darrin and Daniel occasionally attempted to harness some of Gavin's youthful energy, and distribute it throughout the rest of the group.

Gavin had several experiences during his Harvard tenure that had smoothed out some of his rougher edges. However, his tendency to leap before looking consistently had drawn the attention of Darrin, and soon after, Gavin would be under the mentorship of the older, wiser and grounded Daniel Locke.

Gavin's youthful face sported scattered craters from acne endured during his highly active and volcanic teenage turmoil. A healthy mane of brown hair rested atop his head, controlled with heavy doses of Johnson and Johnson conditioning mix. His wiry frame was hidden underneath his bulky desert brown cargo shorts and faded pink T-Shirt from the Newport Aquarium in Connecticut.

Daniel scooted in the booth, eagerly awaiting Darrin's arrival. At twenty-seven, and with a decent four-year advantage on the younger Gavin, Daniel brought a technical advantage to the crew, utilizing his three-dimensional thinking process in the field. He always studied every angle, every frame; every square inch of water came under his obsessive scrutiny. As a seasoned cameraman, editor, producer, and innovative computer programmer, he was solely responsible for the award-winning "money" shots for Darrin's National Geographic specials.

Daniel was bulkier than Gavin, a man fighting inevitable weight gain. His short five-foot-six frame barely supported the two hundred and thirty-five pounds clinging to him like white on rice. His stubby fingers were sometimes a hindrance when it came to editing and preparing the camera for fieldwork.

Nevertheless, Daniel was always pinpoint professional and rarely turned in an amateur project. His details for perfection ignited Darrin's passion as well, and the two men quickly became close friends. The last several specials in particular had brought them closer than before with their deep trust and loyalty to each other. Darrin trusted Daniel with corralling Gavin's rogue behavior, which at times, was reminiscent of Darrin's own maverick attitude when it came to hunting and fishing for sharks.

The diner's throwback pleasant atmosphere became its trademark. A handful of televisions mounted around the diner made easy viewing for the breakfast crowd. Or, for the afternoon and night customers, a healthy dose of sports, news, and other assorted shows.

Red cushioned booths stretched out across the perimeter of the diner, adjacent to the long bar, where many sat chatting endlessly with the bartenders and wait staff. In the center of the diner, tables were scattered about, usually seating up to about four or five people at a time.

Gavin was particularly fond of window seats and scooped up the second booth from the door, enough for six to eight people. Danny was chatting about something he saw in the papers the other night, but Gavin's attention fixed on Darrin's entrance to the diner.

"Darrin! Ashleigh!" Gavin called them over with a short whistle. "I've got a table right here!"

"Do you have to announce his entrance to the entire diner?" Daniel asked, while he turned to greet his employer. "Darrin," he said with a short nod. "Ash."

"So, what's going on?" Gavin asked. "The call was short, abrupt, and I have to admit, a bit intriguing."

The middle-aged waitress came to the table, her white pad ready for the order. Her wrinkled index finger and thumb tapped the pad with eagerness to star the order. "Breakfast? Coffee?"

She addressed the group with a definite sign of job burnout.

"Coffee," Darrin was curt. "Black."

"What a smooth talker he is," she snapped back. "And for you dear?" she asked Ashleigh.

"The same," she said. "And a small stack of flapjacks. Blueberry, if you have them, please." Ashleigh nudged Darrin.

"You got it. And for the two of you?"

"Ah, raisin bran and fresh orange juice for me," Daniel said. "I need a fiber uptake."

"Right," she said. "That was a bit personal, but thanks for sharing."

"I'll have two eggs, over-easy, a coffee with cream, no sugar, and a side of your trademark Maplewood smoked bacon," Gavin gave his order. "Thank you."

"Manners, a lost art," she said, looking back at Darrin with a flick of her pen.

"Anyway, what's up?" Gavin banged the table.

"We might have a problem," Darrin was direct and to the point.

"Problem?" Gavin asked. "You didn't call me out here for just any old problem. This has to be grand-daddy of them all."

"Earthquakes," Ashleigh cut in. "Darrin's afraid the Muppet's patterns have been disrupted."

"Oh, I see, our residential sharks," Gavin said, a bit deflated. He was hoping for something with a little more punch. "You couldn't say that over the phone?"

"I want to be sure they are okay with the sudden 'quakes," Darrin responded. "I don't need the gang going haywire and shifting their patterns. It could have devastating effects on the entire Bay Area."

"That could happen," Daniel joined the conversation. "If they shift a few miles here, or there, they could begin to attack a whole new area without our knowledge."

"Exactly," Darrin said. "We need to explore that possibility as well and attach stronger frequency monitors. We need one with a longer range," he paused, "there's some wicked new technology out there."

The waitress brought the meals over, and once again looked at Darrin. "Would you like another chance?" Her voice scolded him.

"For what?" Darrin raised his head.

"I don't know," she paused. "Perhaps some manners, or an order of eggs?"

"Oh," Darrin said. He stared at the rest of the group, then at Gavin who was sitting directly across from him. He reached over and grabbed up a fistful of Gavin's crispy pepper bacon. "Yeah, better make one of those for me too. Please?"

"That's better," she said, changing her demeanor toward Darrin.

"Thanks." Darrin stuffed more of Gavin's bacon in his mouth.

"What the hell?" Gavin flicked away Darrin's greasy hand.

"Hey, it looked good." Darrin slapped Gavin on the shoulder

"Guys," Daniel broke the mood.

"What's up Danny?" Darrin asked. "Got some ideas for more footage?"

"No."

"What then?"

"Um, take a look at that," Daniel urged the group to watch the television.

"Oh shit," Gavin blurted.

"What?" Darrin spun around and craned his neck, fascinated with the newscast. "Oh shit," he repeated. He shot up, dropping bacon in his lap, and headed over to the bar. "Can you please crank that up?" he asked the waitress behind the counter.

"Only because you said please," she said.

"Come on," Darrin was sharp.

"Whatever," she snapped back. "There. Are you happy now?" She asked, watching as the foursome gathered around each other and stared at the screen, emulating a horde of brain dead zombies. "Okay, this is fucking weird."

Darrin, impatient with the waitress's feeble attempts at turning up the volume, reached over the counter, and pounded the volume button a few more times.

Charlton Coulter the lead anchor for Channel 7 News, burst on the scene with the breaking story. The veteran newscaster was dressed to the nines in a sharp black shirt, black and white checkerboard tie, and a tan only hours completed. Charlton's whitened smile brightened the room; his rocky demeanor did not. A rigid man well immersed in the mid-life crisis portion of his life, he routinely showered his fragile ego with frequent trips to the gym, black hair dye to eliminate the onslaught of grey, and excessive hours under a tanning lamp.

"Citizens of San Francisco, I have breaking news to report," Coulter delivered in a matter-of-fact tone. *"The Golden Gate Bridge became the scene of a grisly death earlier this morning. Local authorities are now diligently investigating, scouring the tragic scene for clues to what happened. Details are sketchy, yet we here at Channel 7 can confirm from the detached remains of a young male, that his name is Trey Darwin of Bodega Bay."*

Coulter momentarily paused while the station displayed live footage of Golden Gate, complete with their flying news copters, floodlights, and random close-ups of the San Francisco Police Department.

"Reports from the SFPD confirm that a brutal accident sent Mr. Darwin's car careening from the bridge and through the now demolished guard rails into the bay below. Witnesses attest to Mr. Darwin's odd behavior, abruptly stopping in the middle of the bridge, and several failed attempts were made to save this young man's life."

Coulter shuffled his papers, staring at the camera, itching for his dramatic close-up. "That's when witness saw them," he *paused for effect. He raised his voice louder than before. "That's right ladies and gentlemen. Channel 7 News has this EXCLUSIVE amateur video capturing the vicious scene in the water. It might be a good idea to shuffle the young ones off to bed before viewing this mature content."*

Coulter took a deep breath. "Okay," he continued. "As you can plainly see, this college student, who prefers to be called "White Doug", captured three rather large dorsal fins breaking the surface moments after Mr. Darwin's car plummeted in the bay. I've never seen anything like this before. The raw magnitude of these sharks, and how they pulverize this young man's car under the water is mesmerizing to say the least. We can catch a glimpse of their shadows, moments before they deliver the fatal attack."

"Now, I urge the citizens to let the San Francisco Police Department do their work as they go through the proper channels in locating and killing these sharks. I understand that with the Fourth of July only three days away the city of San Francisco doesn't need this kind of negative publicity."

After a brief sip from his bottled water, Coulter wrapped up the special report.

"I will be consistent and thorough in my research and dedication to this story. I have been in talks with management to let me roam the sidelines on it. For our next newscast, I will be in the field with the San Francisco Police Department, gathering crucial information, so you, the viewing public, can stay informed and safe for the summer season."

One more shuffling of papers that, although Coulter wouldn't admit it, were always blank. They were merely props for his intellectual bid at stardom.

"This is Charlton Coulter, the official postman of the news. If there's a story out there, I will find it, report it, and deliver it to you."

"Did you see that?" Gavin harped. "Did you fucking see that?"

"Which part?" Ashleigh replied. "Charlton's tan or the fact that three sharks are responsible for that young man's death."

"Well, yeah, I was referring to the sharks." Gavin paced about. "Shit, shit, shit. What if they're *our* sharks?"

"That's exactly why I'm here," Darrin said. "If they are ours, then we have a serious problem on our hands."

"Do we even have a plan?"

"Ash and I will head to the bridge and meet up with the police," Darrin said. "You and Danny-boy head over to the station and see if you can scoop up a copy of that footage. Danny, analyze it, pixel by pixel, and see if we can detail anything about the sharks," Darrin urged.

"Got it," Daniel said. "Come on Gavin, ride shotgun with me."

Gavin called out as he prepared to exit the diner in a rush, "Then what?"

"Meet us back at the research facility on the islands," Darrin added.

"What about the bill? This isn't a dine-and-dash business!" The waitress demanded.

"Pay her, Darrin. I'll square it up with you later." Gavin's voice trailed off in the street.

"Here." Darrin recklessly slid a small wad of money across the marbled counter-top, not waiting for a response, while he hurried outside.

"Do you want change?" The waitress flipped through a small stack of twenty-dollar bills with a surprised look on her face.

Golden Gate Bridge
6:58 a.m.

"**R**eed, what the hell's going on?" Rick Chatham asked. "I'm missing the Luther Castle marathon for this." The rain tapered off, bouncing off the hood of the sheriff's idling patrol car. Reed Davenport killed the engine, jerked the keys from the ignition, and held them in the center of his palm.

"They have one-third of the San Francisco Police Department, and all of the Sonoma Police Department here searching for this poor kid," Davenport said. "We have the bridge's roads, and even the docks covered."

"So, what exactly happened here?" Rick asked, staring out across the bridge, squinting his eyes at the revolving flashing lights. "We have ambulances, police cars, and a fire truck. What the hell happened out here?" He repeated with deliberate impatience.

"According to the call I received, a nasty car accident pushed a car over the bridge and through the guardrails, and then," Davenport paused. "This just aired on Channel 7, exclusively, with that dickhead Coulter reporting it." Angered, he turned the I-Phone sideways and pressed play. The phone displayed an image of the disturbing newscast from moments earlier.

The small video clip displayed the shark attack; a somewhat murky image of the predators in the bay.

"Are those sharks?" Rick craned his neck to catch a better view.

"Supposedly," Davenport replied. "Which means that douche bag, Charlton Coulter will be sticking to the SFPD like a tick on a dog's asshole."

"You really despise that guy don't you?" Rick noticed his friend's distaste for the prominent and pushy newscaster.

"He's just scum. Filthy, barnacle feeding scum is all."

Bottlenecked in traffic, Darrin flicked through the radio stations questing for a decent tune. "Jesus jumping Christ," he slammed his fist on the cream-colored dashboard, grazing the base of the toy Leprechaun. If touched in any way, the small bobble head Leprechaun shimmied from side to side.

"Darrin, please calm down." Ashleigh tried to soothe him. She down shifted the dark red 2008 Ford Mustang into second, hoping for a chance to open up the engines. Her hand released the gearshift that had a silver dog biscuit with 'Warthog' etched in the black knob.

"Would you look at this traffic?" Darrin pointed out, already impatient.

"What do you expect, a clear lane?" Ashleigh asked. "A major crime scene is underway for crying out loud."

"I want to get there and talk to the police."

"Soon enough," she said. "They aren't going anywhere."

"A clear lane would be nice," he said with a chortle. "Or I'm gonna scramble over the roofs of these cars until I get there."

An ambulance screeched through the right lane, two lanes over from their car.

"There!" Darrin pointed. "Follow that ambulance!"

"Are you smoking crack?"

"Give me the wheel," he urged.

"Hold on," she said, diverting her course. A few middle fingers later from the other drivers, Ashleigh skidded her car to the furthest lane, briefly dragging the passenger side against the metal girders of the bridge, dragging red slivers off the door. Sparks sizzled before she regained control of the brand-new car. "Shit Darrin, she's a virgin," Ashleigh slammed the steering wheel. "That's coming out of *your* paycheck."

"Man, I picked the wrong day to quit drinking cough medicine," Davenport mumbled, peering up at the breaking sky. "Here comes the Calvary," he paused, "the news Calvary that is."

"Eh, don't worry about them," Rick soothed over Davenport's flaring temper. "Let's hope," his words were cut short.

He approached the two from behind, like a rattlesnake hiding in the tall grass.

"Gentlemen," his greeting was drama queen-esque, bordering on a runaway egotistical train ride.

"Charlton, you sly fuck," Rick mumbled loud enough for the news reporter to hear.

"I see they finally took off the ankle bracelet." Davenport twisted around, raising his hands in front of his face shielding the morning's sunrise. "Allowed to go out in public, are we now?"

"Quit the shit," Charlton chided. "You haven't liked me since that article I wrote about you five years ago."

"Perhaps," Davenport said. "Or, and let's try this on for shits and giggles." He walked over and faced Charlton. "There are some people I don't like, and some people I do. Wanna know where you fall?"

"I don't have time for this," he scoffed back. "I have a story to report on."

"Then go back to the gym and work on that tan," Davenport harped. "It looks like it's starting to fade."

"I was sent here to cover this story," Charlton addressed him. "And, I'm not leaving until I uncover what happened here."

"Very well then," Davenport seemed to bend, but refused to break. "Grab your stuff."

"Stuff?"

"Yeah," Davenport said.

"Shark repellent, and lots of lotion," Rick interjected. "It's gonna get pretty hot out there on the water."

"Water? I'm going out *there*?" Charlton pointed to the bay. "In the bay?"

"If you want the story, then you're gonna have to get your feet wet," Rick said, "No pun intended."

With both hands, Davenport took out his sunglasses and slid the arms over his ears. "And, keep up. I'm not slowing down for a silver spoon son of the network president."

"Do you hear that?" Charlton asked, looking in Rick's direction.

"Besides your brain smelting?" Davenport chided.

"It sounds like a very fast car," Charlton said, spinning and trying to locate the noise.

"It's a bridge Sherlock, there's nothing *but* cars."

"This one's coming from the west," Charlton surmised. "That would be right behind you," he briefly paused, "Sherlock."

Releasing a craggy cough and mumbling the word 'cocksucker', Davenport slowly turned around, with Rick following his lead. Both men froze, taking in the cherry red vehicle barreling straight for the yellow roadblock.

"Are you crazy!?" Darrin screamed.

"You said you wanted to get to the scene," Ashleigh said, shifting the cherry-red Mustang to fourth, then fifth. "I have an open lane."

"That's because the police closed all traffic to the bridge," Darrin responded. "It sounded like a good idea at the time."

"Hang on," she warned.

"Those are police issued roadblocks Ash," Darrin said, "they're there for a reason."

"I know," she answered.

"If an ambulance can out-run a Ford Mustang--" he said.

"Shut up, shut up, shut up," she ordered. When it came to speed and driving, Ashleigh enjoyed her playground of freedom. She loved opening up along the coastlines with her dog and taking in the California breeze.

"Boss, they're not slowing down," Rick said.

"Yeah, that's a problem," Davenport's response was drier than ink toner.

"I'm going to hang out with the EMT's, and scrape for some info," Charlton excused himself from the hectic scene, and sought out the paramedics.

The Ford Mustang broke through the roadblock, scattering yellow wood everywhere. The driver slammed on the brakes, skidding to a jerky stop on the misty bridge.

Standing several yards away, Davenport and Rick let a sigh of relief escape.

The driver's side door popped open, then the passenger's.

"Is that who I think it is?" Davenport asked.

"Who?" Rick still couldn't make out who the hell Reed was talking about.

"The guy," he replied.

"What about him?"

"Hey!" Davenport shouted out to the two reckless drivers. "What the bloody hell are you doing out here? This is an active crime scene."

"I know!" The man called back. "I'm here to talk with Sheriff Reed Davenport!"

"I figured as much," Davenport quietly replied, just loud enough for Rick to hear.

"Who is this guy? And the girl?" Rick asked.

"Well, Rick," Davenport began, "the girl is our resident marine biologist, Ashleigh Wilkinson, who double dips working for the United States Fish and Wildlife Service."

"And the guy?"

"Darrin Coyle," the man answered back, successfully closing the gap between them.

"Oh, the shark guru." Rick finally put the pieces together. "Sorry, my brain's a bit waterlogged from the alcohol."

"Which means," Davenport said.

"Which means what?" Rick repeated.

"Two things. One, if Darrin's here, and Ashleigh's here, then our situation has taken a turn for the worse."

"What's the second thing?" Rick asked.

"The circus is in town," Davenport added.

"Sheriff," Darrin offered a gentlemanly handshake.

"Yeah, what's all this about?" Davenport quickly returned the gesture. He knew exactly what it was about; he simply adhered to the professional greeting.

"Who's this?" Darrin asked, pointing at Rick. "Can we trust him?"

"He's my right-hand man," Davenport said.

"Oh, he's your deputy?"

"Not quite," Davenport answered. He was beginning to chafe with impatience.

"So, what is he then?"

"Someone who can be an extra pair of hands."

"Okay, enough said."

"Why are you here?" Davenport asked once more.

"We have reason to believe your recent earthquake may have jarred my sharks' senses," Darrin quickly explained.

"Your sharks?" Davenport queried him.

"We've been tagging three great whites the past few years," Darrin added. "Two males, one female."

"I'm not bringing them to dinner," Davenport fired back. "I couldn't care less about their sexes."

"Ashleigh's been working with me, and we've been monitoring their feeding and mating patterns," he continued, "with this recent quake, I fear they might have detoured and quite possibly have caused this attack."

"Attack?" Davenport asked. "What attack?"

"The one on the news," Darrin said. "I saw the piece on the news."

"Well." Davenport rubbed his gruff five-o'clock shadow. "I'm at a loss here."

"I say we let them in," Rick said. "I mean they claim to be shark experts, and if they can help us, then we can all return to our scotch and San Francisco Giants."

"The SFPD's in the process of raising the drowned car from the bay as we speak," Davenport said. "Feel free to take a peek at what's inside, outside, or whatever you documentary guys do. I mean, why not? Charlton's here as well, so what's another two for the ride?"

"I appreciate that, Sheriff," Darrin acknowledged.

"I might have something else for you to take a peek at," Rick diverted his attention to Ashleigh.

"Which is?" She wanted to know.

"A dead body."

"Really."

"Yeah," Rick said. "By the way, I'm Rick Chatham."

"Ashleigh Wilkinson."

The two returned pleasant handshakes as they made their way to the edge of the bridge, looking out over the sun-drenched water.

"Aren't you the famous surfer?" she asked, finally placing the face with the name.

"Yeah, and the former Sheriff of Sonoma County."

"I never noticed," she said. "No offense?"

"It was a rough ride at the end." He watched a patch of seagulls swoop down over the bay and pluck out a school of unsuspecting fish.

"Tell me about the body," she said. She studied the former sheriff. *He doesn't wear a wedding ring, or even a tan line on his left ring finger. His hands are tough, manly. He also wears the rugged beach look well in his denim jeans and a faded orange Hawaiian shirt.*

"Torn apart," Rick said. "If I wasn't blitzed, I'd say it was the Boston Strangler, or Charles Manson, or some sick fuck like that."

"But?"

"But I've patrolled these beaches before, I've witnessed sharks in the water," he said, "I know what a shark can do."

"Really? Are you like a shark whisperer?"

"Can we change the subject?" Rick abruptly ended the conversation. "Do you want to take a look at the body, or not?"

"Yeah, once we're done here."

"Fine." Rick tapped the railing and briskly walked away, leaving Ashleigh to ponder her ill-timed sarcasm.

"Wait, Rick," she tried to call out to him, but he was already back at the patrol car, squawking with the sheriff and Darrin.

Sheriff Malcolm Loomis
San Francisco Police Department
7:15 a.m.

The gathering of EMT's, police officers, several news reporters, and the coroner, divided in two halves, for the Sheriff of San Francisco to come through.

"Sheriff Reed Davenport?" The officer addressed his fellow colleague on the other end of the crowd. His voice dominated the scene. He was the man with the hardest punch of all them combined. No one ever second-guessed, questioned, or butted heads with him.

"Sheriff Malcolm Loomis. What's going on with your search?" Davenport asked. "Any luck?"

"We're pulling up the car now," he said while surveying the scene. His hands reached deep inside his pocket and pulled out a crumpled up black bag of M&M's. A quick reflex popped several inside his mouth. He continued to crunch away on his candy while Davenport answered the question.

"That's always a start. Looks like your Celtics are doing better than my Giants," Reed attempted a friendly barb.

"Another world championship," Loomis said. "That's what? Twenty-four?" He added another round of candy to his waiting mouth, clacking down hard on the colorful treats.

"I guess," Reed said, "does it really matter?"

"The Giants bankrolled their future on Bonds," Loomis replied, "but, they couldn't overcome his ego, or his alleged 'roid use."

"So," Reed diverted the conversation to police business. "Anything else?"

"As a matter of fact, I'm receiving word 'bout another incident." Sheriff Loomis was a man steeped in wrinkles with a shaved head and steady weight gain. A few more years remained before retirement would become a reality.

Loomis, a veteran cop, was brought to San Francisco from Boston, after Davenport slid across the counties, and became Sonoma's new sheriff. Through his western transformation, Loomis couldn't shake his thick Boston accent. A faded, yet still visible Irish green Boston Celtic tattoo, was tucked underneath his short-sleeve shirt, emblazoned on his pale Irish skin. At times, when he waved his arms around, it would peeked out and exposed itself.

"Another incident? Is it water related?" asked Davenport.

"Yeah, it looks that way," Loomis continued. "Listen, I need to wrap my hands around some sort of expert." He ran his hand over his bald head bringing his hands down over his face, then gave a sharp tug of frustration to his anvil-shaped beard. "Do you know anyone?" He finished off the bag of M&M's and stared out across the busy bridge.

"In fact," Davenport paused, looking over at Darrin and Rick chatting up a storm on the other end of the bridge. "That guy over there," he said pointing in Darrin's direction, "is the world famous Darrin Coyle, shark investigator and film maker."

"I'm not interested in filming a shark movie," Loomis snapped back. "I want to solve this case and head back to the office."

"Neither am I." Davenport's dry response always shook Loomis by the roots during their conversations together. "But, he's sort of you know, a shark expert."

"What are you chattering about, Reed?"

"He's already tagged several sharks in our area, and now he fears they might be responsible for this tragedy."

Turning to face the water, Loomis bristled his jaw, dislodging a chipped M&M from his back molar. "Correction," he seethed. "We're facing more than one tragedy."

Across the bridge, Darrin was intrigued by Rick.

"So tell me about yourself." Darrin formally introduced himself to Rick.

"Not much to tell," Rick said. "I'm a former professional surfer, former sheriff, and currently I adorn the breath of an alcoholic."

"And don't forget to mention you've found something of interest." Ashleigh popped up behind Rick.

"Oh, do tell what's up your sleeve, magic man?" Darrin requested information.

"What's with the names?" Rick asked.

"Oh, he does that. You know, stick a quirky name to everyone," she said. "He calls me Ash."

"Anyway." Rick's voice was curt and short. "I found a body, a dead body, on the beach."

"A dead body? Why would that seem interesting to me?"

"I don't really know." Rick's tone turned sarcastic. "Perhaps it's because the body's littered with teeth marks."

"From what?" Darrin pressed.

"I got frisky," Rick snapped back. "My house money is on a shark. A really nasty one at that."

"Why do you say that?"

"I've never seen a body ripped apart like that before, especially in a shark attack."

"You've piqued my interest magic man," Darrin said. "When can we see this body?"

"Soon. After we find out what's going on here."

"Sounds good," Darrin said, leaning forward and stretching out his hand. "I'm here to help, and appreciate you taking the time to tell me these startling things."

Rick quickly returned the handshake. "Yeah, no problem." His hands trembled, a sign he was starting to crave his alcohol intake. He needed a drink in the worst way.

"Tragedies?" Davenport, caught off guard, couldn't absorb the information fast enough.

"That's what I said, Reed." Loomis flexed his fingers, working out the tightened kinks from the previous night's shift. "Why don't you pay closer attention?"

"What makes you think that?"

"My deputy and his boy were out in the Whaler, doing a routine sweep of the bay, when he found fragments of the San Francisco-Alcatraz Ferry."

"Did you just say a ferry?"

"Yea' and it wasn't pretty."

"Explain."

"The ferry was demolished beyond anyone's comprehension," Loomis said. "We've found two survivors."

"Who?"

"The pilot, eh, his name escapes me for a minute, and a small boy named Jack."

"Would the pilot's name be Winston Arkham?"

"Yeah, yeah, that's the guy," Loomis answered, snapping his fingers. "Poor bum's missing his arm."

"From what?"

"I dunno. Maybe a shark? Details are a bit sketchy ya know?"

"After we dredge up this car, we'll take a look at the ferry." Davenport turned his attention back to his own squad.

"Listen," Loomis said. "Once we have the ferry or the remains of the ferry at the wharf, I'll buzz you, and you can bring your expert. I'll also hold off questioning the old man and the boy until you can get there."

"I'd appreciate that," Davenport said. "I have to be honest. We found what looks like a shark attack victim on the beach. Rick

Chatham found the body."

"Chatham? Shit, what's he up to nowadays? Still frisking the bottle?"

"That's none of your concern," Davenport sharply answered. "He followed protocol and notified me, Jonas and Slim minutes after finding the chewed up remains."

"Corpse. Who was it?" Loomis was intrigued.

"We believe it to be Cody Kincade."

"Shit, that's not good. The Pro Surfing Competition's only two days away. We have to work together on this." Loomis again ran his hand over his entire face. "We need to slam a lid on this kettle, before it blows up in our faces."

"I agree. I will keep you informed on my end as well."

"Later." Loomis waved his hand in the air, and headed back to his men.

Davenport called out. "Rick." He briskly walked over to Rick.

"Yeah," Rick answered back.

"Gather the troops," Davenport said. "The new guy and the girl."

"Why?"

"We have something else brewing," Davenport said.

"Besides our dead surfer?"

Davenport lowered his voice. "Yeah, keep it on the hush."

"Keep what on the hush?" Charlton interrupted.

"Nothing. Bug the fuck off." Davenport turned, placing his hand on the reporter's chest, and carefully stepped him away from Rick. "Give us our thirty-five feet of personal space."

"I can smell a story a mile away," Charlton angrily pouted, "and, there's one floating right here."

"I think Sheriff Loomis had some information, go pester him."

"I'll be back to finish our conversation." Charlton stormed off.

"Anyway," Davenport redirected his conversation at Rick. "It seems Loomis has found Winston's ferryboat, and it's being brought to the wharf as we speak. If you want to take a look at it, I'll set up a time."

"Wow, anything else?" Rick's hands continued throbbing.

"Winston and a small boy named Jack survived."

"Are they ready to talk about what happened?"

"Hopefully real soon. Loomis will contact us when he's interviewing them."

"Sounds good. Can I be a part of it?"

"It's fine by me. But I think Loomis still has some reservations about your current state of mind. You know, with the drinking problem, and incessant flirting with the lovely beach goers."

"It's California man." Rick beamed. "What else is there to do?"

"Well, start drinking coffee for one, and pack that pecker back in your shorts, because we have some serious shit going on here. I'm going to need you at a full throttle for this one Rick. Are we clear?"

"Yeah, sure. Clear as the morning daybreak." Rick shook off his trembling hands. "Detox is gonna be a bitch."

"Jesus crickets, Gavin. What do you think it is?" Daniel asked.

Gavin let the black and silver Honda Pilot bump harmlessly against the white sidewalk trim. "I don't know," he said, grabbing the keys from the ignition. "But the boss wants us to take a look at that tape from last night. Between the two of us, we ought to figure out what exactly happened down there." He hopped out of the driver's seat and closed the door.

Daniel scooted out his side of the Pilot and jogged to keep up. "I don't think the tape operator's going anywhere," he said. "He's probably in the middle of the seven o'clock newscast Gavin."

"Better yet," he said, "we'll catch him by surprise."

They entered the studio's foyer through the spacious main doors. Gavin pushed hard against the glass, smearing his fingerprints all over the recently wiped down surface. Daniel made it just as the door began to close.

Gavin's brisk pace continued annoying Daniel, but he refused to become rattled at Gavin's obsessive-compulsive disorder, when it came to completing the task at hand. Daniel's pace continued slowing as he huffed his way across the foyer.

"Good morning, dear." Gavin brought the charm to the idle receptionist.

"Good morning." She replied with a cardboard tone and no eye contact.

Gavin couldn't help but think if her overwhelming sugary sweetness was obtained from hours of watching the orientation videos during the hiring stage if her employment. "I need to speak to the manager of the station. It's very important." Gavin's quirky mannerisms resembled a hyperactive preschooler.

Daniel cut in. "Dude, calm down."

"I'm fine," Gavin reassured him. "I'm relaxed."

"What's this all about, sir?" the receptionist asked.

Gavin chuckled as he stared at her red and blue uniform with the television station's logo plastered across her left chest pocket. "It's concerning Mr. Coulter's sizzling newscast."

"Oh." She paused, and then reached for the telephone. "It was definitely a ratings success. He has such a way with words, and his delivery." She continued heaping praise on the veteran newscaster. "His delivery sweetens the ears, you know?"

"The manager, please?" Gavin tapped his fingers against the

marbled counter and stared at the collection of clocks across the wall behind the desk.

"What's your concern?"

"I really hate to divulge this information." Gavin paused, and leaned in close to the receptionist. He caught sight of her silver name badge. "Mary, can I call you Mary?"

"I guess so. That's my name."

"We work for National Geographic."

"Yeah, okay. I work for Batman." She held up an okay sign with her fingers.

"Honest, we work for Darrin Coyle. Have you ever heard of him?" Mary carried her youth well. Gavin guessed maybe late twenties, at best.

"The shark guy?" Mary's interest perked up.

Ah, yes. Now, we were getting somewhere. Gavin's first impression was right on target. Mary's head had to be full of cobwebs. "That would be why we need to see the footage from Coulter's newscast."

"Rough around the edges, isn't she?" Daniel offered in his two cents worth of opinion.

"Ya think?" Gavin quietly snorted.

"Hold on." Mary picked up the phone. "Mr. Madison? I'm sorry to bother you, but I have some people here who say they are working with that shark guy from National . . . ," Mary's voice trailed off. "I see, sure, I can do that."

"So, what did Mr. Madison have to say?" Gavin asked.

"He's ready for you. Just head down that hallway right there," Mary instructed, pointing to her left. "He's the fourth door on your right."

"I appreciate this," Gavin said.

"No sweat." Mary smiled.

"She was cute." Daniel looked back at Mary as they walked down the hallway.

"I suppose so. She's not really my type."

"What *is* your type?"

"I'd rather not get into it with you," Gavin said.

"Why not?" Daniel asked, while he counted the doors. "Here it is, fourth one on the right."

"Because you'll find it strange."

"Try me," Daniel said.

"I prefer short women."

"Why is that strange?"

"Short women," Gavin again answered, emphasizing the word

short.

"So, what are we talking about? Five-four? Five-three?" Daniel tapped his knuckles on the door's white speckled window pane.

"No."

"Shorter?" Daniel seemed surprised.

"Can we just go in and talk with Madison?" Gavin urged Daniel to drop the subject.

"Come on, I want to know."

"Jesus crickets, Danny," Gavin started losing patience. "I like short women. Let me try and put into simplistic terms you can understand. I have an addiction for little people. I have a thing for midgets." Gavin's voice escalated from annoyance with Daniel's prodding of the personal question.

An uneasy feeling swept over Gavin and Daniel.

Standing there before them was the station's manager, Mr. Rudolph Madison.

"How can I help you gentlemen today?" Madison greeted his stunned guests.

"How much of that did you actually hear?" Gavin asked.

"I'm a trained news reporter," Madison said. "I hear and see everything."

"Shit." Gavin muttered.

"But luckily for you." Madison paused. "I'm not looking at a story about a grown man's obsession with carnival people."

"Oh thank God." Gavin felt relieved and played along with Madison.

"Please, come in." He ushered in his guests. "Darrin Coyle sent you, is that correct?" Madison walked over to his large oak wood desk. "It's a bit overwhelming isn't it?"

"What is?" Daniel asked, pulling up a chair.

"All these awards, accolades, appreciation for my dedication to bringing the Bay Area cutting edge news every day of the week," he said. Madison sat down and withdrew a small bottle from his desk drawer. "Does anyone want a drink?" He shook the half-empty bottle of scotch.

"Jesus crickets, does everyone drink that shit in this town?" Gavin asked. "It's like an epidemic out here."

Madison briefly smiled. "Only the important people." He poured himself a shot glass. He watched them stare over his pictures, wondering how long he was at the station. "To whet your appetites, I've been in this field for over thirty years, twenty-five spent right here at the illustrious Channel 7. Many consider me a dinosaur, but my vision is irreplaceable. And last night, under my expertise and veteran leadership, we courted the best story of the year. Shit, perhaps the fucking decade!" He took a quick sip of liquor. "A fatalistic trio of sharks in the Bay Area, on the eve of Fourth of July weekend." He paused, raising his shot glass in the air. "And we're only days away from the biggest surfing competition in the entire country. You talk about high-octane drama. It's human interest in every sense of the word."

"Wow, it seems you pretty much have your finger on the pulse of 'Frisco," Daniel said. "But let's cut through the self-serving resume, and focus on why we're really here."

"The tape," Madison said, sipping another round from his glass.

"Yes, that's correct." Gavin flexed his hands, cracking out the rigidity in his knuckles. "I want to watch that exclusive footage you claim to have under lockdown."

The three men shared a short burst of forced laughter. All three were playing their own angles in the case.

"Listen, I'd like to be a bit more cautious in such matters, however, since it's been plastered across the entire country, I really have no leverage to keep it from you," Madison said, rising and motioning for his guests to follow. His long frame carried him well as he briskly walked across the room. "I'll bring you to the editing room where the footage is stored on our hard drive. From there the two of you can study each frame until your eyeballs explode."

"You certainly have a way with words," Daniel said.

"Or you'll enjoy the ruthless cycle of boredom. In any case, editing is a repetitive boring process," Madison said.

"Yet it's the backbone of the entire media industry," Gavin pointed out.

"I always hated the scholarly type." Madison enjoyed a friendly spar with Gavin.

Gavin countered with his own brand of sarcasm, "Yeah, me too."

"This is our video operator, Chunk," Madison offered the brief introduction. "It's a nickname we all came up with."

"Because of his weight?" Gavin asked, staring at Chunk's rather obese frame. Each one of his ass cheeks hung over the sides of the exhausted office chair.

"Chunk prefers his condition to be called," Madison fumbled for the rest of the words.

"Genetically superior," Chunk said.

"Yeah, I always forget that," Madison said. "Listen, I need a favor from you."

"Yeah, what's the good word?" Chunk's pleasant demeanor seemed out of place with the rest of the high-octane performers in the field.

"He's a virgin isn't he?" Daniel asked.

"A virgin?" Madison wasn't following the thought process.

"How long have you worked here?" Daniel asked.

"A while," Chunk replied.

"Well, you're still drinking vitamin water, and eating cranberry-almond salads," Daniel said, taking inventory of Chunk's leftovers.

"You can tell all that from what the guy eats and drinks?" Madison asked.

"Yes, I can. And his cleanly shaven face, recently bought clothes, and lack of rings underneath his eyes. I'd say maybe a few weeks at the job?"

"Yeah, you got me man. I'm new here." Chunk relented. "I'm an intern from UCLA."

"You have a sharp eye, son," Madison said, pulling over some more chairs.

"Give him another month or so, and he'll switch over to coffee, a five-o'clock shadow, wrinkled clothes, and rings under those pearly blues of his." Daniel flexed his own muscles predicting Chunk's path of employment destruction.

"Easy Danny," Gavin said, scooting across the floor on the chair. "We need him for right now, at least. After tonight he can search for a new job."

"Funny, real funny," Chunk said. He swiftly moved his sausage-like fingers across the black control bus, bringing up three separate screens of the shark footage.

"Chunk, I'm impressed," Daniel said. "The way you dominate the control board's buttons," he paused, "you remind me of Billy frickin' Joel."

"I am the Piano Man," he said, with a short burst of laughter. "And this is my baby."

"Well then, play your music," Gavin interjected. "Let's see these bastards up close."

"Okay, here's what the amateur managed to catch on tape," Chunk said, bringing up the car on the bridge.

"Yeah, yeah," Gavin impatiently waved on the useless footage. "Get us to the frame when the car crashes into the bay, please."

"It's coming," Chunk said. "Wait for it."

"There," Madison said, tapping the screen with the shot glass still in hand. "They are right fucking there."

The men watched Trey's car careen into the bay. The rear of the car bobbed in the water like a cork for several moments.

"Over there." Gavin jumped from his chair in excitement and tapped the screen. "Check out those fins," he said.

"Looks like two?" Madison squinted at the screen.

"Three, there's fucking three of them," Gavin muttered. "Shit, Darrin's not going to like this one bit."

"Why, what's the problem?" Madison asked.

"Off the record," Gavin insisted.

"Off the record," Madison concurred. "Scouts honor," he said, holding up his fingers.

"You were never in Boy Scouts." Gavin sized up the manager. "You never spent a day outside in the woods, did you?"

"No, no I didn't."

"Okay, then at least you get points for honesty."

"So what's up with the trio of sharks?" Madison asked. "I'm going to run a story on this, but I'll leave out anything said in this room."

"Darrin's tagged three great whites in the area," Gavin said. "He's been watching them for quite some time, and monitoring their behavior patterns."

"Okay," Madison replied. "How does that affect us?"

Gavin tied the pieces together. "That earthquake you had the other day. Darrin feels that could have shifted his sharks' behavioral patterns."

"Does he think the sharks could be responsible for the attack on the ferry?" Madison asked.

"What ferry?" Gavin asked. Before Madison could answer, his cell vibrated. "It's Darrin. He's sent a text message."

"What does it say?" Madison asked.

"He mentioned an accident involving a ferry and said we'll chat later. How's the video footage coming along?" Gavin quickly pounded out a return message to Darrin.

"Is he always this quiet?" Madison asked, referring to Daniel's silence.

"It means he's thinking. He's analyzing data. It drives me fucking nuts when he zones out like that."

"What does it mean?"

"It means he's found something," Gavin said.

"Can we go back to the bridge?" Daniel finally spoke up after minutes of staring at endless frames of footage.

"Yeah, sure." Chunk brought the bridge back up on the screen. "Why?"

"What are we looking at here?" Daniel asked the group.

"Uh, cars," Madison responded.

"I'll bite and play along," Gavin said, with a short grin. "What are we staring at Danny-boy?"

"Chunk, tell them," Daniel said.

"Uh, shit." Chunk grumbled. And then he saw what Daniel was talking about. "I see it," he said, "I see it." He moved his fingers across the control bus, and highlighted the quadrant directly to the left of the bridge. "Yeah, this is what I signed up for." Chunk's voice hardened with confidence. "This is the section right here?" he asked, dragging the box across a large section of water underneath the bridge.

"You got it," Daniel said. "I think it's time you removed 'the intern' from his title and gave this young man the job."

"Why is that?" Madison asked, unable to see what Daniel was referring to.

"He's just found you not only your next story, but the identity of one of the sharks."

I t hit the Golden Gate Bridge with the force of a hurricane. Everyone saw it coming. It was only a matter of time. Moments after Coulter's fierce reporting on the amateur video captured what resembled great whites in the water, the mayor slipped out of his custom-made black Dodge Charger, furiously spewing his apocalyptic political venom at his interns and aides.

Dressed in a fitted black dress shirt with a piano key tie, Mayor Harrison MacTavish made his presence known. A golden wristwatch, a gift from the city of San Francisco's Police Department for his recent crime initiatives, dangled loosely from his skinny almond colored wrist. His slacks were pressed to the point of exhaustion (and his usual obsessive-compulsive mannerisms). The middle-aged politician wasted no time addressing the crowd.

Sheriff Davenport introduced himself. "Mayor, it's a pleasure to see you again, sir." He offered his hand in kind gesture.

"Yeah," the mayor grumbled, shaking his hand meekly. "What the hell's going on here, Reed?"

"We have a situation."

"I saw that early this morning on Coulter's newscast. I nearly choked on my breakfast."

"Mayor!" Sheriff Loomis quickened his pace across the bridge, eager to kiss the mayor's ass.

"Loomis," MacTavish's demeanor changed. He had always admired Loomis and his willingness to do anything the mayor demanded of him. He was, for all intents and purposes, Loomis's puppet master. MacTavish always had the fingers working the strings on Loomis and countless others.

Davenport cut in. "I was about to bring the mayor up to speed."

"Ah, yes." Loomis circumvented Davenport's bravado. "I'll be happy to do it."

"I'm sure you would," Davenport shot back. Leaning in close, Davenport whispered 'ass kisser' in Loomis's ears.

"Anyway," Loomis continued, "where do you want me to start?"

"At the beginning," the mayor said, "and please be quick. I have a luncheon to attend."

Rick grabbed the attention of his friend, "Reed."

"Yeah, what is it?" Davenport was clearly pissed off at Loomis sucking on the mayor's ego like a baby on a bottle.

"Does the mayor always dress like he's at a movie premiere?"

"I . . ." Davenport's mouth curled up, holding back a laugh. "Yeah, I guess so. He definitely fits the bill of a Mafia kingpin, doesn't he?"

"Probably. Why is he here?" asked Rick. "There are no votes out here for him to secure."

"He wants to sniff around the scene, no doubt. Like a dog in search of a bone, he wants to be the first one to deliver the loudest bark."

"They finally have the car up," Rick said, slapping Davenport's shoulder. "Let's go have a look at it."

"Okay, but be warned, MacTavish's fingerprints are going be all over this one."

MacTavish questioned Loomis. "What are they doing over there? Is that the car from the video?"

"Yeah," Loomis said, "they brought it up for us. We're going to study it with our shark guy."

"We have a shark guy? I didn't realize I signed off on that in our budget."

"Well, sir, you can't live in shark country, and *not* have a shark expert readily available as a tour guide."

"That's why you're not mayor, Loomis. You have logic embedded in that tiny brain of yours. Money talks, positions walk. Get used to it. Yours might be next."

"Anyway, that's him over there. Davenport and Chatham are pretty chummy with him. He works for National Geographic, and from what I understand has some solid connections with the local marine biologists." Loomis cradled another package of M&M's in his hands. "It's my lucky day," he said, showing the mayor the bag of candy. "I must've stuffed an extra one in my pocket."

"How fortunate for you and your crazy addiction." The mayor tightened his tie and walked forward. "Well then," the mayor said, and pulled back his face in a forced political grin. "It's time to meet this shark expert."

"What a bang up job." Rick let off a low whistle. "Shit, those sharks were fucking hungry."

"This isn't normal," Darrin said, joining Rick and Davenport alongside the bridge's rail. "Not normal at all."

"What's not normal?" The mayor's voice shook everyone in their shoes.

"And you would be?" Darrin asked.

"Mayor of San Francisco," MacTavish's stubborn tone made it obvious he wasn't one to be played around with.

"Dressed like that?" Darrin asked. "It looks like you're ready for the red carpet."

"I said the same thing earlier." Rick snickered.

"Dammit! Enough already with the comedy hour--If I wanted humor, I'd watch the fucking Comedy Channel. I'm more interested in the shark tank below." MacTavish pointed to the idle bay below the bridge.

"I'm Darrin Coyle. I work for National--" the mayor cut off his introduction.

"Loomis already brought me up to speed. Give me one reason why I don't scuttlebutt your ass back to whatever rock you crawled out from." The mayor adjusted the diamond cuff links on his shirt. "Experts like you are a dime a dozen."

"Because I have three resident great whites tagged in the area, and I believe they could be responsible for this attack, and quite possibly the ferry attack as well."

"Ferry attack?" The mayor bristled. "What ferry?"

"Yeah, I was going to debrief you on that one," Loomis said.

"What's wrong with the ferry, Loomis?" The mayor demanded an answer.

"We don't exactly know sir," Loomis replied. "We think it could be another shark attack."

"Hey, shark guy, what can you do for me?" The mayor stared at Darrin. "Can you navigate me through this minefield?"

"I have some thoughts. I have several options."

"Options. Like what?"

"For starters, you have a national surfing competition beginning in just under two days."

"Your point?"

"My point is this," Darrin said, "if I don't find out what's happening under there," he pointed to the water's surface, "then you might as well ring the dinner bell for those sharks."

"Dinner," MacTavish was abruptly cut off by Darrin.

"In the world of checks and balances, budgets and summertime profits," Darrin continued hammering the mayor, "if these sharks continue swallowing tourists, then you can not only kiss your July Fourth weekend goodbye, but your entire summer season will shit the bed. And two shades of red you don't want to see will be abundant - blood in the water and on your hands, and the red on your business ledger. Your polling numbers will plummet like an arctic chill, leaving you unemployed and looking for your next meal."

The mayor, stunned, fumbled for the right answer.

Darrin raised an eyebrow. "Am I talking your language now?"

"I can keep this under wraps until the competition is over," the mayor fought back. "This was one isolated attack," he paused. "I have a yacht party planned for tomorrow in the bay to kick off the holiday weekend."

"And what about the ferry?" Darrin demanded an answer.

"We don't even know what exactly happened out there." MacTavish shrugged his shoulders.

"And if it was the product of a shark attack?"

"Then we fabricate a story that spins the truth. It's politics after all." The mayor was losing ground in the argument. "This surfing tournament on Friday brings substantial revenue and media coverage to our area. I'm not going to let some shark story thwart my plans."

"You really are a media whore aren't you? What kind of story are you going to fabricate?" Darrin pressed the mayor's buttons.

"I heard there are some killer pods out near the Farrallon Islands," the mayor consistently took refuge in lying when it best suited his needs.

"Really?"

"Yeah, that's what my people tell me."

"I have my fingerprints on everything that happens out here." Darrin closed his distance to the mayor. "And I say your people are full of shit."

"Whale pods," the mayor again repeated. "I can control this."

"Do you really want to be the mayor who fucked up the entire Fourth of July weekend in Bodega Bay?"

The mayor backed away from Darrin. He paced back and forth, vigorously rubbing his tanned face with his hands.

"You're good. You're very persuasive," he replied, shaking his finger. "This has to be the most heated debate I've had since the primary elections."

"I have my moments," Darrin said.

"Then share one of your moments with me. What can we do about this problem?"

"Authorize me and my team full access to anything we need to catch these sharks." Darrin proposed. "You're going to have to open your checkbook a little bit," he continued.

"I hate to admit it, but you just might be the key that can lock the doors on these predators and keep my town in business."

"**A**re you going to fester all day, Cruz?" the man asked his friend.

"Maybe." Cruz shrugged his shoulders. "I just want to get back to the boat."

"A bet's a bet," the man said. He reached down and touched his hairy toes. Stretching his caramel-colored arms high above his head, the younger of the two grinned. "Listen, you made the stupid bet."

"I know, I know," Cruz said. "Goddamn this water's frigid." He dipped his uneven toes in the surrounding water. He shuddered from the biting cold. "I'd like to keep these black swim trunks perfectly dry." He stalled for time. "Can't I take you to the bar, or a club, or an afternoon movie?"

"No." The man walked alongside the prison's walls. "In any case, you said, and I quote," the man taunted his friend, "'The Lakers in five games.'"

"I did say that," Cruz replied. "I thought they'd crush Cleveland in the finals."

"It was your idea to swim from Alcatraz. We're trespassing for sure, so let's hurry up."

"But do we have to swim out there?" Cruz pointed to the calm waters ahead.

"A bet's a bet." The man again paced the prison's rocky perimeter.

"How far?"

"Five miles."

"Jesus, Marco," Cruz said. "I don't think my arms can hold up that distance. I went to the gym earlier."

"Okay, okay," his friend said. "I'll make it four. If you go the extra mile, I'll forget about the hundred bucks you owe from our last bet."

"I should have bet the Cavaliers," Cruz crossed his muscular arms and sucked in a breath.

It broke from the pack, slicing through the dark, murky water. Its senses were high-strung for a predator its size. At thirty feet in length, it was the smallest of the three great whites. The animal's sleek design enabled it to conjure up bursts of speed and power through the water. It honed in on frequent splashing in the distance.

"Cruz, you are crazy," Marco shouted across the bay.

Cruz, already in the chilled bay, felt a nuisance on his lower calf. He half-heartedly entered the water, ripping a thin patch of skin from his calf. A small patch of jagged rocks was the obvious culprit. A series of small droplets of blood seeped into the water.

The shark, only a few meters away from its prey, drew open its snarling mouth, ready to strike. The rapid movement of the water sent him into sensory overdrive. The predator clamped down on the lower half of its prey, spurting blood everywhere and poisoning the blue waters. Twisting, then jerking the stunned prey from side to side, the shark thrashed about one final time before delivering the fatal attack.

A small scattering of cries rushed to Marco's ears. He dangerously pivoted on the prison's rocky perimeter scanning the waters for the turbulent screams. "Cruz! Cruz!" He couldn't find him anywhere.

Marco watched Cruz's blood-soaked head break the red, shimmering surface, a dark pool of blood surrounding his friend. "Swim, Cruz! Swim!" He lurched for the water, ready to swim for him.

Marco cringed while the dorsal fin broke the surface, heading straight for Cruz's flailing body.

"Cruz!" Marco took to the water and dove underneath the surface. His frantic movement alerted the rest of the pack.

Spreading out his arms, Marco sliced through the water, feet away from Cruz.

Cruz's body continued floating in the water, shredded skin trailing behind him.

"Shit, what the fu–?" Marco reached his friend, spinning Cruz's half-eaten body around.

Marco felt something gnashing against his ribs right before a spiral of blood rose through the water.

His father was an experienced fisherman and had told him stories of shark attacks and their ingenious blueprints when it came to hunting down their prey. He knew the swift painful hit was a classic "bump and run" from a shark, a tactic used to determine whether or not he was a threat. Marco knew his chances at survival were running thin.

He began his retreat back to the prison. From the peripheral he caught sight of three dorsal fins emerging from the water, several yards away. They were closing fast on his position, choking off his escape route. Refusing to panic, Marco kept the course, hoping the sharks would move on.

"This isn't right," he said. "They shouldn't be hunting in packs."

The sharks turned and powered ahead, determined to strike.

Marco did his best to brace for the hit.

The first shark slammed Marco with the force of a locomotive, sending him hurtling through the water, landing with a hard splash several feet away.

The second shark, who had initiated the fatal "bump and run", ripped off a moderate chunk of flesh from Marco's lower torso.

Screaming, Marco clutched his side, stabbing his fingers on the ends of his splintered rib cage. His blood spilling by the quart brought the final shark to the attack. The smaller shark's teeth, still riddled with Cruz's skin and bone, clamped down on Marco's legs, severing them right below the knees. Satisfied with the strike, the shark swam away, allowing the other two predators to finish off their dying prey.

For the next hour, Darrin remained fixated on the mayor's stubborn ideals. How could a man with substantial political clout let the bay suffer from multiple shark attacks during its peak holiday season?

"Where are we headed to now?" Darrin asked Davenport while he walked the bridge. "I'm getting restless."

"Darrin, they're bringing the ferry and the car to the landing at the end of Fisherman's Wharf." Davenport said. "Do you know where that is?"

"Yeah, I do," Darrin said.

"Need a ride?"

"Nah, I got Ash and her wheels."

"What's up guys?" Ashleigh rejoined the group. She was careful balanced several cups of coffee.

"Yeah, what did we miss?" Rick asked, reaching for his cup, then nursing long sips of the elixir.

"Are those for us?" Darrin asked, pointing to the white and beige Green Mountain Coffee Styrofoam cups.

"Yeah, we went for a coffee run. Rick said we'd need the jolt of caffeine." Ashleigh handed out the rest of the cups. "Black for you Darrin," she said, holding it out for him. "And for you, Sheriff, I ordered up a regular with cream and sugar."

"That's fine, dear. Thank you." Davenport reached for his coffee.

Darrin felt his cell vibrate in his pocket. "I have to take this," he said, sliding away from the group.

"Who is it?" Ashleigh asked. "Is it Gavin?"

"Yeah, hold on Ash," Darrin said, pressing the cell to his ear. "Gavin, what's up, man?"

"Darrin, we have a problem."

"What's up?"

"Well, we're here at the station with the manager and editor," Gavin said, "and we've poured over the anchorman's newscast."

"What did you find?"

"Daniel was in his zone, and found a quadrant on the videotape."

"A quadrant? How does that exactly help our cause?"

"Daniel found one of the sharks and blew up their face on the screen. You should have it momentarily on your cell."

"Is it one of our sharks?" Darrin asked. A small beep alerted him to a new video text message.

"You'll see for yourself."

"Listen, I'll call you right back. I'm going to take a look at it now."

Darrin ended the call and pulled up the picture of the shark.

"Is it?" Ashleigh asked.

"Not one of ours," Darrin said with a touch of defeat in his voice. He was hoping it was one of their sharks. He turned the phone so she could get a better glimpse of the shark. "I've never seen this one before. It seems to be a different caliber of shark."

"We definitely have a serious problem," she agreed.

"Can I send this to you, and you can blow it up even more at the research center?" Darrin asked.

"Yeah, you betcha." Ashleigh sipped from her coffee. "I can work on that right now. Are you headed out with the guys?"

"Yeah I am. We're headed over to the wharf to study the ferry and the car. Not my definition of hanging out with the guys, but it'll do for now."

"It's the quality time, right?" She grinned.

"Do you need help with the project?" Darrin sipped his coffee.

"Nah, I'm good. Why?"

"I'd like to have Gavin and Daniel with me down on the landing with the evidence."

Ash motioned for him to go ahead with his plan.

Darrin quickly dialed back Gavin.

"I'll call you if I find anything." She raised her coffee in a respectful toast.

"That sounds fine. We're hooking up later anyway to monitor our sharks, so I'll just knock on the door when we get back to the research facility on the islands." He bid Ash farewell.

"What's the plan shark man?" Rick joked, prodding Darrin with his elbow.

Darrin turned to Rick. "I'm going to round up my men, and we will meet you there in a bit," Darrin said. "They're leaving the television studio as we speak."

"What did the mayor have to say about the sharks?" Davenport joined in the conversation after taking a short coffee break.

"Yeah, what did Mr. Fantastic say?" Rick asked.

"He basically blew me off," Darrin said, "until I changed course and began to speak in his forked tongue."

"Economics." Davenport shook his coffee. "That bastard always listens when dollar bills are involved.

"Exactly," Darrin said. "The mayor finally made the correct

decision to give me unlimited access to research the bay and try and save his precious holiday weekend."

"Wow," Rick let off a low whistle. "Talk about swallowing your own set of balls."

"He choked on them, that's for sure," Darrin replied, taking a final sip from his coffee.

"Alright, this is the plan gentleman," Davenport said. "We will be inseparable. The ferry and the car, the two eyewitnesses, we do all of this together. Keep each other in the loop. A tight loop at that," Davenport's demeanor was solid and stiff. "I don't want anyone, especially that cocky Coulter, or even the mayor to get their hands on any information, and if they do, it won't be from our camp."

"Gavin and Daniel have to be in the troop," Darrin said. "As I am quite aware, your deputy will be as well."

"Correct. And Rick and Ashleigh, but that's it." Davenport scanned the bridge for any sign of Coulter. "I'm not running a day camp for shark hunters."

"So what do you think?" Rick asked, approaching the passenger side of the police car.

"Shit, we're royally fucked Rick," Davenport placed his coffee on the car's roof. He then placed his palms down and furiously tapped the roof with his fingertips.

"How so?"

"Think about it."

"Alright," Rick said, leaning over the roof, and craning his neck to listen to Davenport's point.

"Darrin has the mayor allowing free reign for his research team." He paused. "Then we have the ferry crash, where only two people survived, the Golden Gate car crash, and some amateur videotape capturing the shark attack in real time."

"Do you think we could have a major problem on our hands?" Rick knew the answer, but hoped the crisis could be swept under the rug somehow.

"Shit, and Cody's dead body is the cherry on the damn apple pie. Whether it's a shark, or not, something is definitely responsible for all this crazy shit. It could even be a bi-polar whale, or maybe a Frakenfish," Davenport added with a grin.

"You watch a lot of really bad science fiction movies don't you?" Rick asked. "Definitely a lot more than I can ever cram in my waterlogged head."

"Let's see what the landing holds for us." Davenport tapped the hood one final time, then ducked in the car.

Rick bounced onto the passenger seat and closed the door. He worked the seat belt over his shoulder, clicked it, and then turned to Davenport. "Just think, if this shark shit is real, then it will be the first time my nightmares occur when I'm sober."

Fisherman's Wharf added character to the eclectic atmosphere of San Francisco. A history rich in tradition, the wharf now became a home for many businesses and commercialized industry. Television shows, movies, and even documentaries all shared in the historic feel of the area, adding their own theatrical touch. The popular television show *'Nash Bridges'* filmed entirely on location in San Francisco and along the wharf.

Sheriff Davenport pulled in, slipped the keys out of the ignition, and reached for his pair of sunglasses. "Here we go," he mumbled.

He made his way across the hot, black pavement. It was only mid-morning, but the entire area already roasted under the western sun.

"Jonas!" He called out to his Deputy. "Jonas will be spearheading this end of the search," he whispered over to Rick. "It'll keep him out of our hair."

"Thank you," Rick said, keeping pace with Davenport's long legs. "We really don't mix well."

"I can tell."

"You know, Darrin's probably going to want to inspect Cody's remains," Rick pointed out.

"Slim's already on it, like pecker stains on a bridal dress." Davenport sneaked past a wave of teeming citizens and found Jonas smoking a cigarette. "Jonas," he greeted him.

"Sheriff," he warmly acknowledged his superior. He took a thin drag on the cigarette. "Rick," he scoffed, his tone soured for Rick's presence.

"Hey, Jonas. You have a tendency to roll your R's," he chided right back.

"Anyway," Jonas said, flicking the cigarette off in the distance. "The car and the ferry are both in Docking Station A, right over there."

A slight drizzle pranced off the blacktop, leaving behind a thin layer of mist. San Francisco, usually a sun drenched city, now suffered through periodic rainstorms and higher temperatures.

The large ash-colored building, capable of housing many boats, would soon become the central building in the sheriff's ongoing investigation.

Rick entered the Docking Station right behind Davenport and

Jonas, surveying the entire area. The remains of the ferry and the car were sitting in the center of the station.

"Shit, look at that damage," said Rick. "What could've done that?" He walked up close, inspecting the jagged edges of both mauled vehicles.

"I'm hedging all bets on some type of animal, perhaps a shark," Davenport said. "Jonas? Any ideas fermenting up there?"

"A shark's a definite probability," Jonas answered, "I'd say wait for the shark expert to arrive."

Rick's steps were deliberate. The red car was first, the entire chassis of the mangled vehicle had snapped with the delicacy of a wooden matchstick. The remnants of screws, metal shards, fractured glass, and a whitened bone caught in the fabric of the driver's seat alerted Rick to investigate further.

"We have a glimmer of evidence," he called out to Davenport and Jonas. "I'd say a decent piece too." Rick snapped on his plastic gloves to preserve the integrity of the scene, and plucked the bone from the rear of the driver's seat.

Davenport and Jonas leered over Rick's shoulders as he finally wrestled the tooth from its resting place. "Well, can the rest of the class see your discovery?" Davenport chided his friend.

"The triangular shape, and jagged contour calls up my expertise," Rick said, peering at Jonas through the shattered side view mirror.

"Expertise?" barked Jonas. "Are you fucking kidding me? Rick's the residential town drunk, and his version of justice resembles a beaten down tread on Slim's tires." Jonas kicked the car's tires. "Hey, Sheriff, did you notice the damn tires are fucking flat?"

"We're going to have to set aside our differences, Jonas," Rick answered with a sharp tongue, turning around and holding up his discovery. "Because this my friend is a shark tooth, and not your everyday great white tooth. This fucker's from something bigger than our residential whites. And if you keep setting up roadblocks and nonsense chatter when it comes to my expertise in this investigation, then we're going to have a serious problem, junior."

"I see I've frayed some nerves, Rick." Jonas smiled.

"I've seen a great white up close. I've smelled its breath, stared in its eyes, and felt its soul devour my hope." Rick scuffed his feet against the cement floor, "But this tooth--" his words were interrupted by another man's voice.

"That tooth could belong this fellow here," Darrin's voice

echoed from the hangar's entrance, a glossy photograph in his hands.

"How do you know that?" Jonas asked, blocking Rick's rebuttal.

"'Cause when junior here smiles for the camera, he's missing a tooth."

"Really? Do you enjoy mocking my intelligence?"

"Actually, it's quite refreshing," said Darrin. "I honestly believe the shark in this picture could be the owner of that tooth right there." He shook the picture in Rick's direction. "Excellent job, Rick!" Darrin shouted, beaming with a healthy respect for the veteran sheriff.

"Yeah, I thought so," added Rick, both men cutting Jonas off from the conversation.

"That looks like it's about twelve to thirteen centimeters in length," Darrin inspected the object. "A Megalodon's smallest tooth measured roughly 1.2 centimeters in length, and the largest, over seventeen centimeters, close to seven inches."

"I'm growing impatient with this process," Jonas urged Davenport to take action.

"I agree," Davenport answered, sliding a batch of dollar bills to Jonas. "Would you mind heading to Jimmy's Bagel Café and grabbing us some breakfast? I'm lethargic on an emptied stomach."

"Yeah, I need the fresh air," Jonas said, snapping the bills from his boss.

"And, Jonas?"

"Yes."

"Take the scenic route, enjoy the morning sun," Davenport offered a weak smile, political enough to matter, personal enough to rile his deputy.

"Nice move, Sheriff," Darrin said with a quick wink. "I brought my team, I see you have yours."

"Yeah, what have we learned so far?" Ashleigh asked from the rear of the group. "I couldn't stay away. I love field trips."

Rick brought her up to speed. "We've captured a tooth from the driver's seat, and Darrin believes it's part of a missing link of sharks if I followed his explanation correctly. I'm still nursing a bitch of a headache, and the coffee has yet to kick in."

"Here." Darrin handed the tooth to Ashleigh. "What do you think Ash?"

"I can say it definitely, absolutely, positively, doesn't belong to our pack of whites," she answered, turning the tooth clockwise.

"It's also not a Meg tooth."

"That much I figured," Darrin responded with a smirk. "I think we could be dealing with a missing caste system of sharks."

"What are you suggesting?" Ashleigh handed the tooth back to Darrin. She had an idea of where he was going with his hypothesis.

"These sharks could be the missing link between Meg and our modern day whites."

"That would be a historic discovery," Ashleigh countered. "Imagine the possibilities if we were able to capture and examine such a specimen."

"We're going to need to orchestrate a choreographed study of these sharks, preferably before the surfing competition on Friday," Darrin replied.

"This car's a wreck," Gavin surveyed the damage. "It's definitely not one of our sharks."

"Really, do tell." Darrin walked over, with Ashleigh and Rick close in stride.

"Well, the impact suggests these sharks are somewhat bigger than ours," noted Gavin, his hands showcasing the brutalized damaged.

"We concur," Darrin and Ashleigh responded.

"And that tooth Rick yanked out demonstrates what could be the missing chapter in the lineage of the shark."

"I've already covered that idea," mocked Darrin. "Anything else?"

"I'm going to need to go over the car with a fine-tooth comb." Gavin's eagerness energized the team.

"Has anyone checked out this carnage of metal over here?" Daniel's voice emerged from his seclusion by the battered ferry.

"We're making our way over there," Darrin suggested. "Why? What did you find, Danny my boy?"

"Well, something big, really big attacked this ferry, and what's left of it deserves a closer look." Daniel waved them over.

The team approached the mangled ferry, staring at the shredded stern.

"What the fuck?" Rick shuddered at the sight. "There's blood all over these propellers."

"And something else." Daniel used a small pocket flashlight to illuminate the three-pronged propeller. "What does that look like to you?"

"Human flesh?" Rick craned for a better look. "Damn, it's pretty dim in here, ain't it?"

"There's some type of grey matter caught between the blades." Daniel looked over at Darrin. "It looks to have a rough texture to it."

"Shark skin?" Darrin asked.

"Can we draw such luck?" Ashleigh also took a peek at the new discovery.

"I'm thinking so," added Darrin. "Can you get this specimen back to the lab and run some tests against our own group of whites?"

"I'll do that right now," Ashleigh offered, "let me go get my kit."

"You need some help with that?" Rick offered, always searching for a way to work with Ashleigh. His growing fondness for her elevated his desire for getting up in the morning.

"You betcha," she answered.

"Okay," Davenport rejoined the group. "What's going on over here?"

"We were just leaving to grab Ash's kit." Rick slapped him on the shoulder. "I'll be joining her back at the lab, while you play principal with the rest of the group here."

"Lovely," Davenport shrugged off Rick's slap. "Darrin, clue me in." He worked his way toward the team, enjoying their excited chatter.

Rick and Ashleigh soon returned with the necessary instruments for collecting the data. Ashleigh slipped her gloves over a pair of calloused hands, a result of her marine job. Her lips sucked in as a rather cheery Beatles tune hummed through. Rick, although still mired in a post-depressive alcoholic funk, admired her upbeat attitude.

"Are you always this upbeat on your job?" Rick cradled his half emptied coffee cup.

"Oh, are we ready to seduce me with your charm?" She continued securing the DNA sample from the propeller. She knew how to offer a good ribbing. It was a skill she had adopted from her older brothers.

Rick almost blew lukewarm coffee through his nostrils. "Excuse me? Seducing you? Ha!" He peered over her shoulder, observing the process.

"At least that horrid, repulsive scent is gone from your salty breath." Ash offered a meek smile of victory.

"Well now, who's seducing who."

"I do enjoy a good slathering of booze from time to time, but not to the point that my skin bleeds liquor and my breath is flammable."

"Point taken," Rick said. "I fell on the sword of depression and angry passion. That alone would swallow anyone up in its wake of destruction." He paused once more for a drink of coffee. "I've always been in a frenetic search for that elusive elixir to repair my damaged soul."

"I'd say you've encountered such a remedy." Ash tapped the information into her Acer Iconia tablet and continued humming. She gazed back at him with a smile and a heightened flirtatious raise of her right eyebrow.

"Oh, this shark shit? I'm only here out of a complicated friendship with Davenport."

Ashleigh rolled her eyes and turned back around. "We should have some results shortly, back at the lab."

"Lady and gentleman," teased Darrin as he approached them. "What are we looking at with this specific sample?"

"It's still too early to digest the information." Ashleigh paused. "No pun intended."

Rick paced back and forth, still in desperate need for a drink.

Darrin brushed his palms against the side of his legs with rising impatience. "Rick here seems to be missing the bottle, so I suggest we all head to the coroner's office and take a peek at the body. We can analyze this DNA back the lab later over some mushroom and pepperoni pizzas."

"Yeah, that sounds perfect to me." Ashleigh glanced over at Rick. "Can you make it? You know, if you're not too busy with your active social life."

Rick squeezed out a sarcastic grin. "Order me buffalo chicken, and I'll consider it."

"Gavin and Daniel, go spy on that reporter and see if you can unearth anything else we may have missed," Darrin said. "The rest of us will catch up later at Ash's compound."

D aniel and Gavin kept a safe distance behind Charlton Coulter's speeding news van. "Where's he headed to now?" Gavin asked while Daniel rolled the car to a stop. The steeped hills of San Francisco provided somewhat of a decent defense for the duo, keeping their vehicle a safe distance behind the blue and white van, "He must be on a story." Gavin turned to Daniel.

"How can you tell?"

"He's headed in the general direction of The Rock," added Gavin.

"He's probably picking up that ferry scent from earlier," Daniel paused, "the one that was supposedly attacked by a white."

"Oh, yeah, the shark attack on the Alcatraz ferry," Gavin said, slapping his forehead. "I completely blacked out on that one."

"Let's keep a healthy distance between us," Daniel answered, slowing down the vehicle. "We'll grab the next ferry and catch up to him on the rocky beach of the prison."

The morning sun evaporated the last pockets of water from the night's misty rain. Charlton Coulter, never intimidated by any terrain, atmosphere, or other formidable force, casually made his way with his cameraman. "The sun's a raging gorgeous beauty today isn't she, Patterson?" Charlton asked.

"It's a great backdrop for the piece sir," the young cameraman answered.

"I'm going to be the leader for the San Francisco Reporter Award this year. This entire bay," Charlton paused for a brief smile, "is under siege by a savage great white."

"That's a great hook for the story," Patterson said. He continued prepping for the piece, double-checking his camera and equipment.

"Just make sure you have enough film to capture the gritty realism of the 'Beasts of the Bay'." Charlton had coined the phrase for his shark piece. "It has a horrific pull to it, yet it leaves one intrigued and interested in watching the segment." He squinted hard across the bay, soaking in the lazy morning sunshine. His hands cupped over his eyebrows eliminating the glare. He knew something had to remain from the ferry accident.

There had to be a portion of a dead body floating about or a fractured remnant of the ferry itself?

Charlton's impatience rattled many of his colleagues, yet they maintained their false sense of awe in his presence. Patterson was a different entity. Charlton knew Patterson's weakness: youth. Patterson, as Charlton figured, thirsted for knowledge, for that elusive adventure all cameramen and reporters dream about. Charlton capitalized on this.

Daniel and Gavin arrived to find Charlton pacing about the rocky terrain of Alcatraz. "What's that trouser snake searching for?" Daniel jabbed Gavin with his elbow.

"Probably another storyline. Either way, we need to pick his brain."

"If he even possesses one."

"Gentlemen," Charlton's voice echoed across the terrain.

"Fuck me," Daniel sniffed.

"What brings two high school punks to my world?" Charlton chided them.

"We, are not high school punks," Daniel responded.

"We," Gavin interjected, saving the conversation from heading down a path of harsh words, "we've come in a peaceful, professional truce."

"I wasn't squeezed out of my mother last night boys. Get to your point. Is it information you seek? Because if it is, then, well, we are headed down a whole different trajectory." Charlton released his breath in victory.

"Ugh, do we have to?" whispered Daniel.

"Yeah, it's what Darrin wants." Gavin returned his attention back the slithery reporter.

"Ah yes, the so-called shark expert." Charlton mused. "Haven't his tagged sharks done enough damage already? The ferry accident? The surfer? The dead teen in the bay?"

"Darrin's main focus remains the safety of the San Francisco Bay Area, douche," Daniel said with a raised tone. "He sent us here to gather any information you may have on the attacks. You know, since you're the king of the news sleaze."

"Well, at least you've recognized my talents," Charlton answered. "My fellow colleague and I are here to film and report on any development on the ferry attack."

"Don't you mean puppy dog?" Daniel chided the reporter back.

"He recognizes my greatness," said Charlton, "I can't fault him for that." He continued pacing the rocky beach at the foothills of the famous prison.

"If you threw a stick in the ocean, he'd fetch it." Daniel countered. He watched Gavin and the cameraman chat it up on the other side of the beach.

"Listen kid, I have an important piece to finish here and this conversation with you has seriously flogged my brain." Charlton snapped his fingers alerting his cameraman to come forth. "Patterson's raw ambition to be the best intern at the studio has paid off, you little shit. He's attached himself to the highest profile name in the business."

"So I take it you have no newsworthy information for me that an eight-year old couldn't Google on his IPad?" Daniel's eyebrows rose with a flair of sarcasm.

"Daniel, are we done here?" Gavin asked his partner. "I've hit a brick wall with Charlton, Jr. over there."

"Yeah, my stomach hurts now. This predator has no meat left on the bone. Let's head back to the mainland."

Charlton resumed creating his newscast with Patterson, twisting his head in different directions, searching for the perfect angle to deliver his story.

The sun-soaked morning had robbed him of slumber he needed badly after an ill-advised drunken tour of bars across the wharf with a marauding bunch of colleagues. He felt grimy and sweaty and the collection of amber-colored beer stains on his ivory white "Jaws" T-shirt served as a hazy reminder of his hard-core ways. No matter how much he tried to erase the significant parallels between him and former Sonoma County Sheriff Rick Chatham, Deputy Jonas Marsh crawled through the same underbelly of greasy bars, half-naked baristas soaked in alcohol, and rampant, forgettable sexual encounters. Jonas reacted with an immaturity that seemed to infuriate Sheriff Davenport after he received the sheriff's phone call imploring his deputy to scour the bay for further remains of Winston's drowned ferry. Jonas fumed at the thought of being an errand boy for this asshole. First he was going on a breakfast run back at the wharf for Davenport and his cronies, and now he was stuck out on the bay.

"Of all the lame-ass jobs," Jonas sputtered the words, his breath still saturated with beer and a double bacon cheeseburger from the local Whitebeard's Pub the night before. One of the pub's signature items was their burger. They made a fattening, juice-laden burger all the locals craved. Jonas swallowed two of the double burgers after a battle with famine overpowered his brain. A shitty day at the job, dealing with Davenport and Chatham being chatty like a pair of 49er cheerleaders had forced Jonas to drink himself rotten. A strengthened, rolling vomit-saturated hiccup had brought back the stinging memories of last night. Jonas heaved the remains overboard. Another vile eruption splattered across the bay, while a pack of seagulls screeched and circled overhead taking in the scenery below.

The standard thirteen-foot Boston Whaler cruised along, cutting the bay's calm surface in half. A pair of waves rolled with parallel precision on each side of the Whaler. Jonas squeezed his eyelids, blotting out the morning glare, and focused on the approaching prison. The aged landmark now served as a tourist attraction, yet it still became enmeshed in ominous events. He combed through his murky brain and headed for the approximate coordinates of the ferry accident. His hands guided the sleek Whaler along, a few yards from approaching his destination, when a weird holler echoed through the air. Jonas craned his stiff neck and took notice of a pair of intrepid reporters waving him over to the rocky beach of Alcatraz. "What the fuck?" He mumbled weakly. His tired hands returned to the controls, as he guided the Whaler back toward Alcatraz. "This better be good."

Jonas idled the boat and grabbed his black sunglasses. "What's up? I'm a busy man!" He cupped his hands around his mouth and hollered out from the boat.

"Deputy," Charlton answered back with vigor. "Am I to understand your little expedition today includes a ride out the ferry accident?"

"What?" Jonas was definitely bothered by Charlton. "How do you know where I'm headed?"

"Come on Jonas," Charlton said with a foxed grin, "don't play me for stupid. It's a small town with a loud mouth."

"I was thinking of another term," Jonas said with a snide grin.

"It's a small town. Thin walls. Money talks. I could go on and on." Charlton smiled with his victory teeth displayed.

"No, please don't. I've heard enough."

"Five minutes, that's all we ask. A few quick shots for my piece, and we're done."

"Can I shoot you if we go over five minutes? I haven't shot anything in awhile. My fingers are itchy."

Charlton recognized he had won over the deputy. His face revealed a victorious grin. Yeah, I'll even load the bullets myself," said Charlton. "Come on Patterson."

The bay appeared relaxed as it basked in the summer's late morning sunshine. Jonas and his new crew startled the bay's restful slumber with a series of annoying waves from the Whaler's churning wake. Jonas resisted the urge to knock out Charlton's teeth from the repeated verbal lectures on the sharks. Instead, he hummed an old Rolling Stone's tune and blocked him out.

Jonas guided the crew to the scene of the ferry attack about a dozen miles off the shore of Alcatraz. A day had passed since Jonas had rescued the captain and young boy. He hadn't paid attention to the wreckage at the time. Sheriff Davenport had decided to circle the wagons and return back to the crime scene after the survivors were taken care of. A few pieces were retrieved shortly afterwards, yet Davenport was getting heat from the mayor and decided to launch another perimeter search.

"Is this the infamous place the ferry was attacked?" asked Charlton, his hands adjusted his trademark sunglasses.

Jonas snapped back to reality, his ears picked up the tail end of Charlton's question. "Yeah, this is the general area."

"Excellent," Charlton replied with a cocky grin. "Patterson," he said with a snap of his fingers, "start rolling."

Jonas felt awkward. "I don't know, this doesn't feel right." His hands reached for his handgun.

"Relax," Charlton chewed through his crisp, dramatic monologue. "We're fine."

"What do you want to find out here?" Jonas asked.

"We need some establishing shots and maybe a piece of the ferry floating around." Charlton continued prepping. "Or, if we're blessed, a shark fin. Anything that will crush our rival networks."

"Jesus fucking Christmas, man," Jonas growled. "You're willing to risk being severed below the waist for a story?"

"It's the price of journalism, Jonas." Charlton smiled.

"If we come anywhere near a fucking shark, I'm shooting you in the head and using you for chum."

"Funny, real funny." Charlton's smile vanished as he turned to Patterson.

Jonas could hear him whispering something of concern. It pleased Jonas to have rattled this bastard's cage. The Whaler crept to a dead idle as he reached for his binoculars. A break in the surface of the calm bay attracted his attention. A brief hiccup over the side of the boat had finally purged Jonas from his night of hell. A quick wipe of his mouth with the backside of his right hand and he returned his eyes back to the break in the surface. A fractured piece of the ferry bobbed up and down. Jonas whistled a sigh of deep relief. For a moment, he had feared a dorsal fin was the cause of the break.

"I've found something a few feet away," said Jonas. His hands returned life to the Whaler's engine.

"A shark?" Charlton asked as he wrapped up the prologue to his report.

"Nah, it looks like a piece of the ferry." Jonas brought the group closer.

"Yep, that's what it is," Charlton said, disappointed. "A half-chewed piece of boat."

"Yes, but it seems our friends left behind some interesting

teeth marks, and there appear to be several missing teeth embedded in the bite marks. Maybe Darrin can analyze this." Jonas reached for the long pole to retrieve the evidence.

A dark, sullen quiet swept through the bottom of the bay. A pack of sharks roused from their brief rest swirled beneath the bay, hungry and impatient.

Jonas felt a cramp in his arms. "I'm shot to hell, do you mind taking over?" he asked Patterson. "You have some nice long limbs."

"Yeah, sure." Patterson handed the camera to Charlton. "My shoulders need a rest, boss."

"Whatever." Charlton turned the camera on the water to kill some time. "Come on. Show me some fin you punks."

Patterson stretched across the side of the Whaler and slapped the water with the pole, just a few inches from the debris.

The thunderous sound fueled their acoustic senses. A swift change of direction followed as the trio sent a school of meandering fish into a frightened frenzy.

Patterson missed the debris by a few inches, hitting the water with a weak splash. He resumed the process, and again just missed the target.

The fin sliced through the bay as it sped toward the errant splashing of water. The leader of the pack craved the hunt and its methodical swim would prove hard to defend.

Patterson felt the end of the pole's hook clamp catch some debris. A short tug assured his success and the debris dragged across the water. "I got it!" He called back to Jonas.

The shark burst through, its jaws widened for the inevitable strike. The monster's near forty-foot frame erupted from the depths of the bay and snapped off Patterson's right arm with lightning speed. The menace crashed beneath the surface and sent a geyser of red spurting across the bay.

"Shit!" Patterson screamed, his body teetered for a moment before he crashed into the water reddened by his blood.

The brunt of the shark's attack rocked the Whaler violently. Jonas and Charlton both collapsed to the deck in pain. A wave of red water cascaded over them.

Patterson bobbed in the water, his body in shock from the devastating attack. His eyes watched two more fins emerge from below. His legs went numb with overwhelming fear. His mouth tightened and his tongue swelled.

The Whaler had bounced too far away to swim to and Patterson was in no shape to embark on a heroic swim to the boat. His eyes remained fixed on the fins as they drew closer. Blood continued flowing from his wound. As the shadows grew larger, his voice finally echoed to Jonas and Charlton. "Sharks!"

And then it was over.

Patterson felt both legs snap below the knees followed by all warmth escaping his body. The sun grew darker now as his body caved in to the menacing predators. A short gulp of air filled his lungs before internal bleeding choked away the rest of his life and the sharks ripped him apart.

Jonas and Charlton gazed in horror as Patterson's body was yanked under and a short spray of blood scattered across the bay.

"What the fuck was that?" Jonas shouted, his face drenched in the bay's bloody water.

"It looked like a damn shark," wheezed Charlton.

"That thing had to be thirty feet," Jonas said. The Whaler vibrated once more. "Shit, do you feel that?" Jonas yelled.

"The vibration?" Charlton finally caught his breath.

Jonas braced for impact. "It's back."

"What is? The shark?" Charlton needed no further confirmation. A dorsal fin erupted through the waves and steamrolled right for the idle Whaler. "What now?"

"We die." Jonas watched the scarred shark emerge from the water, its mouth agape, and clamp down on the Whaler, slicing the boat in half. Jonas felt jammed inside the shark's mouth as it slammed back down to the bay, spraying the Whaler's remains everywhere. He felt the shark's teeth glide through his skin, filling its mouth with warm blood.

Jonas took a gulp of air before the shark brought him beneath the surface and headed toward the dark unknown. He kept punching and clawing at the beast's eyes, attempting escape.

"You are one ugly motherfucker," Jonas muttered through the water. He felt a slight disturbance and a grey body emerged from the darkness.

It was then Jonas felt the thunderous impact and then a sharp snap just above his waist.

His world spun out of control. A red swirl twisted around his body, only it wasn't his blood. He opened his eyes to find his shark fighting for its life. He absorbed one final image of what looked to be one of their residential great whites attacking the monstrous new predator.

H is hands released the crumpled dollar bill into the vending machine. Sheriff Reed Davenport slept uncomfortably all night and he was on a desperate search for more caffeine. A twenty-ounce bottle of Pepsi Max would do the trick. A few seconds of waiting for it to tumble down the machine, and then he reached in and emerged the victor. A twist of the cap, and a quick drink injected him with the needed boost.

"Any word from the kid yet?" Davenport asked his receptionist.

"No sir, no word from Deputy Marsh." She continued filing the morning's paperwork.

"Rattle your knuckles on that door down there when you hear from him," he said. His throat begged for another cool drink.

"The shark survivors are here and waiting for you in the interview room, sir," she said, never breaking her focus on the paperwork.

"Ah, you never do miss a beat do you?" He made his way down the hallway, exchanging several greetings with his staff on his way. He turned the knob to the interview room and with a gentle nudge the door swung open.

His weary eyes adjusted to room. "Morning," he greeted his visitors. "My name's Sheriff Reed Davenport."

"Sheriff," an elderly man rose to greet him.

"Please, sit." He motioned for the man to sit back down. Davenport quickly took notice of the man's grisly condition. Confined to a wheelchair, his lower torso had been severed from the grisly shark attack, and his right arm was severed beneath the elbow. The boy sitting next to him wore several scars across his face, neck, arms, and legs.

"I'm deeply affected by this entire ordeal," Davenport sucked in his words. His hands rested the soda on the table as he pulled up a chair. "Would you like anything?" he offered.

"Coffee, please," The man answered. "I like it black."

"I'd like two eggs over easy, some bacon, an orange juice, and slightly buttered toast," the boy responded with a small smile.

Davenport looked at the boy with a puzzled look.

"Well, I need the toast to soak up the eggs." The boy shrugged his shoulders.

"Give me a few minutes," He said, his fingers tapped the table.

"I'm guessing your Jack right?" He motioned to the boy.

"Yes, sir."

"And Winston?" He turned to the elderly man.

"Yes, sir."

"Are you sure you don't want some food?"

"Okay, you twisted my arm," Winston answered. "No pun intended. I'll take some blueberry muffins with a slab of butter."

"Now, that's what I'm talking about." Davenport smiled. "I'm feeling better knowing each of you are sharing in some humor today."

"Sheriff," Winston said with a hollow tone, "it's the only way the boy and I can heal from this terrible tragedy. A cloud of negativity will only slow our progress."

"Progress?"

"The healing process, sir." Jack again smiled before his mouth turned rancid with hatred. "It all begins when you kill that son-of-a-bitch that murdered all those people, and my father."

When Davenport returned with food and drinks he was still recovering from Jack's startling comments. "I have a few short questions, if you guys don't mind?" he asked as Winston and Jack enjoyed their meals with a delirious satisfaction.

"Well," said Winston, his hand wiped away a collection of blueberry muffin crumbs from his grey goatee, "we encountered a god damn nightmare out there on the ferry."

"Language please," Davenport replied with a stern look, all indications pointed at Jack's young mind.

"The kid just watched his father die out there in the bay and he displayed his true feelings to you before you left to run your errand," Winston grumbled. "So I don't think for a minute my usage of the word 'damn' will corrupt his mind. He's already scarred for life, the poor kid."

"Ok, point made." He took a sip from his soda. "What happened out there?" His eyes rested on Winston as he retold the horrific event.

"These sharks aren't normal, Sheriff," Winston answered. "These guys are fast, silent, and cunning."

"Not like our residential whites?"

"Not at all. These fuc--, er, I mean, sharks, coordinated the perfect strike on the ferry. They slammed us on all sides. Once the ferry buckled, and those poor souls went overboard, I knew hell had risen from the bay's depths." Winston took a silent drink of coffee, his eyes grew darker. "I don't really want to talk about it anymore, really."

"I understand," said Davenport.

Winston kept chatting however. "Once Jack's dad went under, he managed to drag one of the sharks into the propeller. I bet that one's messed up a bit in the face."

"Good to know." Davenport finished off his soda.

"I served in the Second World War, son," Winston's answer was pitched with a gruff tone. "I take the entire scene in and analyze everything."

"What happened after the propeller attack?" His mind swirled with information and curiosity.

"The ferry began descending." Winston's voice lowered for effect.

"We were trapped inside the captain's box," Jack added after he crunched down on the final piece of bacon.

"Captain's box?" he asked.

"Mr. Winston here made me his Co-Captain." Jack smiled. His face, although scarred and torn apart, retained Jack's infectious boyish charm.

"We were trapped, yes indeed." Winston grabbed the cup, still halfway filled with coffee. His fingers tightened their grip. "I saw them."

"As you were underwater?"

"Yes. These sharks are some sort of freaks of Mother Nature. A genetic mishap."

"Why do you say that?" Davenport inquired.

"What's the average length of a great white?" Winston asked. "Do you know?"

"They usually never exceed twenty feet," he answered, "in some cases twenty-five."

"Correct. These sharks were well over thirty, and great whites usually attack out of stupid curiosity." Winston clenched the cup even tighter.

"True."

"These sharks seemed wired to attack on all cylinders, and kept coming at us with such a relentless pace." The styrofoam cup cracked, spilling coffee all over the table.

"How did you manage to escape?"

"After they crashed through, I managed to pick away at them with my harpoon until everything went black."

"Mr. Winston here," Jack said with a sad tone, "he was attacked first. Jason got him first, right below the waist."

"Jason?" Davenport was puzzled.

"I punched and kicked Jason in the face, and then I must've scratched up my skin on his skin." Jack's eyes welled with tears. "But then something happened."

"What?" Reed was intrigued.

"Freddy and Michael disappeared, moments before another shark slammed into Jason's side. His jaws dropped, Mr. Winston, and I tugged him to the surface with all my might."

"That's where you were picked up?"

"Yes." Jack let a few tears roll down his face. He leaned in to Winston.

Winston returned the gesture and hugged the boy. "This kid saved my life."

"Why do you refer to the sharks by name, son?" Davenport was curious.

"My dad and I used to watch horror movies." An affectionate glow returned to Jack's face.

"Oh," said Davenport. He knew where this was headed.

"Jason, is the biggest shark, then Freddy, then Michael." Jack smiled.

"Oh, I understand," he said with a foolish grin. "You're ranking them based on their horror popularity?"

"Yes, sir," Jack answered.

"Well, I want to thank you for coming in today," Davenport said. "I want to catch up Darrin Coyle, our shark expert, on what you've just told me." He slipped his cell phone out of his pocket. "If Darrin wants to chat some more about this, are the two of you okay with that?" he asked with genuine concern.

"Will we be served lunch and perhaps dinner?" asked Jack.

Winston reached out for the boy, attempting to curb his youthful enthusiasm. "I think we're going to pass."

"Mr. Winston, sir," Jack said, "if we can help the police out then maybe we can save another son or father from these monsters."

Winston took a breath before closing his eyes. He then reopened them and brought the boy closer to his chest. "If that's what you want to do, Jack, I will not stand in your way of saving other lives from these sharks."

"Excellent," answered Davenport. "I will have the Whitebeard Pub serve up some burgers, fries, and soda pop for the two of you."

"Curly fries, please sir," Jack said with a smile. "I'm in the mood for curly fries, a double bacon cheeseburger, and some mac and cheese."

"Jesus," Davenport responded with a grin. "I'll call Darrin and put those orders in."

Winston cleared his throat as if he were afraid to continue talking. "I'll take a some fish and chips."

Davenport nodded his ahead in agreement. "You got it."

H is mind filled with details of Cody Kincade's ravaged body, he failed to notice the room. The tan curtains were tightly drawn to block the dim morning light. Slim Bennings, known for his meticulous design, categorized every bite mark, scrape, tear, bloodstain, and anything else he deemed important to the case. His team managed to rescue Cody's damaged board and had it brought back to the office for a rigorous examination. Slim's sharp mind always hungered for a new challenge. He knew Rick and Darrin were on their way. The office seemed a bit cramped for one person, let alone three people, but that's how he preferred to work. A disorganized, organized mess.

Slim reached for his cold french roast coffee and swallowed the pungent taste with eyes rolled back and Adam's apple tightened. His aged hands tossed the coffee cup somewhere in the overflowing wastebasket. His ears picked up a collection of footsteps approaching the office. His hands grabbed the worn silver knob and welcomed his visitors inside.

"Rick," he grumbled, "I see you brought the shark expert." Slim allowed a small wedge for entry into the tight office.

"Jesus man," Rick said with a shutter of his eyes, "can we turn on some damn lights?"

"The dark provides a clearer image to study." Slim tapped Cody's mauled corpse.

"Really? Is that some scientific hyperbole?" Darrin stretched his arms out, crackling a few knuckles in the process.

"Nah," growled Slim. "I prefer the dark."

"That way you can't see the mess," added Rick with a soft whisper to Darrin.

"I heard that wise-ass." Slim snorted back. "Now, what I've discovered here is, well, quite unusual."

"What is?" Rick asked.

Slim pressed play on his CD player and brought forth the immortal Johnny Cash. "I need to unwind these nerves, you know?"

"By all means." Rick paced around, staring at the surfer's body. "So what did you find, Slim?"

"What's the oddity you speak of?" Darrin tapped the pale feet of the corpse.

"Take a peek," said Slim. His hand unzipped the cover and revealed what was left of Cody Kincade.

Rick twisted his head in disgust, but Darrin remained glued to the unique carnage beneath the sheets.

"This isn't a white attack," Darrin said with a convincing tone. "My sharks didn't do this to him. These marks are unique, and ancient by our standards."

"No, I don't believe it is," added Slim. "I think it's from another member of the great white family. A distant relative perhaps?"

Rick's refusal to examine the body seemed a bit weird to his colleagues. "Ricky boy, aren't you interested?" Slim asked.

"I'm good. I had a heavy breakfast." His throat swelled with nausea as he continued pacing the room.

"A white's bite radius ranges from twelve to twenty-two inches," Slim said. His lips hummed along to the music between their conversation.

"But these aren't from a residential," Darrin answered in reference to his own great whites. "I tagged a trio of whites in the area, and they certainly don't have this biting capacity."

"It's something bigger." Slim stroked his goatee in wandering thought.

"We've encountered some sort of freakish anomaly," Darrin said. "My team and I uncovered a video of a shark attack beneath the Golden Gate."

"And?"

"We have cause for concern that the victim was swallowed whole, or at least severed apart." Darrin walked around the table where Cody's body lay.

"There haven't been any signs of the remains in the bay, or elsewhere," Rick chimed in. "Great whites do not swallow their prey whole, especially humans. They bite them, then swim away." Slim finished humming the song.

"Yet, it's not a Meg," Darrin said. "That I can guarantee with a week's paycheck.'

"How do we know that?" asked Rick.

"Well, they're extinct for one. And two, this bite radius is too small for a Meg." Darrin's eyes widened.

"So what are dealing with?" Rick continued pacing the room, avoiding the body.

"A possible missing link?" Darrin surmised. "In either case, we have a problem."

"Poor boy," Slim muttered. "Can we all decide to keep this

mum for a bit? No sense rattling the public's cages."

"Say what it truly was," Darrin paused, "a shark attack. This area is known as the Red Triangle for the attacks on the seals and occasional surfers. It certainly won't stir a media frenzy unless you throw in the fact that a possible Megalodon was responsible for this." Darrin headed back to the door. "My phone's vibrating hold on a sec," he quickly answered the phone.

"What's up?" Rick walked over to Darrin.

"Jonas, the poor fuck," Darrin said with a glum tone. "That was Davenport. He's en route to the hospital to see Jonas."

"Deputy Marsh?" Slim asked. "What did the schmuck do now? Get his tongue stuck in a light socket again?"

"What?" Rick turned to face Slim. "Are you jerking my chain? Jonas isn't that brain dead is he?"

"True story. I can't make this shit up." Slim shook his head. "He's a bit off the mark, you know what I mean?"

"Boys, Jonas was rushed to the hospital with massive injuries caused by a shark attack." Darrin quieted the men.

"Will he be all right?" Rick asked with genuine concern. "I don't want the kid hurt." He was clearly bothered by the news. "Shit, not like this."

"They have several pieces of him, according to Davenport. It's not pretty and we need to get there ASAP."

"Several pieces?" Slim's attention spiked.

"The shark obliterated his body, we may only have minutes left before the rest of him bleeds out."

Sheriff Reed Davenport led the charge through the otherwise mundane lobby of Bodega Bay County Hospital. Not too far behind his fervent pace, were Darrin Coyle and Rick Chatham. A team of nurses walked by the trio of men with a collection of odd looks, and muted chattering. The noontime sun burst through the hospital's panoramic architecture, flooding the entire lobby with lemon yellow light.

The crescent shaped oak reception desk stationed several receptionists ready for customer service. One of the young women greeted the sheriff with an exuberant smile and sweet charisma. In a well-timed act of teamwork Rick and Darrin immediately went over to the other receptionists and guided them through the same conversation Davenport was currently having with his receptionist.

The desk soon buzzed down the doctor and all three men waited impatiently by the entranceway to the emergency room's corridor. A few moments later, a doctor emerged with a grim look on his ivory white complexion.

"Gentlemen," the doctor cleared his throat in preparation for the news. "Things have taken a turn for the worse."

The men remained mum, not fully understanding the doctor, or perhaps still recovering from the shock of Marsh's grim condition.

"Shall we?" The doctor ushered the men to a smaller waiting room just off the corridor. His professional manner clear, his hands guided over three separate cups of black coffee, and a scattering of bagels. "My name is Morgan Gray and I've been with your friend every step of the way." He sat down in the chair and welcomed the men to follow suit. "He came in here about a half hour ago with severe wounds."

"Am I to understand Jonas will not make it through this?" Davenport asked, his lips tightened with anger. "I was the one who sent him out there, to look for more evidence, to..."

"No one could've predicted this, Sheriff," Gray said, "Jonas was taken by surprise by a monster of these once calm waters."

"If I may ask, what type of monster are we talking about here?" Darrin asked. "I've been in the area for quite some time studying the patterns of the whites out there." He took a fast sip of coffee.

"Thank you, by the way." He held up the coffee in a friendly gesture.

Gray laughed off Darrin's question. "I'm sorry, I don't mean to seem insensitive to your query, but this wasn't the work of a great white."

"How bad?" Rick asked. "How bad is Jonas?"

"This monster, this unknown entity of pure evil," Gray paused, "it nearly severed Jonas into quarters."

"Quarters? What the fuck does that mean?"

"The attack left your friend obliterated. He's barely stitched together from the attack. It's a gruesome sight." Gray answered, "and there's no sign of the reporter he was with."

"What reporter?" Darrin asked.

"Yeah, the slick gentlemen from the news. What was his name?" Gray tapped his fingers on the cup. "Ah, yes, Charlton Coulter."

Darrin swallowed more coffee. "I'm really starting to hate the water, you know that?"

"Shouldn't we be inside with our friend instead out here?" Davenport continued to distance himself from the doctor. "I'll go in myself," he answered with a flash of his badge. "This is official police business."

"Don't mind him, he's a bit shaken by all of this," Rick said as he stepped between Gray and Davenport. "As we all are."

"I will take you to your friend, but prepare yourself for this. Jonas is not the same man." Gray rose and guided the men down the hall.

"So if it wasn't a white, then what was it?" Darrin asked Gray, knowing the answer ahead of time.

Gray led them into the triage section of the emergency room. His trembling hand grabbed the blue curtain. "I've never seen a shark attack like this before, and believe me, I've encountered hundreds of them." He paused for a moment, collecting his senses. "This is the work of the devil." He pulled back the curtain, revealing Jonas to Davenport and his men.

"Jesus Christ." Davenport nearly collapsed to the floor. His hands cupped the vomit escaping from his mouth. It kept pouring from his stomach as Gray called out for immediate assistance.

Darrin diverted his eyes from the image. His years of tracking sharks and talking to shark attack victims had never brought him to this. His body went into shock and powered down in reaction to the grim scene before him. The doctor's definition of quartered was entirely wrong. This was something different. Something horrific.

Rick moved in closer, his entire body pulled to Jonas with some unforeseen magnetic force. Unfazed, a moth drawn to the blistering light of reality, Rick inched close to the side of the bed. His head pounded with flashbacks of his own grisly attack. The room grew darker for the former sheriff. The voices of Gray and the others soon grew silent. Rick reached out for the blood soaked sheets, praying Jonas was already dead. Jonas grabbed his wrist firmly.

It was too late for Jonas.

Rick leaned in close to Jonas's bloodied face. He knew from the severed limbs, deep gouge marks in the skin, and stained spikes of bone still protruding from Jonas, that time was escaping the deputy. "Jonas," Rick's lips moved. "What did this?

Gray went for Rick's elbow. "He's in shock and needs his Last Rites."

Darrin tugged away Gray. "Let him be."

Gray then saw the scars that snaked down the back of Rick's neck and released his hand from Rick's scarred elbow.

"This wasn't a shark was it Jonas? It was something...worse."

Jonas nodded his head, his eyes bounced around in their sockets.

"We will avenge this. I promise you." Rick whispered in his chewed ears.

Jonas shook his head. "No." His words were small and muted, yet still powerful. A fitful cough brought up more blood. "I stared into those darkened hollow eyes..." his words trailed off.

"Rest, rest," Rick urged.

"They never blinked. Then the screaming started. My screams," Jonas coughed up another round of blood. "I want you to walk away from this."

"I can't. It's gone too far. Too many innocent lives have been significantly altered."

"Then Pray to your god," Jonas urged, before a violent twist of pain consumed him. "Because the Devil's minions reside in the bay."

"Jesus." Warmth ran down Rick's leg. His eyes followed Jonas's body as another wave of blood seeped through the sheets and spilled onto the floor.

Moments later Jonas flat lined and became the latest victim of the bay.

Davenport choked on emotion, his throat swelled with defeat and the acrid taste of desolation. The sun's intermittent rays scattered throughout Jonas's room, fractured by the dusty blinds. Davenport sensed the fragility in the atmosphere and cleared his throat for inevitable conversation.

"Doctor, what's the next step?"

"Jonas had some final wishes that if, on the dark side of the coin, he wanted to pass on to you and Mr. Chatham." Gray approached with something cradled inside his hands. The star shaped object lay smothered in a bloody white towel. "This was his badge, Sheriff."

"How did you get this?" Davenport asked, reaching for the maroon stained badge.

"Ironically, it was still pinned to his shirt when Skippy brought him in. He was on one of his routine bird watching trips when he stumbled on the body."

"The elderly man on the beach?" Davenport asked.

"Yeah, he's the hermit who constructs boats for shits and giggles," said Rick, as he returned to the conversation after taking a lengthy moment of silence for Jonas.

"Well, in any case, he's to thank for bringing in your friend." Gray handed over the badge. "This comes with a stipulation, however." Gray's eyes turned toward Rick.

"Which is?" asked Davenport.

"That Rick Chatham be sworn in as your deputy." Gray took a deep breath.

"There's certain procedures," Davenport stated. "It's a complicated process of red tape."

"It was Jonas's last wish, that Rick follow through and end the reign of terror on the bay." Gray took a few steps back. "I have another surgery to attend to, and it's on the same grisly path as Jonas."

"Thank you Doctor," Davenport bid a farewell to the departing doctor. "So," he took a deep breath, "are you ready to rejoin the force?" His eyes swelled with tears for Jonas. "I can't do this alone."

"I thought there was red tape and all that shit?" Rick smiled.

"Listen, I know there was a lot of friction between you and Jonas," Davenport said.

"I know. We certainly didn't pair up well. But I never wanted the kid to go out like this." Rick ran has hands across his sweaty face.

"I think we have a unique situation brewing here," added Darrin as he finished looking over Jonas. "I highly suspect our sharks aren't Megs, but instead a missing evolutionary link between the great white and the Meg."

"How can you be so sure?" Davenport was curious.

"A Meg can swallow your average sized school bus," Darrin replied, "so swallowing a human whole would be very possible." Darrin tapped his chin. "No, we're looking at a missing link that has the agility and power of a great white, with the instinct and ferocity of a Meg. It's a highly violate cocktail of terror, and with the mayor kicking off the Surfer Invitational with a yacht party tomorrow," Darrin brought clarity to the situation, "the dinner bell will be ringing for these sharks. A forty-foot shark will not back down from ramming a yacht or stirring up red chaos in the bay's waters."

Davenport stared back at Rick. "You've encountered sharks before, you know these waters and the layout. Darrin has the intelligence and equipment to end this before it spirals out completely of fucking control. The three of us can realistically put one hell of dent in their paths."

"What the hell," Rick said, his hands reaching for the badge. "I'll personally avenge Jonas and bring down this shark my way. Keep the badge," he said, handing it back. "Consider my involvement as a concerned citizen." He smiled.

"A concerned citizen hell bent on revenge," added Darrin.

"We all have that match that strikes a blaze in our lives," Rick replied with a slap on Darrin's shoulder. "Jonas's death was that strike, and now the fire burns. I honestly don't know what will come of this, but I can say this. It's time to take back our bay, our city, and squeeze every last drop of blood from these monsters."

"**D**id she say what this was all about?" Rick asked as he unlocked the door to his boathouse. "We've been through a bitch of day."

Davenport kept pace with Rick, his head still wrapped up in Jonas's death. "She mumbled something about evidence and a special dinner for all of us."

"This has to be the worst possible time for me to socialize," Rick added with a sarcastic laugh. "Trying to sober up and this entire ordeal with Jonas, I'm fighting back the urge to down a dozen bottles of Jack right now." His hands trembled.

"It's been rough on all of us, Rick. You do know she likes you."

"Who? Your wife?" mused Rick.

"Funny," Davenport sniffed a laugh. "No, the marine biologist."

"Ashleigh?"

"Yeah. So I'd go with that blue Hawaiian shirt with the white flowers."

"Why?" Rick wanted nothing of the dating scene.

"The colors are unique and the flowers display your overwhelming sensitivity for the female race." Davenport slapped his friend's shoulder. "You know, because you're such a caring gentleman."

"Whatever." Rick tossed his shirt and quickly buttoned up the shirt.

"Ashleigh also has some Hawaiian ancestry in her family tree, so going with that shirt makes a great conversation piece." Davenport added with a friendly smile.

"You're such a matchmaker for your friends, but you can't remember shit when it comes to your old lady." Rick laughed.

Davenport changed the course of the conversation. "Listen, we all need a respite from today's unfortunate events, don't we? So let's go crash at Ashleigh's place, have some food and drink, and come up with game plan for tomorrow."

"I agree."

Davenport looked Rick over. "Seriously? You're going with shorts?"

"Yes. I think it's time to crawl out of the shadows of my fears, and embrace the stark reality of the situation." Rick retrieved the green cargo shorts from the closet and a set of brown leather sandals.

The afternoon sun remained strong as the gathering of friends and colleagues arrived at Ashleigh's house. Rick and Davenport brought the Jeep crawling alongside Darrin's crew. The men quickly greeted each other and followed the rocky pathway to Ashleigh's sprawling ranch. The view was tremendous and included the bay's quiet waves and the sunset on the distant horizon. She frequently did her work from home, allowing her easy access to the seal population on the shoreline.

Rick's feet grinded hard on the fractured pebbles and stones of the driveway, and then proceeded to the walkway to the house. He carried a small cooler as requested by the host. Davenport and Darrin also had their own instructions. Gavin and Daniel disappeared around the back with the heftiest of bounties: the pig.

The front door opened and a warm smile greeted the hungry party.

"I'm so glad you guys could make it," Ash opened the door for the men. "Right through those doors, out to the patio please." She motioned them in the right direction. "I was hoping to go over the evidence I dissected today," she continued.

"Yeah, sounds great," answered Davenport as he lowered the cooler to the deck of the patio. "Wow, this is a nice view."

Ashleigh tapped him on the shoulder. "Yeah, I can survey my seals from here with my instruments and down there on the rocky beach," she paused, her finger pointing in the generalized direction, "I can even collect samples. How cool is that?"

"You seem to enjoy your job," said Davenport.

"It has its perks," she then added, "and its drawbacks." She waved over Gavin and Daniel to set up the pig roast on the far end of the patio where the deck had a small pit embedded in it.

"It's been a rough day, may I crack open some demon spirits?" asked Davenport.

"I heard about your loss. I'm sorry. Jonas was a solid guy."

"Yes it's a shock to the system. But we have to move on and fight to save the bay." Davenport pushed away the emotion and popped off the cap to a fresh Samuel Adams Boston Lager.

"I've never seen Rick in shorts," Ashleigh changed gears. "It's different." She watched him assisting the others set up the roast.

Davenport loosened up a little bit. "Rick's a funny guy ever since the . . . ," his words trailed off. "Uh, yeah, he offers a unique look in cargo shorts.'

"What do you mean?' she asked as she clutched a beer.

"Ah, he's just been through the meat grinder." Davenport took another sip of beer. "He's a bit rough, but underneath that shark skin he's a decent guy. Maybe I shouldn't tell you this, but he's wearing his Sunday best for you tonight." He clanked his bottle with hers. "I'll chat later, yes?"

Ashleigh took a needed sip. "Yeah," she mumbled back, still marinating in the thoughts of Rick actually showing interest in her.

"Ash," Darrin hollered out as he made his way over to her.

"Yeah, what's up?"

"I'm eager to hear your findings, but we have to head back to the office and clear up some loose ends for tomorrow."

"What time will you be back? I thought we could all gel together as team tonight," she added, her throat welcoming another rush of alcohol.

"Well, the roast will be ready by six right?"

"About that time, yes."

"We'll be back then." Darrin smiled. "I'll have some news to share with everyone."

"Okay."

Ashleigh couldn't find Davenport or Rick. She scoured the grounds as Darrin and his crew departed. She eventually found the two men down by the beach, with her loyal dog following them.

By the time Darrin returned he was missing the rest of his team. Davenport and Rick managed to carve up a healthy portion of meat from the roast for everyone, and Ashleigh had prepared everything else including salads, desserts, plenty of side dishes, and refreshments.

"Where's the rest of the team?" Ashleigh prodded Darrin.

"They had other obligations, but I've gone over our plan for tomorrow." He sat down with a plate of sizzling pork roast, a beer, red potatoes, and a salad. His fingers kept the fire going in the center of the patio's pit. The sun had finally rested beneath the horizon, leaving a somber dusk in her wake.

"So I was looking over the DNA," Ash said, her hands prepared her own blend of pork, potatoes, buttered peppercorn on the cob, and a salad.

"Yes, and I chatted with the survivors today," Davenport added, his plate full with sizzling pork, corn, potatoes and macaroni salad.

"Darrin and I chatted with Slim about the dead surfer." Rick swallowed down a glass full of soda and picked away at his dinner. His choices were simplistic, a salad drenched in ranch dressing and a mountain of pork roast.

"We have a lot to digest," Davenport said. "I don't think we're dealing with an ancient shark here."

"What makes you think that?" Ash asked.

"The survivors indicated the size of these sharks were larger than our resident whites, yet not quite the size of its Megalodon ancestors."

"I have the findings from Slim that these bite marks are larger than a great white, yet not a Meg." Darrin looked around the group. "But this is all a moot conversation, because the videotape from the bay attack is grainy, the ferry's in complete shambles, and our one solid lead, a dead surfer, hasn't given us much to go on. To make it worse the deputy had no solid word on these predators."

"I hate to burst the balloon, but the DNA we found on the propellers," Ash paused for a hasty bite, "the genetic code remains a mystery. It's inconclusive on the Meg front, and it's not the same as our own sharks. I do think we're dealing with a missing link between the two generations."

"A missing link?" Rick asked. "That would make a world of sense from everything that has happened over these last few days."

"Listen guys," Ash added with a serious tone, "I'm tired of my seals getting chewed up. I'm tired of every time I close my eyes, I hear screams from the bay."

"She's fired up," Darrin said with a deep laugh. "I like that," he said shaking his bottle of beer in her direction.

"Don't mock me," she chided back.

"I'm not. I personally believe all of us need to bring our A-game, and then another level if we are to defeat these sharks."

"I agree," Davenport concurred. "Jonas revealed these beasts are relentless, and that we should pray."

"We need an action plan," Rick surmised. "A solid, no holds barred, kick to the fucking nuts type of plan." He stood up. His eyes adjusted to the fire and he walked away from the group.

"Where's he going?" Ash asked.

"Wait for it," Davenport said with another drink. "He's just getting warmed up."

Rick went over to the cooler and carried over a handful of beer.

"Shit," Davenport refined his thoughts. "He's cracking."

"Listen, time's wasting away." Rick spun off the first bottle cap. He brought the beer to his nostrils, sucking in the fumes. He placed his scarred legs on the edge of the logs. "Darrin, what's your plan?"

"Um," Darrin fumbled for words. He was concerned Rick was crashing off the wagon. "The mayor signed off on a blank check for me so I've assembled a top notch shark cage."

"A cage? Are you fucking insane? These sharks will chew that shit to cracker crumbs." Rick held out the bottle and tipped it to the fire. A blaze erupted to the darkening skies.

"Not just any cage," added Darrin. "This has the ability to withstand even the strongest of jaws. The cage's built-in pressure per square inch ensures my safety. The beauty of the cage, however, is embedded in the rods. They give off a simple electric charge that will attract the sharks."

"Again, are you kidding me?" Rick tipped another drop to the fire. He watched everyone back away.

"If I can attract them to the cage, then you can kill them." Darrin was defiant in his response. "And if they get frisky, the rods will send an electric jolt through their body."

"You'll die." Rick finished off the bottle and watched the fire roar. "If we fail, these sharks will consume the bay, and then feast on our town."

"When these new members of the family come knocking," Darrin added with a wink, "they will either devour the cage and get one hell of a seizure after I overload their senses, or, Davenport here can blast them out of the water."

"How do I do that?" Davenport inquired.

"The mayor has a yacht party planned for tomorrow afternoon," Darrin said. "If you patrol the bay by air, and I have it covered underneath the water, then the only task left is to secure the bay by boat. Which I'm sure Rick and Ash can handle."

Rick swayed left then right. His hands opened up another beer. "So, you're counting on a super cage, Davenport's ailing eyeballs, and my unsteady mental faculties to deliver justice to these monsters?"

"Yeah, it's all we got man. It's down to us, and maybe shore it up with some Coast Guard help. I have some friends I can buzz. But let's face it, by the time they arrive, this entire bay will be red with blood."

Rick poured out the rest of the bottle below, bringing back the raging fire. "Have you ever seen a shark up close?"

Davenport and Ash shook their heads no.

Darrin nodded his head. "Yeah."

"I don't mean on tape, or from the perceived safety of a cage and a weapon." Rick fumed. His hands trembled to unbutton his shirt. "I'm talking about being dragged underneath the bay, and submerged with these beasts, their teeth ready to gnaw you to pieces." He removed the shirt. His entire upper torso was littered with scars from his neck to just south of his waist. Below his knees he was also pocked with scars. "These are permanent reminders that on any day, anywhere, these monsters will attack, devour, and churn their way along the food chain. In some instances they're curious biting you and then leaving you to bleed to death."

Rick watched his restless friends.

"Rick," Darrin began, "I had no idea."

"I was surfing in the competition when I felt a sharp tug and down I went. I clearly remember the shark's soulless stare. Those black spheres refused to blink. They fixated on me. It was clear this shark wasn't interested in a hit and run. He wanted more. This motherfucker clamped down below my knees and began grinding away. I only managed to squirm free when I jammed a fragment of my board through the bastard's right eye. After that, all I remember is being rolled over and over before red filled the bay. I prayed for death." Rick put his shirt back on and peered out across the group. "I want justice. I want these sharks to die."

"In Hawaiian mythology," Ash began, "sharks are the gods."

"I read that somewhere," Rick fumed. "Forgive me if I don't adhere to that religion."

Ash continued. "If you were filled with a evil soul, the sharks would devour you and bring you to meet your maker. However, if you were pure, then the sharks would return you back to the mainland."

"It's that simple?" Rick was still agitated. His memories always riled him up.

"Listen," she said as she reached out for him. "I believe in this mythology. I believe," she paused, "I know deep down you are a good man Rick Chatham. That shark at any time could've severed you in half, yet fate has delivered this chance to you."

"Fate? A shark attack of that magnitude isn't fate," Rick bristled.

"I know second chances exist," she answered with a smile. "You were spared on that day to come to our aid in this fight."

"I'm no hero. I'm a washed up drunk with nothing left on the horizon."

"A maverick. A rogue hero with no ties to anything," added Darrin. "You are exactly what we need." He raised his beer in a friendly toast.

"This is careening off topic, and did I mention insane," Rick growled. "I'm not diving in the water, in fact, I want no part of the water."

"You have to," Darrin pleaded. "You can't fight a war with shark without invading their territory."

"No I don't have to. You have Davenport in the air, you have your cage, and Ash has the bay covered. These sharks aren't going to survive all of that."

"Please," Ash begged.

Davenport cleared his throat. "I've known Rick for some time now, and he's a man of conviction. If he tells you he's not going in the water, then that's it. We will find other means to defeat these sharks. Rick can assist us on the land with supplies and keeping the media at bay."

"It's not up for discussion," Rick seethed. "I wanted to fade into the shadows."

"Well, that's a bit of a chore now, don't you think? The lives of innocent people are at stake and, as a former sheriff, you are forever sworn to protect," Ash countered. "Jonas deserves better, Rick. His life will mean nothing if we didn't avenge his death."

"I understand your point," muttered Rick, "I really do. But things are spiraling out of control. Listen, I need some space right now while you figure out the next step." He walked off into Ashleigh's house.

"You better go talk to him," urged Davenport.

"Why me? You're his close friend."

"That's the reason I can't. He'll see it differently coming from someone else. It's to your advantage to smooth out his rough edges. It will mean even more coming from the opposite sex." Davenport cradled the beer between his hands, soaking in the fire's dying warmth.

"I'll try, but I can't promise anything."

"Tomorrow will be a historic day one way or another," said Davenport, "hopefully it's for all the right reasons, and that means having Rick back at full strength."

Ashleigh left Davenport and Darrin to finish off their beers and converse about tomorrow. Her hands slid open the doors to the kitchen. She added a fresh splash of water for Warthog's thirsty mouth and called out for Rick.

No answer.

She toured the kitchen, then the dining room, and then the living room. On the long couch, Rick stretched out on his back staring up at the ceiling.

"Leave me be," he said.

"Oh, we're still playing the tough guy role?" She sat down next to him on the couch, forcing him to pull up his feet. A few moments later he sat upright and stared over her way.

"I don't know what to say. I had a terrible time just talking about the attack tonight," he paused. "And even a tougher time coming here tonight."

"That's a stark contrast to how I've seen you before," she said.

"What?"

"You were always dressed in jeans and a buttoned-up shirt. I understand now."

"Do you?" His eyes widened.

"You took a big step toward recovery tonight. You sobered up, rejoined the department in some capacity, and now you come to my house wearing your best shirt." She laughed. It was working; she could feel it. Rick was warming up to her.

"You think very highly of yourself. Maybe I just like the shirt."

"Davenport clued me in. It's your go-on-a-date shirt."

"It figures he'd sell me out, the crazy bastard," he snorted.

"We're your friends here Rick. We're not going to judge you based on your scars, imperfections or swirling demons."

"That's a relief. I'm still not going in the water."

"I'm very happy you decided to come tonight," she said reaching for his hand. "I would like to be here for you Rick. A shoulder to lean on, a friend to confide in, a place to just crash and get away from the world for a while."

Rick, although hesitant at first, returned the gesture. They held hands for a few more awkward seconds. "This is weird. It's like high school."

"Whatever. You want a soda or something?"

"Yeah, sure."

Ashleigh soon returned with the drinks. "You know, I wasn't bullshitting you back there about the shark mythology."

"I know. I remember reading up on that after my attack. I went through a whole period of time where I researched the hell out the sharks." He sipped from the glass.

"I do believe you are a hero, returned to us from the depths of the sea. You have a mission to complete, and a town to save."

"I think between Darrin and Davenport have the bay covered.

What do they need us for?"

"We're part of the team. If you still want to remain on dry land, I'll stay with you. I won't go in the bay."

"Really, you'd do that for me? A marine biologist that will stay dry?"

"Yeah," she said with a laugh. "I will."

"So you have anyone special in your life?" Rick asked.

"My dog, Warthog."

"Oh."

"What about you?"

"No, I lost my other half during the whole shark fiasco. It was too stressful for her." He watched Warthog enter the room. "No husband, boyfriend, or boy toy?".

"Nah," she answered. "I do have my sights set on one someone though."

Rick turned a bit red. "Well, he's a lucky guy then. You are a good person."

"Well, he's a bit stubborn and rough around the edges. He won't admit he also likes me. Although, he does appear to have some interest."

"Maybe he needs some more time." Rick finished off his drink, leaned in and kissed Ashleigh on the cheek. "One friend to another. Thanks for the chat."

Ash watched him leave the room and head back outside. "Damn it, Davenport was right. Rick Chatham likes me." She rubbed Warthog's head and gave her dog a kiss. "He likes me."

Ashleigh rejoined the team outside after giving Rick some needed space. "Are we calling it a night?"

"No, not quite yet," Darrin added, "I still have some drink left."

"I'm going to coordinate with the mayor in the a.m.," Davenport said. "We will keep a close lid on everything. He's going to want to go ahead with the celebration."

"It's a mistake," added Darrin. "These sharks will devour everything in their path."

"I'm thinking maybe someone should crash the party." Rick waved his hands randomly.

"Aren't you a pussy when it comes to the water?" Darrin chided back.

"Well, that fear needs to be conquered right? The yacht's a decent sized piece of architecture, it's not sinking to the bottom of the bay." Rick's eyes lit up. "I'm going to need some arm candy," his attention wandered over to Ashleigh. Her attention was elsewhere.

"What?" She finally returned to the group's conversation.

"I'm going to need a date for tomorrow," Rick prompted her. "Are you free?"

"I think I can free up my schedule," she kindly replied.

"We will deliver crowd control on the yacht, while the two of you play in the bay." Rick tapped Davenport's shoulders.

"Guys, I'll be right back," Ash said rising from her seat. "Warthog seems to have run off again to the beach."

"I'll go with you," Rick offered. "You two stay here in case the dog returns."

Davenport and Darrin were heavily intoxicated and seemingly resigned to collapsing on the patio at any moment.

"Does he always take off like this?" Rick asked. He kept pace with Ashleigh.

"He loves the ocean," she sighed, "he's such a child sometimes."

"The moon seems content tonight." Rick looked up at the black sky. A white speck emerged from behind a scattering of clouds. A collection of ivory moonbeams glanced off the water. Rick strained his eyes at a random splash in the water. "There he is," he said. He approached the edge of the rocky beach.

"I'll go get him," she said. "No worries. Really."

"No," he was defiant. "I need to face this fear of the water."

"Not right now." She laughed.

"Then when?" Rick took a step forward. "What's his name again? Warts?"

"Warthog."

Rick spliced his lips with his fingers and let off a low whistle. He heard intermittent barking off in the distance. His feet entered the water. A cool stream of water gushed over his sneakers, soaking them.

Ashleigh followed behind him. Her hand kept a firm tug on the back of his shirt.

The triangular dorsal fin emerged from its slumber beneath the bay. The curious sounds continued to lure the predator closer to the splashing.

"Jesus, how far out does he go?" Rick was up to his knees in water. "I'm having trouble breathing."

"Here, let me go ahead of you," she offered, slipping past him.

"I've done this before. I'm a pro."

Rick felt something awry with the bay. The water appeared calm. Way too calm.

The shark gained momentum, its jaws released open, ready to devour. The splashing grew louder as did a new patch of sounds. The shark closed the thin membranes over its black eyes and prepared to strike.

Warthog swam hard to his owner, his four legs pounding against the water furiously.

Ashleigh reached for him with Rick standing behind her.

Rick saw the fin break the surface, the mouth shattering through the water. The teeth glistened in the moonlight's full glow.

It was too late.

"Ash!" His gut instinct overpowered him as he pulled her away and the shark's mouth collided with the water releasing a spray of red water high into the night air. As both went under, Rick felt the waves rolling over them, turning them over and over again. He couldn't see a thing in the murky black water.

Rick's hearing had picked up what he thought was a muted barking, or a distorted growl. The same growl he heard during his shark attack. His grip tightened on Ash. He powered his legs toward the surface, breaking the bay's eerily calm wake. A sharp pain raced through his left arm.

The barking grew louder.

Rick managed to locate Warthog safely on the beach. He wasted no time in joining the dog on dry land. A severed elephant seal floated by, bouncing off Rick as he continued swimming to the beach with Ash close by his side. "Keep swimming."

Ash was the first one to reach land. Rick retreated for a moment, staring out across the silent bay. A dorsal fin soon submerged in the distance against the full moon's backdrop.

It was then Rick knew what he had to do.

Rick held Ashleigh's hand the entire walk back to her house. He could sense she was shaken from the close call in the bay.

He briefly smiled at Darrin and Davenport both snoring loudly on the patio. "It looks like they've passed out cold," Rick said on returning back to Ashleigh's house. "It's a warm night, it's best not to stir the slumbering bears."

"Yeah, we should leave them be," her words were weaker than

usual.

"Are you okay Ash?" Rick reached for her hand.

"No, I'm not." Her words trembled from the lips.

"Come on, I'll make you some coffee."

"Will you stay for awhile?"

"Are you inviting me for a sleepover?" Rick knew the tension from the near attack rattled both their cages. He deferred to humor to diffuse it.

"The couch. I'll make up the couch for you." She followed him through the patio doors to the kitchen. She pulled a barstool to the inlet counter in the center of the kitchen.

"So where do you keep the caffeine?" Rick searched the cabinets.

"Top one on the right." Her fingers ran through Warthog's fur. "Thank you again for saving us."

"Well aren't you the one who said sharks protect the sea?" Rick poured coffee grounds into the white paper filter. "Warthog is a hero."

"Thanks for that."

Rick filled up the machine with fresh water and pressed the red button. "Okay, we have a few minutes before the java's ready."

"I'm a very strong, independent woman, you know."

"I know. But it's okay to be weak sometimes. I've been down that road before." Rick arranged two ceramic coffee mugs on the counter. He looked into her eyes. "I promise you we will emerge from this."

"I've never been affected like this before," she said. "Of all the studies I've done, all the seal deaths I've watched and endured." Her eyes swelled with tears. "A shark attack has never been part of the equation. Not even remotely."

"I wasn't going to let that demon drag you into the bay." He soothed her with his protective words. "The way I see it, you're just an innocent citizen needing protection."

Ashleigh offered a broken smile. "I really do appreciate everything you've done."

"Me?" He was surprised by the compliment. He reached for the coffee pot and poured two fresh cups. "Aren't you the one that nursed me back to living?"

"I'm drawn to cops, it's one of my flaws," she said with a stronger laugh. Her hands took the cup of coffee and sipped from it.

"I kind of have a thing for sexy marine biologists," he quipped back.

"Can you stay a bit longer, I'm still a bit shaken."

Rick walked over to her and brought her close to his chest. For the first time, it felt good to have a woman rest her head on his broad shoulders. His hands gently massaged the back of her head, filtering her long hair through his fingertips. "This feels so cool."

"Really?" She continued nuzzling her face inside his embrace. "Yeah, it's been awhile."

"I want to be honest with you Rick," Ashleigh said as she brought her head back up, staring at his eyes. "I was going to invite you to stay the night anyway, before the incident in the bay."

"I figured as much. I wanted to time it right and not rush into anything. The yacht idea was clearly my way of asking you out."

"I totally understand that day-to-day philosophy."

"But fate sure has a funny way of igniting relationships with a kick in the balls." Rick looked down at her as they gently rocked back and forth.

"Yeah, fate's a wicked one alright," she said with renewed spirit, returning her head to his shoulder.

Hangover
Thursday
July 3
6 a.m.

His nostrils filled with the glorious scent of bacon and eggs. The sunshine knocked on the windows ready to flood the room with light. He reached over and felt the soft skin of a woman lying next to him. The sweet scent aroused his senses, kick starting his body to get out of the bed.

Rick sat straight up, still clothed from the night before. He was in Ashleigh's bedroom, not the couch as originally planned. His sudden jolt upright stirred her.

"Did we?" he asked with a sheepish grin.

"No," her words were soft and delicate. "Lord knows I tried."

"You're a firecracker."

"I'm happy you decided to abandon thought of sleeping on the couch. It was good to just have someone lying next to me last night."

Rick pressed his lips against her forehead. "It was indeed refreshing not sleep on the broken down wicker sofa back at my boathouse."

Warthog jumped forward and barked off a series of warning shots.

Ashleigh emerged from her side of the bed still clothed from last night as well, and hushed her dog. "I'm guessing from the bacon and eggs the rest of the band is up and ready."

"Hey guys," Davenport greeted the pair. "We figured we'd raid your kitchen and whip up some breakfast."

"Yeah, what he said." Darrin laughed. "Wait, did the two of you, you know."

"No. We had a scary incident in the water last night after the two of you blacked out."

"Are you guys okay?" Davenport asked. "Was it a shark?"

"The dog had a close call, as did Ash here." Rick reached for the plate of eggs.

"You went in the water?" Davenport sipped some coffee.

"I had to," Rick replied as he stuffed more breakfast in his mouth.

"He was great," Ash added. "He pulled me away from the shark and Wart here even managed to survive the ordeal."

"Shit," mumbled Darrin. "Was it a white?"

"Hard to say, it was dark out there." Rick drank his mug of

coffee. A stifled cough indicated the temperature exceeded his expectations. "Damn that's fire-soaking hot!" His fingers caught a few drops that forced escape from his lips.

"It was hard to see." Ash made her own plate.

"It happened so fast," Rick said. "We have a few hours before the mayor's party. If I remember right the festivities start shortly after lunch."

"Yeah, it's being held over at the Golden Gate Yacht Club," Davenport said. "The mayor went balls out on this one. I've seen the yacht. It's a beast."

"Well Ash and I will keep you posted, maybe we'll save you some shrimp scampi." Rick felt the pain return to his chest. He hid the grimace beneath a fake smile.

"Funny." Davenport finished off his plate and placed it in the sink.

"I'll be in touch shortly," added Darrin, as he too returned the plate and his mug to the silver sink. "I'm going to get with Gavin and Daniel and nail down a time for the cage."

"I'm going to tap a pilot for the helicopter," said Davenport. He felt Warthog licking his idle fingers clean of breakfast. "Hungry fellah, isn't he?" He reached down and gave the dog a solid rub on the head.

"Let's reconvene at Fisherman's Wharf at 11am," Rick said. "Does that sound like enough time for all of us to get our shit in order?"

"Yeah," the group replied in unison.

"We need one-hundred percent and then some on this." Rick took a deep breath. He felt Ash's hand slide across his back in support.

"Oh, don't worry, Sheriff," Darrin quipped with his Shaw imitation from the movie 'Jaws' "I'll give this shark a heart attack!"

Rick took a step outside and waved goodbye to Darrin and Davenport. His head pounded with the remnants of his own attack, and how he'd fare again against these sharks. He still feared the water, outside the confines of the shallow beaches, at the mercy of their territory. A section of deep ocean, a bottomless graveyard of teeth and blood, awaited Rick and his men. Another pocket of fear erupted inside his brain, a volcano of emotion seared to the surface. He prayed it was a hangover. The headache's effects continued to chip away at him. The onslaught of memories provided the hammer as it pounded against his will, his psyche, his overall desire to claim victory.

The sky swelled with a sudden burst of color, a rainbow of torment unleashed before his eyes. The blue hue succumbed to a darkened red as it dripped from the clouds, releasing a blood soaked rainfall to the beach below. He knew what was happening. The nightmare returned with a vengeance. His mind kept playing the attack over and over again like a broken record. Rick felt both lungs scream for release, they had reached their limitations. A fierce clutch of the chest would come next, his left arm numb once again.

Rick stumbled forth, his hands reached out for support. He collided with the emptied bottles of beer, spinning them across the patio floor. His balance finally gave way, sending him crashing against the western side of the patio with a thunder, snapping off one of the wooden posts. His face collided with the sandy surface below. Rick's contorted body was still trembling from the heart attack, as he heard the faint screams of a woman in the background, and a howling bark before blackness swept over him.

shleigh's focus spun out of control. Lying before her sandwiched between a collection of demolished sandcastles and broken seashells, Rick Chatman's body left no signs of life. A mad dash back to the house to call the paramedics brought Warthog nipping at her heels, thinking it was another normal run on the beach.

The operator quickly addressed the situation and within a matter of minutes paramedics appeared on the scene. The lead paramedic kept his hands moving in a wild pattern shielding away any type of distraction. Ash knew the outlook was grim, her eyes bounced off the paramedics as they strapped down Rick and administered a variety of life saving techniques.

"Will he make it?" She asked the lead paramedic, her lungs stinging from the lack of breathing.

"If we don't get him to the hospital immediately, then it's going to be a sad day for his friends and family." The paramedic hastened his team away with a whistle. The doors of the ambulance slammed shut and the wheels sprayed a wave of sand as they began their route to the hospital.

Ash managed to catch one of the last paramedics as they hopped inside their Jeep. "What hospital?"

"John Muir."

"Thank you." She waved goodbye and headed back to the house to reach out to Davenport and Darrin.

Sheriff Davenport gulped down another mug of java as he approached the parking lot to the mayor's office. His cell lit up in blue and vibrated against the dashboard. He reached for it and answered the call from Ashleigh.

"Yeah," he greeted the call, his feet emerged from the vehicle, landing squarely on the black pavement. His free hand stretched to block out the blinding morning sunshine. His brain remained saturated in alcohol from the night before and could use a break from the nasty sun.

His demeanor soon soured.

"What the hell happened, Ash?" His voice was rigid and stern.

His head nodded to the right, then to the left, his neck unwilling to crack. "Yeah, I know the place. Was he conscious? No? Shit."

He took a deep breath while he paced the parking lot. "Ash, don't worry about him. He's in God's hands now. John Muir is top-notch talent."

His hand reached for the door to the office building. "Yeah, our plan still remains intact. I'm about to talk to the mayor. Catch you later and keep me updated."

Davenport ended the call with his usual abruptness when it came to dealing with heavy-handed issues. His coping mechanisms appeared to be stoic and lacking emotion. His occupation was partly to blame for that with all the crimes and arrests and in some cases, deaths. Davenport had built up a tough wall, seemingly impenetrable.

"Is the mayor in?" Davenport asked the receptionist, his emotions still smarting from the news of his friend's condition.

"Yes, is he expecting you?"

"He's the one who called me."

"Reed!" The mayor called out from down the hall.

"Mayor," Davenport answered him with a tightened grin.

"You okay?"

"No, I'm not Harrison," he said, "Can we chat somewhere private?"

"Yes, absolutely. Will my office work?"

"Anywhere but the foyer."

"Reed, what troubles my favorite sheriff?" Harrison circled his desk, dragging his fingers across the fresh lemon Pledge finish.

Davenport admired the spacious office with a view overlooking Fisherman's Wharf and the bay. He took a seat to ease the throbbing in his head.

"Are you and your friend still hell-bent on talking me out this festival on the yacht?" Harrison's words were minced with a boisterous ego. "Because for Christ's sake, Reed, it's the fucking Fourth of July, and the National Surfing Competition."

"I couldn't care less about the political testicle grabbing," Davenport chided back. "Rick's in dire straits. He may be dead as we speak."

Harrison fumbled for the right words. "Well, that's quite unfortunate."

"Yes it is." Davenport caught sight of Harrison's family album perched high above the window.

"Yet, it doesn't deter me from going forward with this event later today." Harrison peered out the window and across the bay. "It's going to be a beautiful day today and what a shame it would be to cancel an event featuring so many celebrities and dignitaries."

"Is that your son in the picture?" Davenport shifted gears and went for the jugular.

"Yes, why do you ask?" Harrison kept a watchful eye on the bay. A flock of seagulls hovered by.

"He enjoys surfing?"

"Somewhat. He's into parasailing more." Harrison pivoted on his feet and walked parallel to the window. "I know what you're attempting to do here Reed. It will fail miserably."

"Listen, what happens if one of those sharks grind your only son to bone fragments out there," Davenport lost his cool, which never boded well for the other person in the discussions.

"It won't happen." Harrison felt the brutal discomfort of the sheriff's argument.

"Why? Do you think you've earned enough karma points to sidestep this train wreck that's about to happen?"

"I've bought off that shark expert," Harrison fought for the right words. "That Darrin Coyle character. That's the one who will end it all and preserve my re-election."

"I'm aware of the situation." Davenport rose from the chair. His head reversed the trend and began to recover from the lingering hangover. His clarity returned with a deafening vengeance. "It's stained with your political savvy and distaste for anything logical."

"Coyle has assured me these sharks will not be a problem. His team has bought the best shark cage on the market. He's done this with my money, under my keen watch. Your job's simple Reed."

"You can't dictate terms to me." Davenport closed the distance between them. He knew it would eventually come to this. Harrison MacTavish had only his own interests at heart.

"I'll dictate anything I want to you, Sheriff. I'm your boss you mouthy little prick. I sign your checks. I fund your department, so wise up, or wind up out of a job."

"I don't respond well to bullies."

Harrison ignored the last comment, he was on a verbal tear. "While Coyle's submerged beneath the bay tracking these sharks, you're going to be airborne with your rifle, making damn sure nothing emerges alive from the bay!" Harrison clenched his fists tight. "Is that understood? Or do I need to find another sheriff?"

"I'm in that air for only one reason, and one reason only." Davenport suppressed his emotional fire.

"Enlighten me. Is it for job security?" Harrison displayed his patented smugness.

"To protect the citizens of San Francisco and Bodega Bay." Davenport took a few steps back. His hand rose with the extension of his left pointer finger. "And you better fucking pray I get to these sharks before they find your precious son."

Davenport stormed out of the office and slammed the door behind him, shattering the glass pane.

"That's coming out of your paycheck!" Harrison bent over and seethed at the damage that scattered his name across the floor in sections of fractured glass and wood.

The cell jittered inside his pocket. Davenport reached in and answered the incoming call.

"Darrin," he greeted the caller. "What's going on?"

"We have another problem." Darrin's voice permeated through the small speakers.

"Besides having Rick in the hospital?"

"Not only has the media caught wind of everything, but now, a new release about the effects of the recent earthquake has been given to the media."

"What did they find?" Davenport opened his car door and sat down inside.

"The quake opened up the sea with a vengeance."

"Well how does that impact us?" asked Davenport.

"The other day a science team lead by Maverick Brown triggered the earthquake by accident during a routine drilling activity. The results were devastating and ultimately led to his team's death and the town of Parkfield was destroyed," Darrin said. "Maverick was last seen in the ocean but his body was never recovered, only fragments of his boat were found earlier today."

"What does all of this mean then?"

"It factors into the stark reality of where these new sharks came from," Darrin answered. "But it opens up a new threat."

"It demolishes the landscape of the Bay Area, doesn't it?" Davenport guessed.

"Yes, and that means places like Aquatic Cove, which normally runs twelve to fifteen deep, could possibly be tripled in depth."

"That's where the public swims and moors their boats for the day."

"Exactly, and if this quake did in fact administer the type of damage we're led to believe it did then these sharks will be able to swim and feast inside the cove."

"Has all of this been confirmed?" Davenport asked.

"It hasn't been confirmed about the cove's depth being altered, but earthquakes of this magnitude do deliver a demolishing knockout blow to the area. A news report has quoted several seismologists who believe the aftershocks are on their way as well, which could add another layer of destruction to the Bay Area," Darrin added.

"Oh, by the way, my visit with the mayor was a complete waste of time. He's not budging."

"His agenda certainly has an egotistical spin to it," Darrin said. "He gave me an open checkbook for the shark hunt, but deep down I know he's just creating chaos."

"Exactly."

"Yet, I'm tied to my professional oath of keeping the oceans safe for the public while I gather information on the different species of sharks."

"I understand. I'm only doing this to protect the public as part of my own professional oath as well."

"This entire infection of news will only congest the Bay Area, you know that right? The media hounds will litter the air, shark hunters will roam the bay, and amateur hour will begin."

"I'm not looking forward to it." Davenport was clear in his trepidation for the celebration on the bay.

"I'll keep Rick in my thoughts."

"Thanks Darrin, I appreciate that."

"And to think, he's about to miss all the fun."

Mayor Harrison MacTavish patrolled the busy wharf, a snide grimace stretched across his weathered face. His mandible tightened in a cocktail of anger and hatred for Sheriff Davenport. "That son-of-a-bitch, he's gonna be the fucking ruin of this campaign," he seethed. The chilled bay breeze collided with his heated emotion, almost igniting a steam bath above the boundaries of his temples. Harrison reached for his cell. A feverish pressing of the keys highlighted the intended contact in a blue hue on the screen:

Major Anderson MacTavish.

A few miles outside the wharf, a bunch of grizzled and amateur shark hunters prepared for their hunt.

Harrison squinted from the sun at their shadows while he maintained a firm hold on the cell against his right ear. "Dumb fucks," he mumbled as the ringing finally gave way to a stern voice. "Ah, Major." The mayor's greeting was forced and formulaic. "Where the hell are you?"

The voice directed Harrison to the far end of the wharf where a hot dog vendor, an ice cream vendor and a painter awaited new customers.

"Jesus Christ." Harrison closed the phone in haste.

"What's the problem, Harry?" The Major snickered while he handed over a collection of two-dollar bills to the young vendor. "Two chili dogs, all the trimmings. And a pair of Dr. Pepper's too please."

"We don't have time for this." Harrison still fumed. "I'm on a tight schedule."

"I have all the time in the world," the Major replied. "Here, have a dog, sit down, and breathe brother." The elder brother bounced his feet off the boardwalk.

"Always bossing me around." Harrison smugly swiped away the dog as both men found a bench.

"You are a pain in the ass. But what are younger brothers for? Right?" Anderson gnashed his teeth through the soft bun and bit off a third of the chilidog. "I mean, I'm bald for a reason."

"We have a problem." Harrison returned the gesture with his own hearty bite.

"What's got your panties all tied up in knots?" Anderson

slurped his soda. "You never call me unless you're up shit's creek again."

"These sharks." Harrison bit into the hot dog.

"I heard about them. It's all over the media."

"Shit. I was hoping to contain that."

"Yeah, good luck with that in the digital age of Facebook and Twitter. You do know that little yacht party you're having," Anderson paused for another bite, this time finishing off the first hot dog. "It's gonna be crawling with media scoundrel."

A few tourists filtered through the two men.

Harrison leaned in close. "Brother, I need a favor. You see, I have this pain in the ass," he paused for another bite.

"Davenport?"

"Yeah, how did you know?"

Anderson chuckled. "You're serious? I have eyes and ears everywhere brother."

"Yeah, him."

"The man's a damn hero. His service to our community bleeds blue.'

"He's doubting my judgment." Harrison's eyes narrowed. "And you know how annoying that can be."

"All of us are doubting your judgment. Why would you go through with this yacht shit when the bay's saturated with predators the size of a small school bus?"

"Nothing will happen."

"Jesus, you're fucking stubborn as shit on a bear's wet ass."

"Anyway, I need you to run interference."

"No."

"No? What the hell does that mean?"

"It means I'm not going to be here. I leave for Iran in three hours."

"Do I have to do everything myself?"

"Relax. I already called in the Coast Guard," Anderson paused to finish off his second hot dog. "And," he tried to talk through the shuffling of food inside his mouth, "I have a small band of my best Marines including Kenneth Black and Bud Stephens stationed on Alcatraz Island, and a few more out in the boats with the Guard as well."

"I don't know what to say." Harrison clasped his mouth in amazement. "I mean Black and Stephens are war heroes from Afghanistan."

"Stephens has a keen eye for the rifle. He can thread the needle through any hole, at any distance," Anderson said. "Don't worry,

I have the entire Bay Area under strict lockdown."

"All because I'm your brother and I called in a favor?"

"No. The President actually wanted a small presence at this event since his own nephew, Patrick Ryan, also a nationwide surfing star by the way, will be attending your gala today."

"President Mason Gray has his fingers in this pie?" Harrison was wide-eyed.

"He even thinks your incompetent, how funny is that?" Anderson laughed. You're not the only one that plays political shell games."

Harrison remained firm. "We can't have an incident. Do you understand?"

"We have everything planned out, the only thing that can throw us off are variables to the equation. In every battle, skirmish, even in war, nothing ever goes according to plan."

"I have a shark expert beneath the surface tracking these bastards, and I have Davenport in the air." Harrison squeezed his hands together with nervous energy. "I have all the variables on lockdown."

"The media and these rogue hunters will be the curveball that will determine whether or not," Anderson took a final sip of soda leaving his last remark to sink in.

"Whether or not what?" Harrison lost all patience.

"Whether they're the ones telling the story, or the ones who are the story."

The July sun glanced off the bay, scattering the surface with a glittering, sparkling glow. A low fog continued enveloping the area, choking off the traffic sputtering across the Golden Gate Bridge. Mayor Harrison MacTavish wasn't about to let Mother Nature ruin his party. It would be something else entirely that would threaten to derail his ambitious design of political machismo.

A patch of wandering teenagers filled Aquatic Cove just off the Aquatic National Park's boundaries. The cove served as a swimming area for races and relays, as well as the mooring of several boats allowing tourists to enjoy the park's offerings. The cove enjoyed a boost in business during these summer months, especially the cove's famous restaurant with an underwater aquarium.

"Do you really think we should be entering the cove?" Preston Fillmore asked his best friend. "I mean, with all the tremors and shark sightings, it could be a bit scary."

Dylan MacTavish, the brash and cocky son of the town's mayor brushed off the question. "Shit man, look at the sun. It's a gorgeous sight. And look at the water," he begged Preston to gawk upwards. "She's ready to have her cherry popped today."

"Yeah, I guess so," Preston paused, "but what about those sharks?" The teenager picked nervously away at his expensive lemon gold polo shirt with his fingernails. "The media sure has it plastered all over the newscasts."

"My father has all that shit covered, no worries," Dylan added with a slap on Preston's shoulder. "We've been friends since preschool right? Would I ever steer you wrong?" His eyes told the mischievous stories he had pulled Preston through time and time again.

"Are we keeping track?" Preston laughed, "Because I stopped counting after the third grade."

"Listen, we'll just take a quick skip out on the bay." Dylan stepped forward. He removed the black sunglasses. "If you do this with me, I'll introduce you to Cathy Bixby. *The* Cathy Bixby."

Preston had a crush on the hottest girl in school. "Really? You think I have a chance with her?"

Dylan grinned. "Dude, I will personally make it happen for you tonight on the yacht."

"How so? She doesn't even know I exist."

"Neither do your parents," Dylan mumbled the snide comment.

"What's that?" Preston tilted his head to catch the mumbled reply.

"She will after I slide a few drinks her way." Dylan winked.

"Okay." Preston agreed to the deal.

"So do we have a deal then?" Dylan asked. He played Preston perfectly.

"Yeah."

"I have one more favor to ask." Dylan turned to Preston and placed his hands on his friend's shoulders. "It's going to require some effort."

"What?" Preston knew what was coming next. He was surprised it had taken this long for Dylan to ask.

A cocky smile stretched across Dylan's smug face. "We're going to need to borrow your dad's boat."

Simon and Muncie Everly kept shoveling the chum overboard, watching it splatter across the bay. The two elderly brothers had decided to forgo the warnings of the Sheriff's Department and head out to hunt down the mysterious sharks.

Simon, the oldest of the identical twins, at eighty years old maintained the course with strong steady rowing of the oars. His arms were athletic and well toned for his age. Muncie crunched down on a peanut butter granola bar and scoured the area for dorsal fins. The wiry brothers were the reigning champions of the famous swim to Alcatraz, and kept their bodies in top shape. Simon often teased his brother on the subject, claiming he was the stronger one.

"Damn fog is rolling across the bay," said Muncie, his grey eyebrows furrowed with anger. "We should wait for it to clear up. We ain't going to see shit out there."

"What are you a pussy?" Simon cracked back. "We've spent all of Maude's retirement money on that chum."

"You tend to exaggerate on such matters." Muncie crunched down the remaining morsel of the granola bar. "And the chum's better than her meatloaf. Your cranky old lady can't cook worth a puke."

The two brothers shared a laugh. "Yeah, she's a brutal cook." Simon laughed about his wife's inadequate kitchen talents. "Why do you think you and I stop at Whitebeard's for beer and a cheeseburger almost every night?"

"How big do you think these sharks are?" Muncie scooped up another shovel of chum.

"Media speculates twenty feet or larger." Simon kept rowing.

Muncie licked his lips. "That's a real nice shark steak."

The thirty-five foot shark slithered underneath the water, its appearance hidden beneath the dense fog and floating chum. Its speed slowed down briefly as it reacted to the faint splattering of water just ahead. A fresh patch of water filtered through its scarred gills as it ascended toward the sound.

The long object penetrating the water soon disappeared and the shark rolled back for another strike.

Simon pulled the almond colored oars back out of the water, and let off a low whistle. "Can you take over for me brother? My arms are ready to fall off."

Muncie thought about it for a minute. "You can rest after you give us one more powerful push to where the ferry went down. I'm betting that's going to be a hot spot for these sharks."

"Okay," sighed Simon. "One more row." He plunged the oars back in the bay.

The shark timed its fierce attack with tight precision. Its jaws widened, teeth hungry for the kill, waiting to be stained with fresh blood.

The water ripped with intense energy.

Simon felt a sharp jerk to the right. The oar cracked in half like dry firewood. "What the hell was that?"

Muncie couldn't react in time. His eyes followed the black shadow as it broke the surface.

Simon's deafening screams echoed in Muncie's ears, as the shark's scarred face sank beneath the bay with a blanket of red and Simon's detached right arm throttling between its jaws.

Simon's blood gushed from the fresh wound, filling the bottom of the boat.

Muncie felt something else fast approaching. The fog had now surrounded the boat and the brothers were effectively cut off from any source of help. Muncie's years in the Navy had taught him to understand and feel the sea. His senses knew a dorsal fin had broken the surface somewhere nearby. His hands grabbed the spear gun from the blood soaked floor. His fingers prepared for the kill shot.

The shark Jack had nicknamed "Freddy", had come back for more. The head emerged through the fog with a startling roar and clamped down hard on the boat behind Muncie. In the commotion Simon toppled over the side of the boat and soon drowned beneath the bay.

Muncie was caught off guard and fired off an errant shot while he spun around to face the shark. The shot penetrated the shark's skin, but yielded no damage. "Holy Mother of Christ!" He screamed as he embraced the shark's open jaws and felt the raw power of the shark crunch down on his body. The forceful impact broke apart the boat and severed Muncie in half.

A short while later, the final remnants of the boat sank and the fog cleared leaving no trace of the brother's, except for a small floating trail of red.

10:11 a.m.

"She's an absolute beauty!" Dylan whistled hard at the boat. "How did you manage to score it without your dad hounding your ass?"

"He's at work, and unfortunately he left the boathouse unlocked." Preston felt a bit uneasy. "His fault, right?" He attempted to play it off.

"What's the matter?" Dylan asked. "You seem bummed out. You are about to score with the hottest chick in the school."

"I don't think this idea will work. It has too many variables." Preston bounced back and forth with nervous energy.

Dylan reassured him. "Relax, it will. What could go wrong?"

"The sharks are a good enough reason," added Preston. "Man, you have no idea do you?" His head shrugged at Dylan's lack of clarity for the situation.

"I got that covered." Dylan brushed off his friend's concerns.

"Really? Really?" Preston mocked. "How do you have it covered, genius?" His emotions were easily stirred by Dylan's reckless attitude toward everything in life.

"If you see a dorsal fin break the water, be careful." smirked Dylan. "Actually, sharks don't usually attack humans."

"That's the logic of Dylan MacTavish? Be careful? Sharks don't attack humans?" Preston seethed, his voice mocking Dylan's.

"Well, I'm up in the air, out of harms way. You're in a boat. The last time I checked, sharks don't attack boats either."

"What the hell are you talking about? These sharks supposedly took down a ferry earlier this week." Preston spoke with an angry tone. His hands shot up in the air in frustration. "That's it, I'm not going out there." He shook his hand at the bay. "No. This is a very bad idea."

"That ferry shit? That's probably a fabrication. Do you really believe everything you read in the papers or for that matter on the internet?" Dylan placed his arm around Preston. "The media just wants to stir the pot."

"No, I don't believe everything I read. You're probably right about the fabrication and the media's true intentions." Preston licked his mouth for moisture. "I'm still leery about this whole plan of yours."

"Of course I'm right, I usually am," Dylan paused for a glance at the bay. "It's pitch perfect for parasailing. It'd be a downright glaring shame if we didn't score some waves right?"

"True."

"Come on." Dylan ruffled Preston's hair. "One trip around the bay and then we come back in before we're even missed."

"Well," Preston fumbled for an answer. "Okay, but if we see a fin, we're coming in. No questions asked."

Dylan thought for a moment. "Yeah, no questions asked." He pulled Preston closer with a playful tug of the shoulders. "Preston, I've never told you this, but," Dylan leaned in close, "I've always thought of you as my brother. The two of us, you know, inseparable."

Preston was an only child and Dylan had become his only friend since grade school. They were, in most cases, as close as brothers. "Really? We are?"

"Yes. Yes, we are. Why do you doubt that?" Dylan asked. "With that said, I'm going to need to another favor. A small favor of sorts."

"What?" Preston knew it was too good to be true. "What's the favor?"

"I'm bringing Dawn," Dylan said. "I'm going to need to show her a great time."

"Your girlfriend of the week?" Preston's tone soured.

"And," Dylan continued.

"And another girlfriend for you?" Preston steamed underneath.

"Preston, because I think so highly of you, like my kid brother, I've decided to invite Cathy Bixby."

Preston's heart skipped a beat. "I thought you were inviting her to the yacht party later?"

"Well, I figured the two of you would want to bond a little bit before the party. In fact, they should be getting here right about now." Two beautiful girls approaching the edge of the cove interrupted Dylan.

Preston kept meekness in his attitude. He didn't care if Dylan used him for the boat, and lied to him about being a brother to him. He came through and delivered with his promise of Cathy Bixby. Preston knew deep down Cathy was only here for the ride, and probably couldn't give two shits about him. Preston grinned. For once in his wobbly, nerdy life, he was the one they all wanted. He held the keys to the palace, and the palace was filled with blue skies, crisp water, and a sixteen-foot maroon red and ivory white sprinter called Chum Bucket.

Preston leered uncomfortably at Cathy. It was always a chore when it came to the women for him. He never knew how long a stare could quickly become a creepy leer from a pervert. Her sweetened curvy frame, short curly blond hair and belly button piercing had him fighting for control. Her powder pink and white polka dot bathing suit fit perfectly. Dylan's girlfriend, Dawn fared slightly better. Her reddened auburn hair, freckled skin, and skintight frame also captured Preston's attention. Yet, something else about Cathy reeled him in.

The two girls approached the idling boat with a cooler of beer and sandwiches hugged between them. Cathy looked right at Preston and offered a wink in his direction. "Hi there Stud."

Preston knew she was filling his grave with dirt, and he didn't care. "Hi," his response was soft and weak.

"Oh, he's shy? How sweet." Cathy stepped into the boat and brushed past him allowing him to inhale her scent.

Preston's heart went crazy, and his brain went into overdrive. He kept thinking how sweet she smelled. It reminded him of a mixture of cinnamon and vanilla.

"So what's the plan guys?" Dawn asked, before she placed a kiss on Dylan's lips.

"Preston here borrowed the boat so we could enjoy a trip around the bay," Dylan said, "and I'll show off my parasailing skills."

"You're such a charmer," Dawn added with another lingering kiss. "Always a ladies man aren't you?"

"This isn't your boat is it?" Cathy asked. "Is it your dad's?"

"Yeah." Preston prepared the boat for departure from the cove.

"You have balls." Cathy turned around to face him. "Balls of stone."

"Well, I hope so." Preston went red-faced.

"Preston, you're such a charmer. It's quite cute," Cathy replied. "No, I mean, you have the tough skinned attitude I admire." Her voice deepened.

"Really?" He fumbled for the answer.

"Your dad will probably kick your ass for this right?" Cathy stepped in closer.

"Definitely," Preston answered with an uncomfortable laugh. He could feel the heat radiating from Cathy's body. "He's going to skin my hide for this little excursion."

"So you risked your ass for this trip on the bay? To spend an afternoon with me?"

"You could say that."

"That's so hot," she said. Her hands reached for his shirt and pulled him close to her. A swift kiss on his lips left Preston humbled, excited and ready to embark on the day.

The lingering, lazy white fog gave way to the mid-morning sun allowing for a crystal clear day for summer activities. Preston managed to guide his way through the collecting armies of rogue hunters and media hounds gathering across the bay. "It's going to be an interesting day with all these people crowding the market." He kept the leisurely pace from the cove as the quartet squeezed by a couple of boats.

A few coarse expletives later from the other riders Dylan let out a whistle of disappoint as he inspected the fresh scar on the side of the boat. "Damn, that's gonna leave a mark."

"What?" Preston became defensive. "That shit head scraped the side of the 'Bucket?"

"Scraped?" Dylan laughed it off. "It's more like they gouged it down to the skeletal system."

"Easy," Cathy interrupted the boys. "Let's find a neutral zone out in the bay, crack open the cooler, and unwind. I'm going to need to work on my sunbathing," she said with a short giggle before she leaned in and whispered the rest into Preston's ears. "I'm going to need someone with sturdy hands to rub oil all over me."

Preston managed a hearty grin. "We can head out over there, past the bridge. It gives us plenty of sun and room for Dylan to parasail."

"Smart and sexy," added Cathy. "You're a peach."

Dawn released the frigid beers from the silver cooler and cracked off the bottle caps. "Drink up boys."

"So Preston here thinks there's some danger out here." Dylan motioned to the bay with a beer in hand. "Don't you?"

Preston felt the immediate heat of Dylan's statement.

"Danger?" Cathy perked up. "Oh baby, I'm drawn to danger."

Preston fumbled to avoid the answer.

"Well, aren't you going to tell the girls about the danger lurking beneath the bay?" Dylan kept prodding his friend as he twisted off another cap. He flicked the bottle cap overboard.

Its senses picked up the faint noises and splash in the bay.

The bottle cap drifted down, spiraling through the bay before it glanced off the tough skin of a nearby shark several feet below the boat.

"What danger, Pres?" Cathy begged him for an answer.

"There's a media rumor, and some eyewitness stories, that some brutal shark attacks have happened out here." Preston exhaled and poured the beer down his throat.

"But we're safe right?" Dawn asked.

Dylan embraced her. "Yeah baby, we are. Preston here won't let anything happen to us."

"I'll try to live up to that." Preston finished off the beer and returned the bottle to the cooler.

Dylan tossed his empty bottle to the water.

Fifty feet below the boat the shark glided methodically. Its snout felt the odd object bounce off. A vise-like clamp with its teeth shattered the bottle, sprinkling glass throughout the dark bay. A few jagged pieces ripped the shark's gum line, forcing out a small droplet of blood.

The four shared one more fast-paced round of beers before Dylan prepared for his jaunt across the bay for parasailing. Dawn adhered to the safety rules and made sure her boyfriend was secured, safe, and sealed with a kiss for added comfort.

Cathy slipped out of her pink bikini and revealed her curvy

frame with eye-appealing 36 C's. A healthy tan covered her soft flesh and made Preston nearly fumble away the bottle of oil over the side of the boat. "I'll just stretch out right here," she said imitating a fake stretch giving Preston a full glance of her well-known beauty.

Preston squeezed a small amount of oil on the grain of his sweating palms and approached Cathy with nerdy reservation.

"Don't be shy," she answered with a laugh, "lather me up, cowboy." She pressed her face against the cushion of the bench and waited for the royal treatment.

"You two almost done over there?" Dylan chided the group. "I'm ready."

Preston finished up the rub on Cathy's back and headed back to his duties as Captain of the Chum Bucket. "Hold on, king," he started the boat. Within a few seconds Dylan was soaring high above the water. The 'Bucket kept a steady pace as Dylan enjoyed the view from high above. Preston calmed the boat, sliding it to autopilot and let the winds carry his friend for a while. It was becoming the perfect storm for him. A writhing, naked girl arched out in limber invitation, his dickhead friend high above without any interference, and Dawn in a zombie like trance, mesmerized by Dylan's slick skills and daunting machismo.

"When will you need to restart the boat again?" asked Cathy, her head tilted to the right to catch a passing glance at Preston.

"The wind's blowing with a double edge. He'll be able to glide up there for a while. I'm busy with other matters right now." Preston's confidence grew as he massaged the oil deep into Cathy's muscles, working her over with cool masculinity. His ego surely benefited from Cathy's desire for his attention.

"Oh God, you have the hands of Zeus. So strong and powerful."

"I understand you're making fun of me, so I'd appreciate it if you would stop the snide remarks." Preston still had some reservations about her true intentions.

Cathy immediately changed her tone. "Preston, I'm being quite sincere with you. I've always been attracted to you in tan odd sort of way." She offered a smile to smooth it over.

Preston held firm with a sarcastic tongue. "Please, I can feel the vomit swirling in my throat."

"You've always treated me with respect and kindness, and never judged me," Cathy answered back. "That means the world to a girl like me." She smiled.

"Well, you deserve it." Preston continued his magic on her back. He felt a little better after she ironed out the wrinkles.

"All the guys want from me is some sort of sexual favor, or worse, a trophy girlfriend." She sighed.

"And how do you know I don't want that as well?"

"Because of the way you're sweet with your words and actions, and the gentle way you're massaging my back," she observed. "You take great care in treating a woman. And, from the looks of things, you are one hell of a friend to that dickhead up there." She pointed to the sky referring to Dylan.

"I never knew. I've been in the dark all these years," Preston was humbled by Cathy's honesty.

"Preston, are you going to stand there and reminisce about your nerdy past or squirt oil all over my back and come and finish the dance?"

"We're not going to need the oil. I've got what you need." Preston tossed the oil to the side and caught Cathy by surprise in a powerful lip lock. He felt another surge of machismo as she let a satisfied moan of pleasure escape.

"I'll take the wheel while the two of you suck face." Dawn regained control of the boat and guided her boyfriend through the bay. "Of all the hot guys in the school, she picks the nerd."

Dawn felt turbulence against the side of the boat as a patch of fog rolled over the teenagers. "Did you feel that?" she asked.

"Feel what?" Cathy answered, her head coming up for a brief respite from Preston's passionate kisses.

"That bump against the boat?" Dawn peeked over the side and eyed the silhouette of something ominous descending further underneath the bay's surface.

"Preston's a bit rough, maybe it was him?" Cathy chided back with a giggle.

"No, it wasn't him," added Dawn. Her fingers slipped off the wheel as another rock of the boat sent her reeling backward, and Cathy and Preston landed entangled with each other on the floor of the boat. "Now, did you feel *that?*" Dawn growled back.

The three peered over the edge of the boat and witnessed a large shadow escaping once again from the boat.

"What about Dylan?" Preston asked. He reached to kill the engine on the boat.

"He's above the fog, it's impossible to communicate with him." Dawn stared straight up. "Let's wait for a clearing and we'll bring him in."

Dylan had felt the jolt from underneath. "Hey guys! What's going on down there?" He attempted to gather a clear picture of what was happening through the thick fog. Nothing emerged and he soon dismissed the mild jostle from below.

Preston and Dawn were engaged in conversation when Cathy walked backward into them. "What's the matter, Cath?" Dawn asked.

Cathy remained silent, frozen like a half-naked statue of fear. Her body trembled, skin covered in goose bumps, her fingers pointed to the stern.

Preston and Dawn followed Cathy's frenetic pointer finger.

Cathy's lips trembled, sucked inward, and then escaped with sound. The dorsal fin broke through as the ominous silhouette emerged. "SHARK!"

Another shark crashed through the surface on the eastern starboard side. "SHARK!" Dawn screamed. Cathy followed again with another verbal echo of the word.

The first shark, thirty-five feet in length, brought its mighty jaws down hard on the rear of the boat, splintering the fiberglass and forcing the bay to flood the boat.

The second shark, the smaller of the pack at thirty feet, timed its attack differently and barreled head first against the starboard side, cracking the framework. A steady stream of water broke through, adding more water to the sinking vessel.

"Motherfucker," Preston slipped in the water, stopping his fall with a hard grab of the steering wheel.

The sharks retreated and patiently bided their time.

"Shit, what are we going to do now?" Dawn yelled. "And that mouthy bastard severed the line to Dylan."

"As long as there's wind Dylan's safe up there," Preston answered, his eyes attempted to peer through the fog at Dylan's whereabouts. "Dylan!" He shouted, but was cut short by the larger shark breaking through and clamping down on the stern of the boat once more.

The rolling fog obstructed all visibility and Preston's shouts for Dylan became muffled. "What the hell is going on?" Dylan felt freedom from the boat. "Shit, the line snapped." His reaction swift, his hands soon manually adjusted to the situation, using the handles to guide the parasail. The wind remained strong and he kept pace through the fog and misty rain.

"They better be drunk as hell, because I'm going to ream all of them new assholes." His eyes squinted against the streaking sunshine.

Dawn lost her footing and slid down the sinking boat. Preston reached for Cathy, but it was too late. Dawn's lower torso became entangled inside the beast's mouth and a series of wild kicks yielded Dawn no reprieve. The shark sank its teeth deep and dragged Dawn bloodied and frightened beneath the bay's blood red water. Dawn gargled a few more screams before blood and water flooded her lungs.

Preston fought to save Cathy in the chaos but her sudden disappearance concerned him. He reached to the starboard side of the sinking boat. His eyes scoured the desolate patch of water. A hard crash of the surface brought him to terrifying attention; it was Cathy. She was a solid distance from the boat. Although the boat endured extensive damage, it was the only hope for Cathy. "Cathy! Swim! Swim, Cathy, Swim!"

Preston searched the boat for some sort of weapon. His hands threw off the top of the bench and removed a few things in haste, tossing them over his shoulder. A bead of sweat trickled down his face, then another, then another. Preston returned to Cathy for a moment to check on her status. "Swim, Cathy, Swim!" He found his father's prized hunting weapon at the bottom of the makeshift storage compartment. His fingers clutched the harpoon gun and prepared it for firing. His other hand secured the flare gun and he wasted no time firing off a warning shot clear of harm's way.

The boat continued sinking into the bay. "Fuck, where is that bastard?" Preston searched the bay. Nothing. After a short pause, the dorsal fin broke through behind Cathy. The fin sped through the water, cutting it with precision and spraying water across the bay.

Preston raised the harpoon gun and steadied his shot. "Faster Cathy!" He hollered. "Faster!" He knew she was losing energy, and probably injured from the attack. He squinted his eye and waited for the shark to emerge once again.

Another splash from behind alerted him to what was coming next. He knew it was the other shark, and time was clearly short.

Cathy ducked under the water for a moment, and then returned screaming, her mouth filling with blood. Preston couldn't hit the elusive shark, but he diverted his attention and whistled the shot clear through Cathy's heart ending her nightmare.

Preston reloaded for the second shark. He pivoted around, his feet sloshed in the waterlogged boat.

The shark's snout shattered the calm surface, its teeth ripe for the kill.

Preston swallowed a deep breath. He knew from his father's fishing expeditions the best way to kill a shark was to not rely on the obvious design of the kill. "A little bit more. "Come on! Let me see those black eyes of yours," Preston beckoned the shark to stare him down. His finger rested on the trigger. He had his plan set. He was going to bury the harpoon deep in that monster's brain right through the eye and make his father proud.

The fog soon cleared and Dylan peered down at the horror scene below. The boat was obliterated, spread across the bay like matchsticks on a tabletop. There was no sign of Preston, Cathy, or Dawn. Dylan felt his throat swell with fear. His mind ran amuck with the possibility of Preston's shark scenario. It had to be the reason for the carnage below. Dylan felt the wind dying down and fear crept up his body some more. There was no conceivable landing spot for him. If the wind didn't pick up, he was headed straight for a hard water landing. His hand reached to his pocket for his cell phone. It slipped from his grasp and hurtled into the bay below.

Dylan's eyes widened in despair as the bay grew closer. He braced for impact. His feet took the brunt of the crash. The water felt cool against his fractured sun burnt skin. The refreshing feeling soon soured, as he knew a bone had burst through somewhere. His mouth unleashed a howl of anger as he tried to fight through the excruciating pain.

Dylan's intelligence may have been sub-par when it came to the core subjects, but he knew even a milliliter of blood attracted sharks. His arms still ensnared inside the collapsed parasail, his legs kicked wildly beneath him. He felt the bone eruption just above his left ankle. The adrenaline vanished and pain riddled his entire leg.

He ducked under the water for a quick peek. His ankle was shot and a small swirl of blood twisted clockwise away from the wound. His blurry eyes focused on a group of shadows that seemed to come from all directions. His head burst back through the surface, water ran down his face. His body still wrapped up in the parasail provided constant friction and limited his escape.

The dorsal fins broke through one by one.

Dylan stopped counting after five. His head submerged once more and he watched the group gain ground on his location. The three sharks leading the pack were definitely not of this area, but the other two were the residential great whites.

Dylan dislocated his left shoulder as he struggled to untangle himself from the parasail. The first dorsal fin submerged and he felt the shark scrape by his ribs, opening a new wound with its tough skin. Dylan knew the procedure. The shark had opened the buffet table. The next shark grabbed hold of Dylan by the feet and pulled him under. His screams were muffled underwater, his bubbles rose to the surface. Those black eyes rolled back and the monster severed off the rest of his feet.

Unable to maintain balance with his mauled legs, he made one final lunge for the surface with a kick-start of adrenaline, only to find himself completely wrapped up in the parasail. The next shark punctured his lungs and brought him down with a forceful scream. His eyes caught sight of the pack clamoring for a piece of him. The sight of the sharks, reducing him to the suffering prey, devoured Dylan's machismo. To make matters worse his body was a bloodied puppet hanging from the parasail underwater, arms knotted in broken angles, his body still buckled inside the safety belt, and his head tilted in defeat.

A pack of seagulls flocked across the bay as the parasail disappeared beneath the water with a harsh tug. They plucked up the remains of Dylan's brains and ripped flesh as the dorsal fins retreated and the bloody pool dissipated leaving no trace of Dylan MacTavish.

The silent hum had caused his Boston Celtics I-phone case to bounce about the wooden table. A short breath and a brief wave encouraged the members of his party to take their seats.

"Good morning Harrison. What does the mayor want from the SFPD?" His free hand brought the crystal glass of water to his lips. Loomis refused to wait for an answer. "Harrison, I can't stress how busy I am at the moment."

Sheriff Malcolm Loomis tapped the blue and white menu with his free hand encouraging his party to glance over the lunch menu. His hand reached for the warm basket of bread the waiter brought him earlier. He parlayed a quick glance behind him at the underwater aquarium, a glamorous design of the restaurant's architecture. "I'm about to enjoy quite the power lunch with some world-class friends." He snapped off the biscuit heartily. "What's all this about?"

"I'm having a yacht party," the mayor's voice crackled through the phone.

"That's the point of this insane call? What the fuck does that have to with me?" Loomis polished off his biscuit and took another drink of water. "The citizens of San Francisco elected you to run the city, and you want to interrupt my lunch for a yacht party?" He tossed the breadcrumbs across the table. A few scattering glances caught him by surprise.

"I have some concerns," Harrison continued.

"Make it real short, Harry," Loomis chided the mayor. "You're on a short leash here."

"These sharks could pose a problem."

"The whites?" Loomis asked, not really interested in the conversation.

"No. The others."

"I chatted with Darrin on the bridge after the crash," Loomis said with a growl. "He's all over this."

"I know. I have him in the bay. I also have the military and Davenport on patrol."

"You have the military on call." Loomis laughed it off. "It must be your crazy ass brother calling in a favor."

"It doesn't matter Malcolm," Harrison answered with a grit to his tone. "Will you be able to assist me? Because you see, the entire bay will fall apart this weekend if these sharks continue to hunt our residents."

Loomis blew a breath of aggravation. "I honestly have no idea what you want me to do."

"I need extra muscle."

"Even though it's my jurisdiction, you seem to have all the corners covered Harry." Loomis waved over the waiter. "I'm going to eat my lunch and close all of the loose ends you've left hanging for me."

"Like what?"

"That car crash off the bridge, the dead surfer, and the ferry accident. It appears the survivors of the victims are pissed off and want to sue the city for every damn nickel in our treasury."

"Well, that's why I have you on my payroll Malcolm," Harrison said with a snickering laugh. "I suggest you get to work, and then come provide security at my party."

Loomis ended the call with a hard press of his fingertip and slid the phone across the table in a rush of anger.

"I'm sorry for the phone call," Loomis said to his party. "The mayor has impeccably bad timing."

The two lawyers shook their heads in agreement.

"Anything you want on the menu," urged Loomis, "go ahead and order."

Loomis took another peek at the aquarium and smiled. He took pleasure in sea life; especially the diversity San Francisco had to offer. "So the two of you are lawyers from the top firm in the city?" Loomis swirled his water and clacked the ice cubes together.

"Yes sir," the younger man answered. "We are with the Winston Group."

"I'm Albert Rojas, and this is Valery Delgado."

"Well, nice to meet the two of you," Loomis answered. "I'm sure we can all come to an acceptable agreement on these lawsuits. It's been a tragic few days with the earthquake and the shark attacks to say the least."

"What are your plans for these sharks, Sheriff?" Albert reached for his appetizer - a bed of steamed clams, a lobster tail with a dish of yellow butter sauce, and a Sprite Zero. The husky lawyer had an insatiable appetite.

"Yes, how can we soothe the parents and loved ones of those innocent victims?" asked Valery. "How can we assure them everything will be different, safer, and most of all, wipe away these recurring nightmares?" The younger lawyer reached for Al's clams only to have his hand smacked away. "These citizens are living in a reality where the terror remains clear and intact."

"Don't touch my food," Al said. He stuffed the clam inside his waiting mouth, saliva dripping onto the white napkin below.

"As a matter of fact, the mayor himself has orchestrated a decisive plan," Loomis took another bite of a second biscuit. His eyes steered away from the portly lawyer and his lethargic looking partner, and focused on a series of shadows looming inside the aquarium.

"Do tell." Val sprawled his fork across his recently arrived dish of loaded baked potato wedges garnished with mushrooms and bacon.

"He's enlisted the assistance of another sheriff, a local marine biologist and her shark team," Loomis paused for another bite. "And gentlemen, if that wasn't enough, the fucking mayor has Marines staged across Alcatraz Island. Yes, the fucking Marines. Nothing will slip by those guys." Loomis winked and placed his half-eaten biscuit back on the plate while he waited for his porterhouse to arrive. He rose from the chair. "So can we agree to a monetary value here? I'll give a series of public service announcements, create scholarships and fundraisers in memory of those innocent, innocent victims." Loomis curled his lower lip to feign affection for the dead. He knew these two neophytes would buy anything he offered them. They were star struck just to be eating clams and lobster in the finest restaurant on the wharf. "So, do we have a deal?"

"I'll have to run it by our boss, but I don't see why not." Al took another gulp of clams, nearly choking as we watched the shadow approach the viewing glass.

"Excellent," said Loomis, his back to the aquarium. "Hey kid, what's the problem with you?"

Al choked down the clam and took a hard drink of soda. "Are you sure those sharks are under control?"

"Yes, I just confirmed the mayor's plan. Weren't you paying attention?" answered Loomis, his anger level rising and patience thinning.

"Are we safe in here?" Al and Val rose from the table echoing the statement in eerie unison.

"Fuck yeah, we're in a restaurant." Loomis turned his head to the aquarium to see what they were looking at. His eyes tracked the shadow, as it scattered away the smaller fish and approached the glass with blazing speed and accuracy. "Holy hell," he whispered, his hand already unlatched his Glock from its holster.

"It can't break through that, right?" Al asked. He and Val were already backing away, heading for the exit.

"It's virtually shatter-proof," Loomis assured all of the curious guests as they all stared at the tank in amazement. "Jesus Christ, it's polymer boys. It doesn't break into tiny pieces like stressed glass. It just bends and bows."

A series of screams erupted as the shadow revealed itself with a thunderous impact against the tank. The entire room rattled. Loomis aimed the gun at the forty-foot menace. "Son-of-a-bitch." He watched the tank give a little, bending and bowing from the impact. He flicked the safety off and felt for the trigger. A wave of pandemonium spread throughout the restaurant, people trampling others to the exits. "Everyone calm down, I have everything under control. They can't just crash through the restaurant. It's not possible." Loomis spun to face the restaurant and delivered his speech, but his words were lost in the chaos of people rushing to escape.

The shark soon retreated.

Loomis withdrew the gun and turned back to the crowd. "See? Nothing happened. That ugly bastard swam away after those black eyes saw this," he said raising the gun. "I'd like to see that shark come back for more. He'll be chewing on lead after I get done with him---"

Loomis felt the hairs on the back of his neck bolt upright, mere moments before his eyes caught a glimpse in the bartender's mirror across the room of three sharks rampaging toward the tank. A cold, bitter wave of water flooded the restaurant, drowning the entire building in the aquarium's contents.

One by one the sharks entered the restaurant, growling for prey. Al and Val never made out of the building, their legs caught beneath debris and their lungs ran out of air. Freddy soon ended their problem; his mouth widened and engulfed both of them with one chomp of his jaws.

Michael's size enabled him to cover the most area. A speedster and ruthless killer, the shark picked off the confused swimmers rolling back his black eyes back with every sinister saw of his teeth. A few moments later his dorsal fin reached through a thick blanket of red as he retreated back to the bay with a satisfied appetite.

Jason, the largest of the group, kept a fierce pace through the dismembered bodies and carnage.

Loomis swam for the nearest exit, startled, confused and second-guessing his decisions. His lungs were about to burst when he swam past a series of floating lifeless bodies. He knew his weapon was a state of the art Glock 22 Gen 4 that allowed for underwater shooting. He was an avid scuba diver and used the weapon for protection when necessary. He would have to time his shot perfectly; he only had a two-and-a-half-foot margin of error.

Jason stretched out his mammoth jaw and clamped down hard on the flailing prey ahead of him.

Loomis let off a howling scream. His ankles severed completely off, a slurry of blood filled the water. His body shifted around, as he held his gun, ready to fire. His eyes met those of the shark. The black piercing eyes refused to blink. Loomis, in his usual stubbornness, refused to back down from a fight. There was no time for words. His lungs screamed for air, the left one reached its full capacity. He felt it pop. A sly grin added to the drama as he pulled back on the trigger. A bullet tore through the water and embedded itself directly in the snout of the shark.

A patch of red blood emerged. The shark closed it eyes for a moment.

Loomis couldn't move. His feet were gone and so was his balance. He readied the Glock for another crack at the shark.

Jason reopened his eyes and snarled forth, clamping down on Loomis's waist.

Loomis felt the shark's teeth grind down as he felt a rush of energy overtake him. His hand kept beating the shark on the side of the head with the gun. He unleashed an errant shot through the water.

Jason sped out of the wrecked restaurant and gained momentum as he headed for a series of docked boats. His mouth released its grip on its prey at the exact moment of impact.

Loomis was sent screaming to his death as Jason released him against the hull of a docked yacht with the intensity of a sixty-mile-per-hour bus. Loomis's head exploded on impact. A stream of bloody brain matter smeared across the surface.

Jason soon returned to enjoy the remains of Sheriff Malcolm Loomis.

Off in the distance, the severed hand of the sheriff, Glock intact, settled to the bay floor with a quiet displacement of sand and pebbles.

Mayor Harrison MacTavish welcomed his guests with a grin and a false gentleman's handshake. His eyes monitored another yacht a few piers down being rocked violently, but thought nothing of it as he turned his attention back to the crowd. A collection of surfers, including Patrick Ryan, the son of the President of the United States, emerged. A patch of Secret Service followed closely behind with black tinted sunglasses and tuxedos that mad it obvious who they were.

Robert Roy, an independent filmmaker from New Hampshire, pulled the mayor to the side. "Hello sir," he greeted him. "I'm Rob and this is my special effects and make-up assistant, Watson," he introduced the mayor to his slender and very pretty colleague.

Watson fixed her sliding glasses as she nodded toward the mayor. Her voice was sweet and to the point. "Hello."

Harrison feigned the desire to care. "And what do you want today, Mr. Roy?"

"What's the deal on the sharks?" Rob adjusted the strap to his camera and rolled a piece of Trident gum inside his mouth. His uncanny resemblance to actor Bill Murray caught several by surprise, and he was fine with that. A recent weight loss added to the glaring role of celebrity status for the director of countless gripping films.

The mayor leaned in toward Rob. "As the most talked about independent director of the last year, are you hungry for a new storyline?" His recently whitened teeth displayed that 'winning' political smile of his. His mental engines were in full gear for the event and it seemed nothing would derail his ambitious design for a fundraising tour de force.

"I'm privy to a shark movie with real footage," said Rob as he adjusted his stance to let other guests pass by onto the yacht. "It adds more depth to the story."

"The sharks aren't going to be a problem. I have my best men containing the situation and making this event a historic one." Harrison slapped him on the shoulder. "Now, if you'll excuse me, I have other guests to greet."

"Yeah, sure," Rob said with a sour tone, his confidence deflated by the mayor's smug attitude. "He's such a jackass."

Watson brushed aside her red and purple hair with a quick flick of her small fingers. "Yeah, he blows. We can get our own footage."

"Aren't you afraid of the water?" Rob joked with her.

"Well, yes. I'm terrified of deep water, but since we're on a yacht, I think we're safe from any type of apocalyptic disaster." She smirked, briefly displaying her innocent grin, before it was wiped away with an evil twist of her lips. "I'm not afraid to go into dark places, you know that Rob. But this bay may be the darkest chasm we've ever seen."

Rob nodded his head. "I know they're out there waiting for us. The mayor has no clue what he's doing."

"So why are we here if you think the mayor's off his clock?"

"Adventure filming is the most exhilarating experience in the world," said Rob. "If we're able to capture real time footage of these mammoth sharks and splice it into our movie, it will be gold."

"You do know how to get a girl excited don't you? I love the tease of a dangerous adventure." She smiled once more and ran her hands over her body in a shivering tease of satisfaction.

Rob grabbed the passing waiter by the arm. He reached over and took two shots of whiskey from the silver plate. "Here's to our movie." He handed Watson a shot glass. He downed his shot with ease.

"Here's to one hell of a party." She swallowed down her shot with one swift action, her eyes lit up from the whiskey's punch. "Ah, that's the shit right there."

Harrison continued his rounds with the other professional surfers that made their way on board, a wrestling superstar in David "Scotty Flash" Lewis, a few musicians and their female lead singer Miss Tina K. Harrison's jaw ached from the conversations, yet the power of speech soon filled the yacht and departure time was nearing. The crowd kept mingling and chatting with one another much to Harrison's delight.

"Ah, Miss Tina K," Harrison smooched her freckled hand in affection. "You are a red-headed maelstrom of musical talent."

"Why thank you, Mayor," Tina replied in kindness. "You're a political gem as well, and it's my pleasure to perform here tonight to raise funds for the area."

"I look forward to the performance." Harrison's attention diverted to the skies as Sheriff Davenport shot a wave to him from the helicopter. "Asshole," Harrison muttered under his breath.

"What's that bird up in the sky for, Mayor?" asked Tina. Her eyes were glued to the sky as well, tracking the path of the helicopter.

"Yeah, what's the chopper for, Mayor?" Watson asked from the group.

"I have my capable sheriff patrolling the area," he said attempting to diffuse the nature of the questions. "He's been instructed to keep the bay safe."

"Is he watching for the sharks?" Tina's voice was filled with concern that was echoed by other guests who were gathering to see the helicopter.

Harrison went into full-blown recovery mode. "If they are reckless enough to surface, then my sheriff will plug their tiny brains full of bullets," he paused, "and then we'll change tonight's menu to shark steak!"

A short round of laughter and applause ensued.

Tina and Watson were concerned and conversed together over the applause about the state of situation.

"What brings you here?" Tina asked her.

Watson took a breath and smiled. "Rob's shorthanded and he begged me to make the flight out here. What about you?"

Tina waved down a waiter and scooped some clams from the silver platter. "Ah, yes, well my young lady, I'm the entertainment for today's party." She sucked down the clams and prepared for another round, but couldn't catch the wandering waiter.

"That's neat." Watson kept peering around the crowd. "This mayor seems a bit off the compass doesn't he?"

Tina nodded. "Aren't all politicians?"

The two parted and each went about the yacht in search of more food and drink.

A few feet away the mayor kept his mouth busy trying to coerce his guests into forking over their hard earned money.

"Now please feel free to donate some coin to the cause, enjoy some great seafood and drinks, and don't worry about the sharks. I've got all the angles covered. In a short time, the lovely Miss Tina K will sing from her outstanding library of music. Until then, spread out and enjoy the afternoon." Harrison took a step back and watched the crowd mingle and chatter among themselves.

The mayor forced his way to the bar for a desperately needed drink. A quick snap of his fingers brought the bartender over. "Whiskey on the rocks." He impatiently tapped the counter so hard it made his gold watch bounce against his slender wrist. He drowned his swelling apprehension with the whiskey and prepared for another round, but a voice derailed his train of thought.

"You are a man of great rhetoric," the man said as he poured himself a drink from the bar.

Harrison sized him up while he cradled his drink affectionately. He was a man in his late thirties with a thick beard of grey and a sunburn. "You aren't from around here are you?"

"Nope." The man kept drinking. "Michigan."

"Aren't you that guy?" Harrison tapped the bar for the next phrase. The name of the man escaped him. "Shit, I can see your name on the damn billboards."

"Yep." The man finished off his scotch. "I am him." He smiled.

"The famous horror author." Harrison got closer to remembering the name. "You've been the country's most prolific writer for the last decade."

"Sawyer. Tom Sawyer," the man played the James Bond routine with perfect sarcasm.

"Isn't that name a bit overused?" Harrison chided back, a bit frustrated for not remembering it sooner.

"It still plays the right chords with the ladies," Tom's answer was glib.

"What brings you to the festivities today?" Harrison prodded further. He placed his emptied glass back on the bar. "I'm hoping being a staunch Republican and having your pockets lined with coin is a start to our friendship."

"I'm picky when it comes to friends." Tom tapped the bar. "You will receive the healthy benefit of my intended donation," he paused, "not for politics, but for the town's sake."

"You could've donated it through a wire transfer," Harrison was smug. "Why the dramatic public appearance."

"I'm interested to see what happens here today."

"What do you mean?"

"I've figured you're either dumb as a box of wet rocks, or, you have no hint of human decency in your genetic code."

"You could've said that in a letter or an email." Harrison fumed. "You didn't need to come to the party for such antics."

"I'm going with the latter." Tom added a full grin and another shot of scotch to his remark. "I'm a writer and the ending to horror stories are usually bathed in grimy filth and traipsed in blood and chaos."

"That particular ending will not come to fruition today, I can guarantee you that."

"I really have no dice on the table when it comes this floating casino of yours," Tom shook down another shot glass. "I really don't."

"I'm wasting my time here with you." Harrison went to shake Tom's hand. "Thank you for the support and have a great time today."

Tom twisted Harrison's tanned hand around and pinned it firmly to the bar. "I'm only going to say this once you grimy fucker. You can blow those smoke rings up everyone's asses here and tell them it's all going to be okay, and the sharks aren't coming." Tom sighed. "But we both know those beautiful creatures are headed straight for that beating heart of yours. When their razors purge your heart free of its blackened soul, you will survive not in memory, but in ridicule."

Harrison wriggled a few times, forcibly struggling to free himself. "I have everything covered." His face exploded in a red anger and embarrassment. "You, my friend, are overreacting."

"Yes, you keep saying that. Your hollow cries are a broken record repeated to a deaf crowd." Tom held firm. "The intelligent guests know there's something not right out in the bay, but they are here because you've filled their ears with such dribble," he paused for a drink. "As a writer, I've come to notice a few flaws in your logic."

Harrison grumbled back, his head tilted to the left in definitive boredom. "Do tell. I'm dying from boredom."

"Your sheriff in the sky simply can't cover the entire bay. You factor in these new super sharks along with the residential whites, and it doesn't compute. There's going to be a loophole where these beasts emerge victorious."

"I have other means. I never leave wiggle room for my enemy." Harrison smirked.

Tom again sighed in despair. "Unless you have a Matt Hooper with amazing super powers underwater in a shark cage," he paused for another sip. "Which in my creative opinion will be a speed bump to these sharks. These creatures have you pinned down."

"I have the military!" Harrison's tone turned defiant and desperate.

"You have nothing!" Tom shouted back. "Your fantasy land will come to a crashing halt, a chaotic end to your run here as mayor. You need to call this whole thing off."

"I will not!"

"Listen, I've tried to talk sense into you," added Tom. "There's no way you will come out the winner. If the rumors are true and these sharks are over forty feet in length, do you really think they won't attack the yacht?"

"You're crazy," Harrison scoffed back. "This is the Titanic compared to those sharks."

"And what sank the Titanic?" Tom growled back. "Icebergs, you fool. You have three of them out there roaming about and a yacht filled with breakfast, lunch and dinner for these predators." Tom's voice escalated. "Why can't you see you're bringing them right to the mess hall?"

"We're safe." Harrison kept his stance.

"You know what, I was wrong about you," Tom said as he released his grip on the mayor. "Wet rocks are smarter than you."

"Get off my yacht!" Harrison bellowed. He attempted to regain his balance, staggering as he tried to hold on to the bar.

"Now, now," Tom chided him. "That's no way to treat your guests, especially the richer ones."

"Then stay out of my way and keep your witless analogies to yourself." Harrison brushed him aside and headed out to the deck.

Tom sat back with another round of scotch and hummed a familiar tune underneath his moistened lips.

Harrison kept a brisk pace sharing a few pieces of conversation with some of the passengers before reaching the yacht's bow. A few short moments later he initiated a call to the sheriff.

"How's things up there?" Harrison peered upwards watching the skies for the sheriff.

"Murky," the sheriff said. "We have a situation in the bay."

"So take care of it. We have a situation here as well. Some tremors seem to have taken down the aquarium; it's destroyed. There's also some damage along the docks inside the cove."

"The aquarium? Is that the final word? I heard through some backdoor channels it was something else, quite possibly our sharks, and that Loomis is feared dead."

"There will be casualties in war, son. You know that," Harrison's answer was glib. "In any case," he fought back the anger in his voice. "Take care of our situation."

"Don't you want to know about what I found?" Davenport pressed the issue.

"No, that's why I'm paying you to keep everything under

control and out of my line of sight."

"Are you that blind? People are dead. The San Francisco sheriff is dead."

"Well then, I suggest you do your job, especially with these hungry sharks headed right for you."

Davenport ignored the pompous remark, and attempted one more time to speak to the mayor. "Sir, you really need to hear this, it concerns your s--" Davenport's message ended with an abrupt close of the cell phone.

Harrison stuffed the cell deep inside the pocket of his slacks and returned to the gathering crowd of guests with a fake smile stretched across his face.

"That bastard hung up on me." Sheriff Davenport stared down at the phone in disbelief. "Is he really that self-absorbed and cocky to refuse the phone call? His son is dead. Poor Dylan's beyond dead, he's mutilated."

The pilot shrugged his shoulders.

"Land over there, where Skippy is waiting," Davenport instructed.

The pilot made a soft landing on the water.

"Keep an eye peeled for fins." Davenport tapped the pilot on the shoulder. "You see one, you get the hell out of here. I just got off the phone with the aquarium back at the cove, it seems our friends smashed through and caused quite a scene."

"Any casualties?"

"Some yes, including Sheriff Malcolm Loomis," Davenport paused. "And the funny part is the mayor was right there in the yacht club a short distance away from the attack, and didn't even blink an eye. He brushed it off as tremors from the earthquake."

"What a shithead," the pilot added. "I'm glad I voted independent."

The water's calm and tranquil slapped against the stern of Skippy's sleek boat with lazy intentions. "Sheriff," he greeted Davenport's as he boarded the small boat. "I was out and about doing some rounds when I came across this."

"What do we have here, Skip?" Davenport looked over the bow of the boat. "Is that a red parasail?"

"It was one. It's chewed up pretty good, sir," Skippy paused. "But it's what's underneath that frightens me."

Davenport gently peeled away the ripped parasail. "Jesus Christ---," Davenport fumbled for words. His face drained of color, a stinging burp erupted within his esophagus and rocketed for freedom. One clear minute later, Davenport choked off the rest of his vomit and turned back to the mangled remains of the teenager underneath the parasail. "I've never seen shit like this before. There's hardly anything left of him."

"That's what I told you over the phone, Sheriff. Should we tell the mayor?" Skippy asked.

"I tried and the bastard hung up on me." Davenport stroked his face. "We still have to tell him. If not for the obvious, then for the fact that whomever went out with Dylan MacTavish hasn't returned yet either."

"Do you think they've been swallowed as well?" Skippy peered out across the bay. "In all my years living here, I have to say this is one fucked up Fourth of July weekend."

"Let's get this back to the yacht and show the mayor once and for all that these sharks are a real threat." Davenport turned back to the helicopter.

The pilot waited calmly and gave no hint of problems with the sharks.

"By chance have you heard from the Muncie's today?" asked Davenport, his hands on his hips as he scoured the bay.

"No, as a matter of fact I haven't." Skippy rustled what was left of his hair and let off a low whistle. "They always return to shore by now from their morning jaunt across the bay."

"What route do they usually take?" Davenport asked.

"With all this fog, they probably kept close to the bridge."

A patch of boats appeared. "Get some lunch, refuel and come back and get me in an hour," Davenport alerted the pilot through the headset.

The pilot exited the bay and vanished above the thin layer of fog.

"Would you look at these assholes and their recklessness?" Davenport's tone soon sounded defeated. "The mayor has simply crippled the entire city with his boorish intentions."

"Want to alert these amateurs about the sharks?" Skippy asked, his hands already on the steering wheel.

"Only because it's my job," Davenport said. "Do you have anything to catch their attention?"

"Underneath the parasail there's an air horn."

"For what?"

"Safety purposes," Skippy added with a grin. "You know, besides the flare gun, an air horn's the next best thing."

"I have to reach under there?" Davenport ached at the thought of fumbling through Dylan's mutilated remains for the horn. A squeamish stomach once again rolled with venom and fire waiting to purge its contents. He held firm and recovered the air horn from the bloody remains.

"Didn't you just violate a crime scene, Sheriff?"

"Are we concerned with protocol right now? There's hardly anything left for Slim to study back the morgue." Davenport raised the horn. "Get me a few feet closer."

Skippy guided the boat closer to the pack of shark hunters and sightseers.

Davenport sounded the horn alerting the hunters to his arrival.

"Listen to me," he began. "All of you are in trouble out here."

A whispering grew within the circle until one man spoke up.

"Sheriff, in all due respect, isn't it legal to hunt?"

"Not sharks. Not in the bay without a proper fishing license, and not under such dire circumstances."

"Sheriff," the middle-aged man spoke once more. "It's a free country and there's no reason to think our safety isn't our prime concern. Because it is, trust me. We only want to end the threat of these sharks to our community."

"What's your name?" Davenport now had the boat idling side-by-side with the man's. The other hunters soon formed a circle around the sheriff.

"Nicholas."

"Have you been drinking?" Davenport caught a whiff of alcohol.

Nicholas grinned and rolled his eyes. "Maybe a few licks from the ol' bottle."

The others laughed.

"This is why you need to let the professionals control the situation," Davenport pivoted and chatted with the rest of the group. "These sharks real and they won't hesitate to devour everyone here."

"Come on, Sheriff!" The group echoed. "You're being a bit dramatic aren't you?"

"Listen---" Davenport's voice trailed off. It was no use chatting with these Neanderthals and their boozed up brains.

"Have you seen one up close and personal?" Nicholas asked. "Were you able to smell its breath?"

"No," Davenport responded. "I haven't."

"So how do you know they are even out there?" Nicholas's defiance impressed the crowd.

"We should go, Sheriff," Skippy interjected. "Let them learn their lesson."

Davenport grew impatient. "I have the mayor's son in my boat gnawed, ripped, eaten to shreds by these sharks."

The chatter echoed through the water, permeating the depths of the bay. The sharks diverted their course and swam toward the sound waves.

"That could've been done by the whites," Nicholas said. "Whether it is the whites or these newer sharks, it doesn't matter. We will find these sharks for you, don't you worry."

"I'm telling you, there's more than great whites down there, and I'm not keen to scooping up your remains with a bucket."

"It's the thrill of the hunt," added Nicholas. "I promise you another hour and I'm done. I'll be headed to the mayor's yacht party to support my author Tom Sawyer after we're done here.

"That should be fun." Davenport tapped Skippy on the shoulder. "Fine, I can't arrest all of you and throw you in the boat."

"Thank you." Nicholas brushed away his long, curly black hair and smiled back at the sheriff.

"If all of you are still here in fifty-five minutes, then everyone will be thrown in jail. In the meantime I'm going to talk the mayor out of this yacht party."

Michael, the smallest of the pack at thirty feet, slid quietly beneath the bay with keen stealth. The shark's fin broke the surface behind the group.

"You're gonna fuck that up too?" Nicholas snapped back. "All due respect, Sheriff--," Nick's words were cut off, interrupted by a violent jolt from underneath his boat. He teetered into the water.

A series of bumps rippled through the group overturning several of the boats and sending the hunters scrambling to stay out of the bay.

The shark continued plowing through the center of the group until it disappeared, leaving a trail of chaos and uncertainty for the hunters.

Davenport took notice of the thirty-foot shark as it glided by his boat. Its black eyes, rough skin, and strategic attack filled him with fear.

"You see? This is what happens when you don't listen!" Davenport chided everyone.

He and Skippy frantically aided the others as they scrambled to get back in their boats. "Everyone's accounted for sir," Skippy said.

"Shit," said Davenport.

"What?"

"Not everyone." Davenport reached for his trusted Glock and unlatched it from the holster.

A few yards out, Nicholas bobbed up and down in the water, fazed and seeking shelter from the sharks. "Hey, Sheriff!" He called out. "Over here!"

"At least he's easy to spot in that horrid orange shirt," Skippy said. "It strains my eyes just looking at that thing."

"Bring me closer," urged Davenport. "He's too far from his boat. He won't make the swim with those bastards out there." The sheriff took a quick count of the others and felt better as they all headed frantically back to the wharf and the cove.

"Sheriff," Skippy called out. "Starboard side, there he is!"

The fin sliced through and sped toward its prey.

"Nicholas, are you bleeding?" Davenport shouted.

"I think, I don't know. I feel a scrape on my knee," Nicholas called back, his voice simmering with a nervous anxiety. "That's bad isn't it?"

Skippy shook his head in defeat. "He's a horror publisher, and he's asking if that's bad? How ironic is that?"

"Shit," Davenport urged Skippy to hurry. "Sharks are attracted to a milliliter of blood. He's a sitting duck out there." He raised the Glock to fire at the shark. His fingers squeezed off a shot, just missing the fin. A thin spray of blue water erupted.

Nicholas screamed in fear of the gunshot.

It had bought some time for Davenport. The fin submerged briefly. "Can you swim and meet us halfway?"

"I can try." Nicholas began swimming back to the boat. "My muscles are tensing up."

"He's going to have to swim faster." Davenport watched for the fin to re-emerge. He finally spotted it thirty feet behind Nicholas's scrambling body. He fired another shot and thought he hit its torso.

The fog lifted and the helicopter appeared and hovered right above Davenport. "Down here!" He alerted the pilot.

"Got it," the pilot responded, offering a blockade between the shark and Nicholas.

"Nicholas, get in the helicopter!" Davenport shouted, his hand motioning to the chopper above. His eyes remained fixed on the shark whose mouth was inches from exploding through the surface.

Davenport, on the other side of the chopper, held his aim steady. "Hurry!"

The pilot touched down for a brief moment, a few inches above the water. The bay rippled with madly from the speed of the approaching shark.

The shark's mouth stretched open and prepared to clamp down on Nicholas from behind. The monster, mere inches from taking down the helicopter, prepared for the final attack.

The pilot pulled up at the last minute.

A short distance of roughly fifty feet separated the sheriff and the roaring predator.

Davenport felt time suspend for a minute. Skippy ducked for cover in the boat as Davenport pulled back on the trigger. His actions spoke louder than words, burying countless rounds of bullets in the center of the shark's face, forcing them deep into its brain, and in the process obliterating countless rows of teeth.

"That's for Winston and Jack," Davenport's words echoed meaning and victory. He had the momentary pleasure of watching as the shark sank beneath the bay to its death in its own chaotic mess of bone and blood.

Black Tie Affair

11:32 a.m.

H arrison MacTavish continued offering up more subtle handshakes and greetings to the growing crowd with the sole intention of lining the city's pockets with their money. The yacht, a gift bestowed on the mayor months after his re-election campaign ended in a landslide victory, rocked gently in its place at the club. A sparkling specimen of architecture, the yacht was the premier craft in a new line. The mayor always charted his career to have the best of everything, from wine, to women, to expensive toys.

Ashleigh made her way through the bustling crowd in her search for the elusive mayor. A last minute departure from the hospital where Rick remained in stable, yet critical condition, allowed her to board the yacht and mingle. A flowing black strapless dress hugged her curvy frame and a necklace of shark teeth, a birthday gift from Darrin, hung from her neck. She kept an eye out for media hounds as part of the plan that Darrin and the sheriff had devised the previous evening at her house. She would provide damage control and, if necessary, offer a buffer zone. She would much rather have attended the party with Rick, but soon found the company of another friend sitting at the bar.

"Good afternoon," the man greeted her. He pivoted on the bar stool, his face caked in nervous sweat. "I'm never good at starting conversations, especially when a stunner walks in."

"Hello," Ash greeted him. "Rum and coke please," she ordered her drink from the bartender. "A stunner?"

"Yeah, you are very beautiful." He raised glass. "Are you here to donate to the mayor's nefarious cause?"

Ash swirled the ice in her glass before taking a needed drink. "No, I'm actually here to derail his plans."

"Really?" The man perked up. The last several minutes of absorbing expensive liquor had submerged his brain in a murky swamp. "Let me introduce myself," he said while clearing his throat.

"Tom Sawyer." Ash finished off her drink.

"You know of me?"

"Who doesn't? Your mug's plastered all over San Francisco." She smiled. "I actually enjoy your work. I'm pulled, perhaps even dragged, toward the horror genre. You know, the darker side of the coin."

Tom beamed. "Thank you, Miss--?"

"Ashleigh Wilkinson."

"Ah, the marine biologist, and her merry band of tagged great whites."

"Oh, you've heard of me?" She seemed surprised. After all, his famous run as an author had easily overshadowed her mundane work.

"I read," he paused, "I read a lot, especially about the decaying health of the planet. The papers offer a lot of interesting tidbits in these fine parts." Tom smiled.

"I'm in a complicated relationship," Ash warned him, "I'm not interested in a horizontal dance. So keep the slick one-liners to yourself."

"I wouldn't dream of it," he said taken aback by her response. "I actually admire those who fight for the planet and the wildlife. You've written some powerful articles in the science journals detailing the elephant seal's train wreck to extinction."

"Thank you." She took another drink. "It's satisfying when someone other than my parents and my dog recognize and appreciate my hard work.'

"My intentions were to force the mayor to cancel this whole event." Tom rose from the stool.

"How did that go?"

"Shitty. He's a cocky bastard." Tom's tone was deflated.

"Well," she paused to rise from her bar stool, "this whole yacht will be adrift soon in the bay. I have to work interference with the media and keep this whole thing from erupting across all the social outlets, if that hasn't happened already. The accident at the aquarium is drawing every media outlet."

"What happened there? I overheard the mayor chatting about residual tremors."

"The tank erupted in the restaurant and mostly everyone is dead, including Sheriff Loomis," Ash said. "The aquarium is built with polymer and netting to allow it to bend or bow on impact."

"As a writer of the genre, I'd say it took a pretty decent impact to break that tank," Tom answered finishing off his drink and placing it on the counter. "Earthquake tremors wouldn't do that. It had to be something bigger."

"There's an eyewitness who claims to have seen three sharks the size of school buses come crashing through." Ash polished off her drink as well.

"And did they buy those goods?"

"The paramedics treated the witness for shock and nothing further was made of her statement. I was in the hospital when they brought her in, but I was there for someone else and couldn't afford the luxury of leaving my friend."

"That impact would defy the laws of natural physics for sure." Tom looked around the room. "I bet the restaurant is beyond recognition."

"Yep, pretty much. The police have locked down the entire scene because of Loomis's death, it's a crime scene of the highest priority."

"So you want some help with your agenda? I mean, if you want. I'm bored and enjoy watching the mayor squirm."

"I don't see why not." Ash headed for the exit.

Tom reached for her elbow and withdrew the program card for the day's events. "So I managed to secure the events for the mayor's big yacht party. We have the opening remarks, the musical concert featuring Miss Tina K., then the introduction of the surfers in the competition tomorrow, followed by the firework display at the end of the ceremony off Alcatraz Island." Tom smiled and tapped the program guide. "Which one do you want to crash?"

The Cage
11:56 a.m.

D arin Coyle instructed his team where to bring the boat to an idle stop. "This should do." His hands tapped the starboard and peered out across the silent bay. "Daniel, Gavin, are we secured and ready to go?"

"Yes," Gavin answered as he lowered the cage into the bay.

"Are you sure about this, boss?" Daniel asked. His hand kept a busy pace preparing Darrin for the cage dive.

"I don't know. We all made a deal last night at Ash's house."

"This is insane. These sharks are bigger than the whites. They'll devour this thing in one bite." Gavin finished securing the cage to the beams. A few more clicks of the hoist and he gave the thumbs up sign.

"That's the plan." Darrin slipped on his dark blue wetsuit. "Ah, there goes another media chopper," he said pointing up to the sky. "Damn rats to a sinking ship they've become recently."

"What do you mean by that?" Daniel shot back.

"It's a one-way trip for me boys," Darrin added while he tested his equipment, adding a wad of spit to his goggles. A hasty rub with his fingers cleared away the smudge marks and brought his visibility back to normal for the underwater task.

"I don't understand." Gavin stepped in closer to Darrin as if to hit him.

"This cage is not your grandfather's model." Darrin's voice changed in tone. It became serious, brooding, and intelligent. "It has some futuristic modifications."

"It's not? It's a fucking cage man, plain and simple. It's chopsticks for these fuckers down there!" Gavin unraveled. The entire team knew of Gavin's hero worship of Darrin. "You can't do down there on a suicide mission."

"The beauty of this cage," Darrin paused to tug at the wires, "is its ability to give these sharks a jolt. A nerve induced overload that will either trigger a heart attack or fry their brains." Darrin took a deeper breath and held it far longer than usual. "I'm scared, I admit that. But our town, our citizens, they can't be held hostage by these monsters any longer. Sherriff Davenport has the air, Ash has the yacht, and I'm the eyes beneath the surface."

"It's a fucked up plan, if I do say so myself," added Daniel. "I side with Gavin on this one. You are out of your damn mind."

"My mind rolls with ideas of on how to save our ecosystem and preserve the balance." Darrin pulled the goggles over his face. "If these sharks survive, they will devour the entire underwater caste system, and send the entire aquatic world spinning out of control."

"That's a valid point." Daniel agreed. "But we still have our whites. What about them?"

"Shit, that's the easy part." Darrin smiled. "They are tagged and tracked. Kermit, Miss Piggy, and Gonzo have their routines set and aren't looking to destroy the human population, or take down the entire seal population in one bite. These monsters are capable of a huge appetite and who knows where that will end? I'm going to put one hell of a kink in their plan and take out one of them with this cage."

"How do you know it will work?" Gavin asked.

"Well, it worked in '*Jaws*'." Darrin smiled.

"Wise-ass," Daniel ripped back. "That was a movie."

"These sharks will come to me. I know it. They want a fight. They're the bullies of the bay."

"So what happens if all three attack you?" Daniel inquired.

"Then I take all three out with one hell of a dose of electrical shock therapy."

"What about us?" Gavin asked, doubting Darrin's plan.

"Get the hell out of here if you can. Shoot off a flare, scream for help. Try and wave down Davenport's chopper if all else fails." Darrin entered the water with his harpoon for defense. "We will all laugh about this back at the diner with Ash and Davenport, and Rick too."

Gavin and Daniel shrugged off the positive speech knowing their lunatic boss was on a one-way ticket to his grave. They lowered Darrin into the water until he became a blurred image beneath the bay.

"Damn it's grainy and dark down here," Darrin grumbled. His left hand held the slender harpoon with a firm grasp. His eyes followed a small patch of fish meandering by. A shadowy image emerged from the right side of the cage. "Is that you Jason? Freddy? Michael?" Darrin recounted the names Jake had given the sharks.

The shark soon emerged, but it wasn't any of the monsters that had the bay in their terrorizing grip. It was Gonzo, one of Darrin's tagged sharks.

"Hey, boy," Darrin called out to the shark.

Gonzo floated by with a lazy stare, his black eyes filled with curiosity about the new item in the water. His head was turned slightly to the left; his mouth was ajar displaying his well-worn teeth. A piece of seal still adhered to the lower rows, a blood stained tooth stood out on the upper plate. A flimsy string of flesh caught between several teeth floated about.

Darrin firmed his stance. Gonzo seemed attracted to the cage's slight current change in the water. If he made contact with the cage it would trigger sensory overload throughout the shark's Ampullae of Lorenzini.

"Come on, swim away Gonzo. Swim away."

For a minute Darrin thought the shark had gotten the message. Gonzo's mouth closed and his head turned back to the right, away from the cage.

Freddy, the thirty-five-foot menace of the pack slammed into Gonzo and obliterated the cage on impact. Both sharks were left stunned as a pair of weary boxers at the end of a prizefight.

Daniel and Gavin surveyed the bay and blinked in unison as they tried to pinpoint one of the dorsal fins. They fought to maintain their balance as the boat rocked from the vicious attack beneath the surface. They remained glued to Gonzo's shadow as he glided underneath the silent bay adjacent to the cage. The fin sliced through the bay and darted straight for Gonzo's location, a few feet below the boat.

Darrin and the cage caught the brutal violence of the two sharks colliding. Gonzo's body opened up releasing a sprawling stream of fresh blood into the bay's depths. Muted, but not yet defeated, the white careened off course and opened its jaws in a defensive maneuver. It waited for the finishing attack from the other stymied shark.

Darrin craned his neck upwards and witnessed the series of splashes above as his crew fell into the bay screaming and cursing. Freddy regrouped and dismantled Daniel with a jarring snap of its serrated jaws.

Gonzo's senses gravitated to the smearing of fresh blood. The shark, too late for the prey, glided past Gavin and opened up a sizeable wound across his lower torso with a quick bite of curiosity that emptied Gavin's stomach and intestines. Darrin scrambled to grasp the harpoon, but was faced with the inevitable task of averting his own death in the face of untimely attacks on his friends.

A harpoon whistled through the clouded water and knifed its

way across the approaching shark's face, dragging a new scar along the tough skin. Gavin's lifeless, mauled body drifted off until a series of other sharks ripped him apart, enjoying the fresh kill.

Darrin loaded for another shot, his cage battered and barely sustainable beneath the bay. His shark regrouped, and prepared to demolish the rest of the sizeable cage. "That's right keep those eyes locked on mine," taunted Darrin. His mind rattled with scurrying images of his departed friends. His eyes narrowed, adrenaline surging, he locked on his target. He knew if he could fire a kill shot through the shark's eye, the cage would finish the predator off with the electric sensory overload.

Darrin's life was a victim of Murphy's Law. He knew somewhere in the design of things this plan would implode.

As the red cloud beneath the water dissipated, the identity of the shark was revealed to Darrin. The shark opened wide, its mouth inches ajar for the attack. On each side of the beast's face was a complicated series of recent scars. A small stream of blood escaped from the newest wound inflicted from the harpoon grazing across his skin.

"Freddy," snorted Darrin. "The kid was right after all." He pressed the trigger releasing the harpoon. Murphy's Law kicked in and the shot went errant inside the bay's blackness. Freddy, now a few yards away, pulled apart his jaws and slammed down on the cage.

Darrin bounced around inside the imploding cage as the thirty-five-foot monster ripped it apart. The electrical field fractured Freddy's attention, forcing a howling grumble through the shark's chattering teeth. Its snout caught at an awkward angle between the cage's bent bars and snapped with murderous intent at Darrin's flailing feet.

With the harpoon gun lost, Darrin reached for his knife moments before Freddy dug his jaws in Darrin's feet. A frenetic stabbing poured out another wave of blood right above Freddy's snout. Numbness grew below his knees and he refused to watch his own blood fill the bay. He released the knife as Freddy's monstrous jaws tore at him. The red blade of the knife soon scattered out of view and disappeared in the darkness. Darrin's throat closed in a tight knot, forcing the blood back down his esophagus. His oxygen tank still attached and functional, he reached for one last heroic blow.

The kill shot. Darrin's own version of the end game.

His legs still tangled inside the shark, Darrin reached for the cage, if only to stave off death for another minute. His fingers grabbed one of the bars that was now bent and aching to snap free. Freddy pulled back with every intention of severing Darrin in half. Darrin closed his eyes, then reopened them with a sharp snap of clarity. A brief moment revealed time slowing down for him.

Darrin used this newfound adrenaline surge and dislocated the bar and buried it through Freddy's searing gills. The shark rolled about, its mouth still wrapped around Darrin's legs. "If I'm going to die here today, so are you." Darrin paused, "And, this," his voice roared while tilting his head back, "is for my friends." Darrin's voice gargled a few more incoherent words while he jammed the piece further through the shark as the two fought each other in their bloody descent.

A shleigh and Tom made their respective ways across the deck of the yacht admiring the multi-colored balloons and the blue and red banner welcoming the surfers. The mayor barred no expense when it came to this fundraiser.

"Hello," Patrick Ryan, one of the professional surfers, greeted the couple. "Welcome to the party."

"Hello," Ash returned the friendly greeting.

"Good afternoon," said Tom.

"What's going on?" Felicia joined the conversation. She finished off the lobster meat from her nimble fingers while steadying a drink in the other.

"Hey," Ash said with a nod of her head. "Aren't you the best woman surfer in the entire world?"

Felicia kept her drink steady in her hand balancing the yellow umbrella while she stared off across the bay. "Yes, I am. It's quite the chore to sustain that ridiculous momentum." Her short dirty blond hair bounced with the slight breeze. A typical build for a surfer, her body maintained a svelte figure that warned off any sign of fat. "A healthy regimen of exercise and diet is absolutely critical in this profession."

"I agree," Patrick added. "I hate exercise."

"I bike with my husband whenever I can," Felicia kept the flow of the conversation going. "Or a nice hike up through the reds."

"Ah, yes the redwoods," Ash said with a grin. "They are exceptionally beautiful this time of year." She was happy to see another equal to chat with, although their professions were different in scale, Ash welcomed the balance of the sexes.

"I also strongly believe in keeping in touch with my spiritual side and reflecting with meditation from time to time," Felicia added with a charming wink. "It's good for the mind and body to keep its balance."

"What brings each of you here today?" Tom asked as he too cradled a drink of a different sort. His drinks now consisted of tonic water or flavored seltzer.

"The good mayor wants all of us to join in the celebration before our big competition tomorrow," Patrick said.

"Of course he does," Tom replied with a sarcastic spin.

"Why the tightness in your voice?" Felicia asked.

"The deceptive mayor needs an infusion of capital for his re-election campaign, and the public relations press for this will be off the charts." Tom sipped his drink. "I'm going out on a limb here, but it seems that unlike our surfer neophyte Mr. Ryan here, you've been to quite a few of these before."

"Very perceptive," Felicia noted. "Yes, I've been a part of such parties for a few years now."

"Patrick's the unfortunate son of the President, and it remains he's the social draw for this event," Tom took a step forward, "as you can ascertain from the men in black patrolling the yacht and providing safety for Mr. Ryan." Tom sucked in a breath. "I don't want to sound demonic or spin your delightful day out of control," he paused, "but once this yacht departs for the bay, all of us are headed for disaster."

"How so?" Felicia was intrigued.

"Tom and I are certain those sharks are out there," Ash added.

"Yeah, so?" Patrick questioned them. "We are on a yacht, and there's nothing that will prevent us from enjoying the mayor's gracious hospitality. The mayor has it all under control. His thumb's on the pulse of this entire town."

"Well, I have faith the mayor will do everything in his power to ensure your safety is his top priority. Since he and your father share the same political views, I'd expect an answer like that from you, son." Tom tapped Patrick on the shoulder with his drink as he walked by.

"Really, you actually agree with that?" Patrick was caught off guard with the response.

"No. No, I don't." Tom walked across the deck and approached the railing.

Ash bid farewell to Felicia and Patrick and joined Tom at the railing.

"Did you have to mix politics and pleasure back there?" Ash asked. The wind caressed her black dress with a sensational cool breeze.

"They have a right to know the mayor's intentions are bathed in rogue selfishness." Tom peered at the skies. "Well, look up there my fair lady." His finger pointed to the helicopters scattered across the blue skies. "There's your media circus."

"Can't we just enjoy the party?" Ash asked.

"Oh, I intend to." Tom gave a quick glance to her as he walked off. "I intend to."

Ash watched him submerge himself inside the gathering crowds until he disappeared. She returned to the railing and thought fondly of Rick as the yacht jostled free from the pier and embarked on its voyage across the beautiful bay.

Mayor Harrison MacTavish swerved between the guests moments after the yacht had departed the club. He held his cell phone firmly. "Mr. Stephens is it?"

"Yes?" the voice came through with a mixture of static. "Who is this?" Stephens asked.

"The Mayor," he said. "My brother Major Anderson MacTavish referred you and your impeccable services." Harrison paced back and forth.

"I am aware of that, sir," Stephens answered. "I've had the chance to meet you brother. He's a wonderful man, a hero for this country."

Harrison weaved the cell phone about attempting to gain a better reception. "Yeah, yeah, whatever. Listen, I have no clarity on this end," he paused, "where are you situated?"

The static cleared for a moment as Stephen's voice came through. "Alcatraz Island."

"How many men are with you?" Harrison asked. "We've just set sail and I need solid eyes on the yacht at all times."

"Myself and Mr. Kenneth Black, sir," Stephens again offered the response respectfully. "What do you need protection for? Isn't the Secret Service on board?"

"My brother alluded that as an added precaution you were adding another layer of security to the President's son." Harrison found a spot on the deck to continue the call without further interruption.

"I've grown fond of my rifle, sir," Stephens assured the mayor "As you draw closer to the island, I will have the entire yacht in my scope. Nothing will harm you on my watch."

"It's not the yacht I need you to watch." Harrison leaned over the railing and caught the shadow of a shark sliding beneath the bay.

"Then what am I watching out for sir?"

"Sharks. A pack of prehistoric killing machines, according to various reports. They have taken residence in our beloved Bodega Bay." Harrison turned his glare back to the approaching crowd. "I have to go now. Don't hesitate to open fire. If a fin breaks that water, obliterate it." Harrison closed the cell and ended the conversation. He slid the phone back to his front pocket and shook another round of hands.

"Hello, Mayor," Rob greeted him. "When will the show start?" Rob asked as he found the mayor through the crowd. "I have quite the affection for the music industry."

"Within the hour," Harrison urged the crowd to remain calm. "The production company has been working diligently since we departed, setting up the area for the lovely Miss Tina K."

"Mayor! Mayor!" The voices heightened.

"I have some business to attend to," he briefly placed his fingers to his lips to mute the crowd. "I prefer everyone to unwind in the meantime. Have some drinks, enjoy the sun and the beautiful bay."

"**S**kip, slow down," Sheriff Davenport requested. "What's up sir?" Skip killed the engine gliding the boat to an idle stop. "Ah, like skimming a rock across the ocean, smooth as silk."

"These are the coordinates Darrin gave me earlier," Davenport paced the boat from stern to bow, and to the east and west starboard. "I mean, you know, within a few degrees."

"Calm as a sober man's hands out here, Sheriff."

"That's just it. Darrin's team would be in this area. There's no sign of their boat, or his cage." Davenport retrieved his pocket flashlight and skimmed the water. "Can you bring me closer to that debris over there?" He pointed in the general direction.

"How far?" Skip brought the engine back to life.

"A few hundred feet out, I think. But go slow. I don't want these sharks to become attracted to the engine's noise."

"I hate to break the bad news to you, Sheriff," Skip said. 'But, these guys are attracted to slightest disturbance in the water."

Davenport didn't care. He was on a mission. "Like I said, be real cautious."

"That seems to be part of a boat, Sheriff. A real gem of one too."

"That would be Darrin's," Davenport answered. His tone was glum and defeated. "Damn it!"

"How do you know?"

"The mayor footed his bill. I'm rolling the dice and thinking Darrin went bananas on the boat and the cage."

"Maybe they found their shark and went home."

"No. We had a deal last night." Davenport attempted to quiet the angry storm swirling in his mind.

"Out on the black market these sharks are worth a fortune. I bet close to a sweet million dollars for one these rare beasts."

"I don't buy it. Darrin's not the shady type." Davenport waved his flashlight closer to the debris. "I can see something shiny beneath the bay. Do me a favor and cut the engine completely."

Skip throttled the engine, bringing the boat to a dead calm. "What is it?"

Davenport strained for a decent look. "I can't tell. I think it's metallic."

"Can we move on from this?" Skip begged. "Bunny needs her medication, and I was only out for a quick peel on the water."

"Give her a call and explain the situation. Your wife will understand your involvement in this dark and dangerous matter. You, my friend, are embroiled in official police business." Davenport stripped off his weapon and placed it on the bench. "You carry extra clothes?"

"Yeah, under the bench." Skip blew a hard whistle. "You're insane."

"We can debate that later." He placed the waterproof flashlight between his teeth, leaned forward and executed a precise dive into the bay.

The noon sun pounded the rocks of Alcatraz Island. Sergeant Dwight "Bud" Stephens and Kenneth Black patrolled the famed prison on strict orders from Major Anderson MacTavish. Stephens had risen through the ranks of the Marine Corps with blistering pace. A recent tour in Afghanistan with Black resulted in various medals and successful missions, but their bodies paid the price. Black suffered several flesh wounds, while Stephens incurred serious mental damage and welcomed a return to the states with open arms. His young body's health eroded rather quickly from cigarettes and the grueling lifestyle of the Marines, and this respite proved the perfect elixir.

Stephens shook a pack of Marlboro cigarettes hard against the palm of his hand forcing one to rise above the others. "Want one?"

"I'm good, thanks." Black replied. "Why the hell are we out here anyway?"

"The major's brother is the mayor, and that yacht over there has the President's son on board." Stephens dragged a puff of smoke and pointed in the general direction. He felt the slight breeze against his crisp, shaven face. "Nice day today. Hardly any wind."

"So we're babysitters now?" Black reached for a cigarette. "You know what, gimme one of those."

Stephens tossed the pack to his friend. "There's some unusual shark activity out there as well. The mayor has these sharks on high priority."

"Sharks? Are we frickin' marine biologists now?" Black cracked a solid orange flame across the tip of the cigarette.

"We're the safety valve," Stephens said.

"Whatever. Are we calling in the Coast Guard as well?"

"I chatted with the major. His brother already called them."

Stephens paced the prison's wharf. "You know, if the yacht can make it to that point over there," he said waving his finger, "I can pick off anything within a thousand meters."

"With that rifle of yours?" Black laughed.

"That rifle of mine?" Stephens smiled. His cheeks wrinkled up a bit and his pupils dilated. "That rifle of mine saved our asses quite a few times back there."

"Yeah, I know. You took out a small band of insurgents in the streets from the rooftop, without even being noticed." Black took a drag from the cigarette. "I was dead in my tracks in that jeep. How many did you pick off that day?"

"Seven."

"All with that rifle of yours," Black added with a smile. "Pretty damn impressive."

"It's a Remington m40a5, 7.62 by 51 caliber and that thing packs a punch." Stephens smiled while he rattled off the statistics.

"Yeah, I have no doubt you'll be able to pick off any type of threat on that yacht, or a shark in the water."

"And you forget my friend, you took that bullet to the side of the head saving my life," added Stephens. "That's loyalty and I'm forever grateful for that."

"No sweat. You saved my life first. It was the least I could do." Black walked to the end of the wharf and flicked the cigarette into the bay. "I mean you didn't want me taking care of Susie for you right?"

"Hell no." Stephens walked up to Black.

"How's she doing?" Black leaned over and caught a glimpse of a shadow lurking beneath the bay.

"Susie? She's great." Stephens strained to see what Black was peering at.

"And the baby?"

"Brand new." Stephens finally saw the fin break the water.

"Trisha right?" Black remembered the details.

"Yeah. She's got me wrapped around her little fingers." Stephens took another drag before he flicked the cigarette to the ground. "She's a gem."

Both men stared at the yacht off in the distance and the projected path of the shark.

"We're going to need all hands on deck ASAP. That thing's headed right for the yacht." Stephens gnashed his teeth, preparing a plan in his head.

Black raised the binoculars. "That bastard appears to be a

different breed of shark," said Black. "The fin alone creeps the shit out of me."

"It's not a white. It's gotta be thirty or thirty-five feet." Stephens peered through his own binoculars at the shadow gliding beneath the surface. "The mayor mentioned these things were Jurassic."

"Jurassic?" Black answered with a sharp rise of his eyebrow.

"Not of this day and age? I don't know, he said they are pretty fucking big." Stephens stood firm and prepared for the situation.

"I'd argue it's almost forty-feet." Black whistled in amazement.

"We need a plan and quick. Any thoughts? The Coast Guard's too far away."

"We're going to need a bigger weapon than that pop gun you've brought to the party. Yep. We're gonna need a bigger cannon for that bastard."

Davenport inspected the demolished cage. His hand waved around the flashlight before a needed breath of air forced him to the surface.

"Do you see that?" Stephens asked.

'What do you see?"

"That idle boat out there with the old man." Stephens peered through the binoculars.

"Yeah? So? It was there before," Black stated.

"True, but that was before that shark appeared, and now they are in its direct path to the yacht." He squinted tighter. "There's someone treading in the water." Stephens took away the binoculars. "How far do you think that is?" He reached for his rifle that rested across his back.

"A lot more than you can reach with that rifle."

"See if you can reach that boat on your talkie," instructed Stephens. His forearm flexed as the newly acquired tattoo of "Sue" stretched and twisted with the process.

"Are you thinking that's the sheriff out there?" Black switched on the talkie.

"That boat's idle and they aren't fishing." Stephens monitored the wind. "It's worth a shot, right?"

"Fuck yeah," Black answered with a grin. He knew when his partner had that tone, that look, that feel for the hunt, there was no stopping Stephens. You just stepped aside and marveled while he worked his magic with the rifle. Truth was, Stephens was a deadly shot, and although Black teased him, he never doubted Stephen's uncanny accuracy.

Stephens already had the rifle loaded with five rounds and pulled back the bolt to fire the weapon. "I'm thinking that boat's about half a mile east of us."

"Don't hesitate man, take the shot if you have it." Black continued his attempts to locate the frequency of the sheriff's radio.

Skip heard static from the bench and reached for the sheriff's talkie.

"Hey!" Davenport called out to Skip.

"You're talkie's acting all weird. I think someone's trying to reach you."

"Probably the mayor. Ignore it." Davenport urged him to pay attention. "I found the cage. No sign of Darrin, or the others."

Skip placed the talkie back down moments before a voice broke through the static.

"No answer." Black said. "I think it went through."

"Yell."

Black tried to reach the boat, but it was no use.

Stephens fired off a warning shot at the starboard side of the boat.

"Jesus!" Skip shouted. "Someone's shooting at us."

Davenport pivoted his head. "No. It's a warning shot."

"How do you know?" Skip kept his head down. "I didn't sign up for this."

Davenport entered the boat. "That man on the island. He's gotta be the Marine they talked about. He's not here to kill us."

The fin broke the water and headed straight for the stern of the boat.

"What's he here to kill then?" Skip turned, his face drained of color. "Mother--."

"Start the engine!" Davenport threw on some clothes and prepared his weapon.

A shock riddled the Bay Area.

Davenport lost his balance and crashed back to the boat, his gun fell to the floor.

"That's an aftershock," Skip warned, still trying to bring the engine to life. "She's not purring! She's dead, boss."

"A warning shot?" Black shouted. "Are you nuts?"

"They got the message, the sheriff looked back at me. It's the aftershock that just hit us that concerns me." Stephens pulled back on the bolt.

"Why?"

"It moved the target further away." Stephens tightened his vision and released another round. It seared through the air and nicked the fin of the shark. Another pull of the bolt, another round released. The shark dipped beneath the water as the bullet skidded across the bay.

"Shit, where did he go?" Skip asked, his aging hands still trying to ignite the engine.

Davenport scrambled for his weapon. "That Marine only has a few more feet with that shot of his. We're going to be out of range in a blink of an eye. We cannot absorb another aftershock."

"There it is!" Skip warned. "Starboard side."

Davenport couldn't get a shot off but something else diverted the shark's path. "I don't believe it."

"What?"

"The whites just rammed that bastard hard."

"And that's good?"

"Anything to buy that Marine some more time."

"It's back again," Skip alerted him. "The stern and coming fast."

"We're the last line of defense before it reaches the yacht." Davenport raised his weapon. "So now might be a good time to start that engine."

Stephens's next shot pelted the side of the shark through the water. A red mist of blood escaped.

"You only have one more shot left before reload," Black warned.

"I know, I know," Stephens was cool and collected. "I've hit it, but it's not enough." A bead of sweat ran down his cheek. His forearm once again tightened. He was ready. The thrill of the kill.

"Just give me one clear shot," begged Stephens, "right between the eyes."

He monitored the shark approaching the stern of the boat. Stephens took the western angle from the prison's wharf to guide his shot. "That's it. Break the surface." Stephens's razor sharp focus sealed the shot.

The fin broke through the water, the snout of the shark soon followed. Davenport held firm. A series of teeth sprang forth, its eyes rolled back ready for the kill.

Stephens released the round at the mammoth shark. The bullet found its mark, and brought the beast crashing back down to the water in a wave of red blood.

"Nicely done," Black congratulated the kill shot. "Shit, there's no sign of the boat. Maybe the sheriff managed to squirm free and get away."

"Perhaps. I have a feeling that shark's not dead though." Stephens warned. "Did you see the face on that monster?"

"Sure it is. You plugged its brain with lead. There's no way that shark survived."

"We're going to need the Coast Guard here to inspect that area and fast. I won't rest until I'm enjoying shark steak tonight." Stephens returned the rifle back to its holster on his back. "I need a smoke. That was scary as hell."

Aftershock
1:09 p.m.

His wet hands fumbled for the doorknob. His brain replayed grisly images of Cathy's death and Dawn's demise. They shattered his psyche. Preston fidgeted a few more times with the doorknob with no luck. He knew it was the mayor's personal quarters from the time he had spent on the yacht with Dylan when his dad was away on business.

Poor Dylan. Preston watched the entire event unfold as the sharks pecked away at Dylan's body, tearing and ripping away at his friend as he watched helplessly. He had to remain hidden from the sharks. His chances of survival increased after he managed to escape with a daring shot of the harpoon gun and a little luck. His ears swelled with their voices, their cries for help, the bloodcurdling fear in their pitch. Preston blinked hard and cupped his head to silence the pulsating madness. His mouth roared a high-pitched scream of anger as he raised his left foot, still inside a waterlogged sneaker, and slammed the heel against the wooden door.

The frame gave way, splitting across and releasing the door with a creaking whinny. He knew exactly why he was here. He approached the mayor's oak desk and tugged at the drawers. One by one they opened exposing their contents inside. Preston ransacked the entire desk, rupturing everything, and scattered the remains across the aqua blue rug. "It has to be here somewhere," he snarled. His scratched fingers tossed away random papers, pictures, contracts, boating magazines, and a box of cigars. Off in the distance, it laid waiting for him to discover it: its power, its beauty.

Preston slipped on a bottle of seldom-drank Vodka, before reaching the glimmering object. The silver husk of the weapon dared him to romance it with his bloodthirsty lust for revenge. He swallowed down some vodka and continued. He bent down in agonizing pain and clasped the weapon.

A 9mm handgun, fully loaded and ready to destroy the enemy.

His fingers clenched the vodka bottle before a final taste calmed his frayed nerves.

He sent the bottle crashing against the wall, splintering into pieces, and soaking the rug.

**

"Miss Tina K!" The mayor roared across the gold-plated microphone. His anxious feet paced the makeshift stage, arms stretched to the skies in a triumphant sign. Hip-hop music filtered through the yacht as the partygoers and guests enjoyed dancing and the afternoon sun.

Miss Tina K exploded onto the stage, her crimson red hair flowing left, then right. Her lipstick cherry red dress flowed with the beat, never leaving her skin, a perfect fit. Fireworks exploded high above the yacht, painting the sky. The vibrant music rocked the yacht with rhythmic intensity. Miss Tina K glanced across the dance floor. Men, women, teenagers, even seniors all partook in the festive mood.

Scotty Flash earned his reputation through the smooth ways he treated the ladies. A brutish wrestler, Scotty still found time to sweep women off their feet with his slick moves. His eyes never left the bevy of beauties surrounding him as he pulverized the floor with his feet, a synchronized demonstration of dancing genius. His dramatic flair soon swept Watson up in his tornado of moves, leaving her breathless and ready for more.

Preston made his away through the crowd, his clothes matted and caked in blood. He was looking for the mayor, and it wasn't going to be for a handshake.

The majority of the people were entranced by Miss Tina K, and to a certain degree, Scotty Flash. Yet two people weren't that interested the music. Their minds wandered elsewhere.

Ashleigh and Tom sought after the departing mayor, eager for more answers. The mayor disappeared amongst the dancing partygoers. Ash peered above as the media choppers circled the skies, virtual vultures waiting to pick the yacht clean.

"Shit, it's only a matter of time before they create an inhabitable vacuum of annoyance," Tom whispered to her.

"I still have a few questions for the mayor," Ash said. "Where did he go?"

Tom scanned the yacht for him. "Over there," he answered with a wave of his finger. "Did you feel that shock before?"

Ash kept a steady pace. "Yes, and it usually triggers another series of them."

"Do you think your friend has taken care of the sharks?" Tom was curious.

"We can only pray."

"Do you hear that?" Tom tugged at her elbow.

"No, I don't what is it?" Ash looked to the skies.

"Not them," answered Tom. "It's a patch of voices in argument."

"How can you even tell that onboard a yacht full of people?" Ash was impressed. "A yacht filled with music and dancing nevertheless."

"I'm a writer remember? I've trained myself to rely on my senses to gain an advantage. I've spent some time as a part-time reporter for the Sacramento Bee."

"So Sherlock, where's it coming from?"

"Over there. Come on, I have a feeling this is going to be very interesting." Tom made a beeline for the escalating argument.

A cigarette dangling precariously from his lips, Stephens reloaded his rifle with seamless precision. "Are they coming?" His eyes shifted to Black. His hands made quick work of the rifle.

"No worries," said Black. "Here they come now."

The Coast Guard approached the wharf. The captain addressed Stephens and Black with a friendly greeting. "Gentlemen, please, come aboard."

Stephens and Black were approaching the craft when another minor tremor rocked the bay. Stephens took notice of the helicopters hovering around the yacht. Their patterns were thrown off course for a few seconds. "Those media hounds have to be called off. They are dangerously close to that yacht."

"Have you secured the bay, Sergeant?" the captain asked.

"I've managed to drown one of them with a healthy amount of lead." Stephens grinned a bit but was still unsure of victory.

"You doubt the success of your kill?" The commander pivoted his head to the yacht's coordinates.

"That shark delivered one hell of a punch to that poor sheriff's boat." Stephens sat down and ran his fingers through his jet-black hair. "It's possible it survived. There was so much going on."

"Sheriff?" Another voice reacted from the crowd. "Was it Sheriff Davenport?"

"I don't know, but whoever he was, I think he escaped with no serious damage." Stephens rose to greet the new voice on board.

The man's voice echoed from the rear of the craft, hidden behind a wall of officers. He found his way to Stephens, parting the officers one by one. "I'm very fortunate you were able to postpone the inevitable."

"The inevitable?" Stephens was confused. "I'm somewhat confident that shark is rotting on the floor of the bay by now."

"I doubt there's even a remote possibility of that," the man continued. "You see these aren't your ordinary sharks. My team has data indicating there's three of them." The man sighed. He ran his hands over his head.

"Three? Shit, that does pose a serious problem." Stephens grew impatient. "What's this to you anyway?"

"These sharks are a missing link. Their senses are sharper, faster, and keener. That yacht full of music will draw them to it with a vengeance."

"I must've missed it the first time. What's your name?" Stephens felt another rumble from beneath the surface.

"Those aftershocks are growing, and with it our window shrinks for saving that yacht." The man took a deep breath, his hand covered a rising cough. The white medical bracelet had given Stephens his answer. "My name is Rick Chatham. Once I heard my old friend here was coming out play on the bay, I jumped at the chance. I'm recovering from a nervous breakdown and a recent heart attack scare, and I've been grinded on the teeth of a great white. And, to top it all off, my girlfriend's on that yacht." His tanned arms reached for the skies, crackling his stiff joints.

"I haven't seen any signs of the others," Stephens said. "Isn't the pack of sharks a myth?"

"I wish. All three are a brutal reality. We had a plan. Darrin, Davenport, Ash, and myself were to keep an eye on the bay in spite of the mayor's party. I can only hope Darrin and Davenport were able to eliminate the rest of the pack." Rick paced the boat. "How big was the shark you claim to have defeated?"

Stephens fought hard to remember. "Shit, it was well over thirty-feet."

"About forty, sir," Black answered Rick. "It had to be the leader right?"

"Yes." Rick's hands tightened around the starboard railing of the craft. "We have to stay close to the yacht and hope Davenport's in the area as well."

"What for?" Stephens inquired.

"Well, unfortunately, if you saw Davenport in a boat, then our plan has been altered. His task was to patrol the bay from the sky, and alert us to anything suspicious, and fire on the sharks at will." Rick watched the yacht with growing concern.

"I'm sure he'll do just fine down here with us."

Rick nodded in agreement. "Perhaps, but that doesn't change the fact that this craft alone will not stop that shark. It's a toothpick to that beast. The yacht actually remains the safest place for now. We need to keep an eye out for people in the bay we can save, and keep track on these sharks. If you can call in a favor to your superiors to bring some extra firepower," Rick paused, "that will at least level the playing field."

"So we're fucked either way?" Black asked, irritated.

"It's a matter of degree, but yes, unless something unforeseen happens and fate joins our side, then we're royally screwed."

"I'll place the call." Stephens dialed his cell.

"I'll get more boats out here ASAP," the commander also followed Rick's advice.

"I'll be damned if anything stands in my way of saving Ashleigh."

Ash tapped Tom's arm. "Hey, look out there, by Alcatraz's shoreline."

Tom followed Ash's line of vision. "That's the Coast Guard."

"Someone must've tipped them off. That's a good thing. We need the extra protection out here." She strained her eyes. "Do you see that guy leaning over the rail?"

"Where?" Tom couldn't locate the man.

"The guy in the blue Hawaiian shirt," Ash lost her voice. *It couldn't be him. He was lying in critical condition in the hospital.*

"Sorry, I don't see him." Tom shook his head.

"Never mind," she sighed. "My mind's playing tricks on me." Ash wiped her eyes. The man was gone.

"Come on, let's join that verbal fight over there." Tom pulled her away.

"What do you mean, he's dead?" The mayor yelled.

"You sent us out there to die!" The voice bellowed back.

"Preston, relax, breathe," Harrison urged him to follow his orders.

Preston clenched his severed fingers inside bloodied fists. His clothes wet and soaked in blood and seaweed fueled the air with an unforgettable stench. His face was pale and scratched with deep wounds that were still visible to the naked eye. "You have to pay for what you have done!" He took a few steps closer, his Nike sneakers squishing red water cross the floor. In his other hand, the 9mm was firmly pressed against his right thigh.

"Now let's not overreact." Harrison fought for a solution.

"Your son is dead. Our friends are dead!" Preston raised the gun. "You have no remorse do you?" His teeth chattered the statement.

The music filtered through the bay creating vibrations deep beneath the surface. Its eyes adjusted to the darkness and stared in the direction of the vibrations. Its mouth swallowed another round of blood, engulfing the last of its flesh wound. The shark managed to fend off several interested attackers with quick work. The schools of fish dispersed as the shark gained momentum and sped toward the origin of the sound.

Miss Tina K brought surfers Patrick and Felicia on stage, as well as Rob and Watson, to join her final act. The dancers mingled across the Plexiglas floor, hand in hand, heads tilted for a view of fireworks streaking across the sky.

Scotty Flash, the hulking wrestler, took a woman in his arms as they glided across the floor.

A dark shadow emerged below.

Preston unloaded a hard right to Harrison's face, another one followed suit. A direct hit to the jaw line dropped the mayor to his praying knees.

A mob scene soon gathered around Preston, including Ash and Tom.

"This scumbag has brought all of you out here to die today." Preston kicked Harrison in the face repeatedly, rolling him over.

"Hey, let's talk this over." Tom weaved through the crowd.

"Back off," warned Preston, gun drawn and cocked for release. "He's mine. He let his own son die out there. He knew the sharks were in the bay. And he did nothing!"

"That's not true!" Harrison stood back up with a cautionary stare at Preston. "I hired the best team I could find to patrol the bay."

"Not good enough." Preston pointed the gun to Harrison. "I

lost a potential girlfriend out there today. I watched her ripped to shreds by those teeth. They grinded her to bits. Her name was Cathy Bixby."

"Ok, I'll create a charity in her name." Harrison offered.

"Then Dawn went in the water and never returned. I can still hear her screams."

"I'm sorry," Harrison pleaded.

"I was next. My entire body caught in some twisted mechanism of death. My limbs forced to crack, bend, and twist. I refused to die out there. I fought back and somehow that beast released me from its clenched jaws."

"I don't know what to say," Harrison fumbled for words. His defeated look soured his guests on him and they riddled him with obscenities and vile discourse.

"That brings me to your son." Preston licked his salted lips. "Dylan the poor fuck, he never saw it coming. His entire body wrapped up in his parasail after our boat sank. I watched him being torn limb from limb, his contorted body pinned in the harness, upside down in the water."

"No..." Harrison grew angry. "You watched him die. You're such a hypocrite. You could've saved him."

"That's not my job. That was your responsibility when you made the call to go ahead with this shindig today. You wanna know the sad part?"

Harrison's eyes welled with tears.

"He never once talked about you in a positive light. The last scream that spilled from his mouth before his world grew dark, was for his mother. Not for you."

Harrison crumbled to the floor. His fists pounded the floor in anger. The knuckles separated in his hands from the thunderous beating.

"It's coming for you, Mayor. A lot sooner than you think." Preston pressed the gun to the mayor's temple. "If you're confused right now, don't worry, it's going to end soon. That beast is coming for you. It's coming for everyone here."

The bay buckled with a series of brutal aftershocks that tilted the yacht, and caused a commotion amongst the mob.

And then it happened.

Another thunderous rock of the yacht yielded to a flurry of high-pitched screams from below.

Ash and Tom scrambled for a view as Jason burst through the Plexiglas and the bay flooded the yacht. It sank to the depths with Scotty Flash in its teeth and a swirling whirlpool of blood in its wake.

Miss Tina K felt the water rush over her legs, a slight sizzle soon followed from the stage's electrocution. A sharp pull to the right pulled her to safety.

"Are you okay?" Patrick asked.

"Yeah, I think so." She rubbed her head. "What the hell's going on?"

"We're sinking. The shark obliterated the hull."

"Where to now?" She blinked her eyes at the sky. "What about them?"

"The helicopters?"

"Yeah."

"It's worth a shot, can you walk?"

"A bit. It hurts but I'll manage," she replied.

Another hit from the shark brought the yacht further into its watery abyss.

"Hurry," Patrick ushered Tina along.

The yacht's architecture groaned in pain. It wouldn't be able to survive another jarring impact from the shark.

On the deck of the yacht, now off balance and teetering survival, Preston and Harrison remained embroiled in their brutal standoff.

Patrick and Tina safely approached the deck, waving down the helicopters for rescue. They managed to catch the eye of the police chopper.

In the ensuing madness, the riotous mob forced Preston to juggle the weapon, releasing an errant shot upwards that pierced the media helicopter's windshield.

The pilot's face exploded in red, smearing the cracked windshield. His hands slipped from the controls and swerved toward the pack of media helicopters sharing his airspace.

His blades caught the side of another chopper, bringing both careening onto the yacht. One of the chopper's blades snapped off and pelted the side of the luxury craft with a significant jolt. The first chopper exploded against the side of yacht in a roaring fireball that swallowed up most of the scattering mob. Preston fought hard for his own life in the escalating madness. His eyes followed a few people racing toward the police chopper. He launched his body, now ignited in flame and screaming for death into the bay below.

Harrison recovered in the chaos and turned the weapon on Preston burying a bullet in the teenager's sternum. "You could've saved my son." He straightened up and turned his head to the left, right into an errant blade whistling through the air. "Motherfuck--"

Harrison flew through the air and landed with a hard red splash in the bay. He fought hard for survival, writhing to free a piece of blade piercing his chest. A red spurt of blood spewed forth, spilling down his chin. Gasping for life, his hand still clung to the jittery gun. A wave of cool water washed over his stained face as he began to tilt backward beneath the water. He forced himself up for a swallow of air. A few feet away a dorsal fin sliced through and barreled straight for him.

He watched the yacht sinking in a fireball of chaos, screams still heard from within its confines. His fellow citizens, most of whom loyally voted for him, dove to the water for cover from the flying debris. His hand raised the gun and aimed straight for the approaching shark. "Nobody destroys my family."

The shark opened wide for the kill.

Harrison felt the soft whimper of the gun. It jammed from exposure to the water. The shark plowed through Harrison with swift justice, taking away the body inside its jaws allowing the severed head to float in a frightened scare before smaller predators feasted on their fresh kill.

Patrick and Tina approached the edge of the fractured deck to wave down the police. The chopper glided close to the sinking yacht. The pilot waved the two of them on.

Mother Nature pelted the bay with another aftershock that separated the chopper from the yacht's vicinity, making the jump impossible for Patrick and Tina.

Passengers stormed the edge of the yacht. Patrick and Tina were shoved aside as the pack of scared citizens leapt off the boat and straight for the chopper.

The chopper absorbed the brunt of the weight, but not for long. As the people swarmed over the chopper, some beheaded from the blades, others falling to the bay below, the chopper flew out of control and careened for the water.

The fin cracked through as Jason rose from the water, drawn to the whirring noise.

The sudden crash erupted a wave of water as the shark clamped down on the chopper and gnawed its way through a horde of fearful citizens, severing limbs and bodies with fluid motion. The beast incurred damage to its snout from the dismantled, whirring blades. Jason growled in pain as he retreated to the depths with the chopper in tow.

"Ash, are you okay?" Tom asked.

Ash rolled across the deck in pain. "I'm a bit battered, but I'll manage."

"We need to get out of here," he urged.

"Where?"

"Anywhere but here." Tom searched for a way out. "Do you see the Coast Guard?"

"Do you think they're still coming? That shark just took down a yacht."

"How rich is the mayor?" Tom asked with a wink.

"Richer than God." Ash answered.

"So what would a selfish, cocky bastard own on a yacht?"

"A tanning bed?" Ash struggled to stand. "I don't have time for games."

"A personal jet ski."

"How are you so sure?"

"I found it earlier on the stern of the boat."

"Yeah, great idea, Sherlock, but we're sinking fast. That jet ski will be submerged soon enough and totally useless," warned Ash.

"Then we'd better hurry."

Rick fought hard to contain his emotion. "I told you," he warned the rest of the Coast Guard. "That son-of-a-bitch hit that yacht with the force of an atom bomb."

"We can circle for survivors," Stephens offered.

"That's our only hope. The damage is too severe to mount a rescue near the yacht. The debris alone restricts our path. Any word on some military help?"

"They are tied up with the president's appearance in downtown San Francisco," Stephens answered. "I'm sorry, but we're it for now."

Rob Roy had his entire body pinned to the floor. He searched for Watson. She was out cold on the other side of the dance floor. A wincing pain shot across his face. His hands reached for the culprit. A shard of the Plexiglas floor embedded deep in his lower leg forced droplets of blood from the wound. "Damn it!"

"Here, let me help you." Felicia offered. Her hands worked diligently to free him.

"That shark's coming back. My blood's in the water. I'm good as dead." Rob knocked her hands away. "Go save yourself."

"No." She worked hard to release Rob from his location. Rob's eyes widened with fear.

The dark shadow emerged from beneath the water and burst through. Its jaws opened and snapped down hard on the remains of the yacht's floor. The force splintered wood and metal debris everywhere, throwing the yacht further off balance. The beast soon retreated and out of sight in a spray of water.

Felicia lost her balance from the shark's impact. Her feet slipped across the collapsing floor. "Help!" her words were lost in the chaos. Rob's hand reached for her, but his leg restricted his motion.

Felicia's fingertips glanced off Rob's. Her hands fought hard on the slant, unable to gain traction. "Help!"

Felicia felt someone tug violently at her arm.

"Hold on," yelled Watson. She had one arm cradled around the top of a table, and held Felicia tight in her free hand. "You're going to rip my arm off Hercules. Let's hustle."

Rob watched the shark emerge from the water, its face sliced and bloodied from the chopper attack. Its hunger relentless, its teeth snapped out and prepared to drag Felicia down to her watery grave.

Felicia refused to look back, she could see the reflection of the shark in the broken dinnerware scattered across the floor.

The table began to give from the weight of Watson's daring rescue. Her purple hair saturated with water, her body ached from the accident. The creaking continued until Watson's fingers couldn't hold on to Felicia any longer.

Watson let go with deep regret. "I'm so sorry," she called out to Felicia as she went sliding down to the bloodied serrated jaws below.

A loud whistle went off and Felicia felt a cool splash of water drench her body.

Tina stood firm on the deck above the destroyed dance floor.

Her hand lowered the flare gun. Patrick offered assistance to Rob and Watson.

The shark's snout retreated back to the bay beneath a ripple of water.

"Everyone okay?" Tina asked.

"Yes, but that shark will be back." Felicia warned as she climbed back to Rob and the others.

A burst of flames rocked the yacht.

"What was that?" Tina looked at the others.

"It's probably a delayed explosion probably from the chopper's impact." Rob limped over to Felicia.

"I think the shark hit the fuel chamber," Patrick stated. "I smell gasoline."

"I have one flare gun left," added Tina.

"What are you suggesting?" Rob asked.

"A Fourth of July barbeque," Felicia answered with a short laugh. "That shark will return and when it does, we explode the yacht."

"That means certain death."

"If we enter the water, we're dead anyway. If we stay here on the yacht, we're dead." Rob tapped his head with his finger. "Do the math." He tapped his temple. "We have no solution where we survive this hell." Rob walked over to the gaping hole in the floor. "If you want the shark to come to the party, all you have to do is invite him back." Rob clutched his leg and squeezed blood from the wound into the water.

"Have you lost your mind?" Felicia bellowed. "This is insane."

"Get your shot ready, Tina." Rob peered at the calm water waiting for the beast to return. "We're going to send that devil back to Hell screaming in fire."

Courage
2:14 p.m.

"**W**e're not going to make it, Tom." Ash slowed her pace. The pain consumed her lower body.

"Yes we will," Tom urged her to continue. "We're almost there."

"Do you think anyone else survived?" Ash asked as they made their way to the stern of the boat through a watery stairwell.

"Maybe. Keep pace and follow me."

"Wait. Do you hear that?" Ash begged him to stop.

"The voices?"

"Yes."

"Probably the dead fucking with your head."

"No," she said. "It's her voice."

"Who?"

"Miss Tina K. We have to go back," she pleaded.

"No. That jet ski's our only hope." Tom remained firm and stubborn in his quest.

"Not anymore," Ash warned him of the chaos ahead. "It's all submerged on the other side."

Debris blocked the stairwell exit. A hard knock came from the other side.

"Shit," Tom urged. "Go back, go back!" He watched the debris rustle and rock from the relentless pounding. "I'm right behind you."

Ash fought hard to find her way back to the voices she had heard earlier.

Tom's foot tangled up in heavy debris limiting his movement.

"Tom, let's go!" Ash returned her gaze back to Tom.

The entire stairwell flooded with fresh water.

"Tom!" Ash cried. The stern now submerged in the bay made it difficult for her to locate her friend. "Tom!" She yelled once more before retreating with guilt.

The yacht groaned and growled as it fought hard to stay afloat.

Ash approached the small group in the center of the dance floor, where Rob stood awaiting the shark.

"What are you doing?" She hollered.

"We're going to blow this thing to hell." Rob's eyes widened as a shadow approached the opened hole. "Hold steady," warned Rob. "Fire when you see the bastard's face." The crown of the water broke.

Tina held firm, her finger ready to release the flare.

"Don't just stand there, give me a hand," Tom screeched.

"Tom! You're alive!" Ash was relieved.

Rob pushed him aside to a safer stance. He turned to face Tom. "We thought you were--" His sentence went unfinished as the shark exploded through the water, twisted its jaws around Rob, and dragged him into the bay.

"Holy shit!" Ash yelled.

"Fire it, fire it!" Patrick screamed at Tina.

Tina never heard a word. The flare escaped the gun moments after Rob's encounter with the shark. Rob's body lit up first, swallowed inside a hue of orange flame. The heated streak of flame engulfed both Rob and Tina in an indiscernible fireball. The stunned group followed the final act as it sizzled beneath the water, before the explosion rocked the remainder of the yacht, splitting it in half.

The stern sank below the bay, dragging the bow with it.

Ash fell hard from the explosion. Her head swirled with searing pain. Her adrenaline surged and brought her back to wobbly knees. A few feet separated her from the bay and possible rescue. A horrid sound of metal screeched toward her. The flagpole gave way and careened straight at her.

"Ash!" Tom screamed for her. He ran hard to save her, arms stretched out. His adrenaline peaked and he hit her with the power of a freight train.

The two landed hard in the bay, as the yacht erupted one final time, showering chunks of debris across the bay.

Watson broke through the bay with a violent gasp for air. Her hands melted from the intense blast, shards of skin peeled away in the water. She made the painful swim away from the collapsing yacht and exploding debris. A few metal sheets landed a few feet away from her position, spraying water across her scratched face.

Her legs powered her toward the distant boat. She could make out the Coast Guard and shouted out a cry for help. A tight patch of fog rolled across the bay and obscured her line of vision. "Please, help me!" Her voice was loud and desperate. A softer whisper followed, "I hate deep water." Her teeth chattered the cries for safety. A stream of tears rolled down her cheeks and landed gently on the water.

Jason crept beneath the shadow, his senses picking up on the weak disturbance from her tears. His grey skin burnt and raw with blood, the monster kept his senses and headed for the kill. The jaw kept crunching, eager for his impending strike.

Watson kicked against something razor sharp then felt a string of her skin rip off. Her mind exploded with the image of what it could possibly be. "No, no! Please God, no!" Her fears became reality when her right foot lodged between a series of jagged triangles. A short pop later Watson's screaming voice disappeared beneath the blanket of fog and sloshing water.

Rick Chatham cringed as the yacht vanished beneath the bay, a casualty of the explosion. "She has to be out there somewhere," he called out her name. "Ashleigh! Ash!"

"It's no use, man." Stephens gazed out across the debris littered bay. "It's a needle in the haystack out there."

"Wait," Rick said, his eyes secured a patch of people to the east. "Can we swing this boat around and pick them up?" He addressed the commander.

"Yeah, absolutely." The commander instructed his team to set the course for the survivors in the bay. "We'll be there in a flash."

Rick found another shadow emerging from beyond the dying embers of the yacht. "Well, I'll be damned, it's Davenport." Rick called out to his friend, but they were still too far away to be heard.

"It looks like we've gained some added punch in the rescue mission," Stephens said. "That's the same boat from earlier. I'm going on the assumption your friend is the sheriff."

"Yes." Rick walked the boat in excitement. "She could be in that patch of survivors."

"Yeah, that would be cool if she was," added Stephens with a burst of positive energy.

"Skip, swing this piece of shit around," ordered Davenport. "Now!"

"Boss, she took on quite a bit of damage from our forty-foot friend. Our stern's cracked and we've taken on enough water to sink us."

"Ah, that bastard took a small bite from the stern. We're still floating aren't we?" Davenport squirmed in the boat. "Is that the goddamn Coast Guard?"

Skip followed Davenport's voice and located the Coast Guard. "Yeah, that's them. It appears they're headed to those survivors over there." He nodded his head in the direction of the people.

"Well, we've got some people over here as well. Can we help them?"

"No." Skip was firm. "The added weight will impede our ride back to shore."

"We're not going to let them drown out there are we?" Davenport tapped the starboard side of the boat.

"Of course not." Skip changed course.

"If we can help them get on the boat, then the Guard can swing by and relieve us."

"That's a good plan. Any sign of your friends out there?" Skip bobbed his head back and forth checking for Davenport's friends.

"I don't see them, but I don't want anyone in the water with the possibility of those sharks still out there."

Skip steered the boat closer to the floating survivors, vigilant of the roaming sharks and floating debris. "It's going to be tough navigating through this minefield."

"Keep your focus." Davenport reached over and stretched for the first survivor. "Come on," he urged her. "What's your name?"

"Felicia." She climbed on board. "I have a few other friends out there."

"Where?" Davenport asked.

"I think they're right behind that large metal frame." Felicia sat down on the bench and took a breath. Her feet touched the blood covered tarp. "What's that?"

"Uh, that's the mayor's deceased son." Davenport shrugged it off. "It's a long story."

"I witnessed the mayor's gruesome death," added Felicia. "Why are you keeping the body?"

"We were headed back to the yacht to bring the mayor to his knees with our findings," Davenport paused allowing what Felicia said to sink in. "The mayor suffered a gory death?" Davenport's attention peaked. "How?"

"I thought I saw a few broken blades sever him and knock clear to the bay."

"I wouldn't wish that on anyone. But he had his coming to him for some time." Davenport blew out a whistle. "Karma's always going to push until it wins."

"That's what crashed into the yacht, the media choppers," Felicia said. "The aftershocks didn't help either."

"We thought that too, but our position was caught inside a rolling fog," answered Skip. "We were rendered helpless for a short period after the Marines sank that shark that attacked us. Hey, over there, sir." He pointed to the debris.

Davenport and Skip dodged more metal carnage and arrived at the destination suggested by Felicia. "Jesus," Davenport's mouth stretched open with awe. The yacht's remains bobbed and weaved with the waves. A few unlucky passengers were melted to the metal surfaces, while others were forced to drown without the use of their limbs. "This is an aquatic graveyard."

"That one over there," Felicia said, "my friends are alive over there."

Davenport welcomed a few more on the boat. As the introductions continued, one young man suffered the greatest injury of the survivors.

"We're going to need to get him to shore," Davenport urged Skip. "What's your name son?"

"Patrick Ryan." His voice was drained of energy. "Am I going to make it?" His eyes followed the survivors on the boat. "Felicia, Tina, you made it." Patrick's teeth chattered uncontrollably.

"So will you." Tina rushed to him.

"It's nothing really," Patrick answered with a weak grin. "It's a simple flesh wound."

"That piece of metal's lodged clear through your abdomen, son," Davenport inspected the grim situation.

"I'll make it." Patrick's face drained of color. His body shuddered and convulsed before unleashing a stream of blood from his lips. "Did we kill it?"

Tina held him close. "I believe so, yes." Her bloodied hands pressed his face tightly to her chest, muffling the last moments of his life. "Listen to my heart Patrick, let it take you away from this horror."

Patrick's head went limp, his arms weakly collapsed to his sides.

"Where's Ashleigh and Tom?" Felicia asked.

"Ash is alive?" Davenport remained optimistic.

"She was before the explosion." Felicia watched the Coast Guard off in the distance. "Maybe they have her?"

"Perhaps." Davenport tapped Skip on the shoulder. "Get us home."

Skip refused to move.

"What's the matter now?" Davenport asked.

Skip grabbed hold of Davenport's head and turned it toward

the direction of the Coast Guard.

"What am I looking at?" Davenport strained to locate what Skip was fascinated with.

"There!" Felicia and Tina hollered.

Davenport followed their voices. "Shit," his words drained of emotion.

The group stood in silence as Ashleigh broke the surface, and began her swim toward the Coast Guard.

The bay's quiet slumber soon shattered as the fin sliced through and sped toward Ashleigh.

"She's not going to make it," Davenport said. "We're too far away."

He could only watch as the shark closed the distance on his friend.

"There, there she is!" Rick hollered. "Swim Ash, swim! Jesus Christ, come on Ash!" He waved his hands frantically to encourage her.

Stephens already had his rifle drawn and locked in on the target.

"What the hell are you doing?" Rick demanded. "You'll hit her!"

"No I won't." Stephens looked at him and pointed with the rifle. "You don't see that fin behind her?" Stephens pressed his eye to the scope.

Rick's face cracked a slick grin. "Yeah, that's the badass. Bury it in the ocean, Sergeant." He took a deep breath. "She's too far away. She's not going to make it."

"I'll buy her some time." Stephens released a round.

Rick watched it whistle over Ash's head and enter the water behind her. "Did you hit it?"

"Hard to tell. This is one tough bastard." Stephens unleashed another one that blew off a chunk of the shark's fin.

"You did it," Rick said. "She's separating from the shark."

"He won't stay down for long." Stephens blew a hard sigh.

"You're probably right," said Rick. "We're not going to make it to her in time."

"We're still a good distance away." The captain raised his binoculars.

"Hey! You need a boat!" The voice hollered from the stern of the Coast Guard's boat.

"Davenport?" Rick ran to the stern and greeted him.

"We don't have time," Davenport warned. "We dropped the survivors off with the other Coast Guard boat by the bridge." He and Skip boarded the Coast Guard boat.

Rick stepped on board. "I'm riding solo on this one Reed."

"She won't last long Rick," Skip added. "She's taken a beating."

"How's our friend?" Rick hollered back.

"He's still down," answered Stephens. He turned around and gazed out across the opposite side of the boat. "This day keeps getting worse."

"Why?" Rick turned around to see what Stephens was talking about.

Three more fins broke through the surface.

"We're gonna need a bigger boat." Stephens raised the weapon. "I have a few more rounds left. Your call."

Rick twisted his head back to Ash. The maimed fin once again appeared. The forty-foot shadow glided beneath the surface. Rick fixated on the larger shark, then back to the three fins that approached the boat with reckless speed.

"Just cover me," Rick hollered back. He started the boat back up. "Save your bullets. I have an idea."

"Are you insane?" barked Stephens.

"It's natural selection," said Rick. "I need to lure them past Ash and straight for that bastard that's chasing her."

"Yeah, I'll cover you." Stephens tapped his rifle.

"Me too," Black chorused in raising his own weapon.

"Good to see you alive." Davenport winked. He tossed Rick his Glock. "Now go save your girlfriend."

Rick caught the Glock in one hand and steered the boat with the other.

"What the hell does that mean? Natural selection?" Stephens asked Davenport.

Davenport filled him in. "Those three fins belong to our residential great whites. Miss Piggy, Kermit, and Gonzo. Tell me, what happens when someone terrorizes your neighborhood, threatens your family, and disrupts the balance of your life?"

"You fight back." Stephens suddenly realized Davenport's logic.

"Keep your rifle on the larger shark. If I'm right, then Ash is the least of their concern. They will swim right by her and attack Jason."

"Jason?" Stephens was confused. "Does everyone name their sharks out here?"

"One of our survivors, a young boy, named the sharks after horror icons, and the largest one, well, he named it Jason."

"How fitting." Stephens raised his rifle and prepared to fire. The men followed the three fins as they descended beneath the craft with cannon speed straight for Ash.

Rick powered ahead, but the boat lost momentum as it coughed out water. "Almost there, hang in there." He turned to watch the three great whites gain ground. He returned back to Ashleigh who crowned through the surface a meters off his starboard side. "Ash!"

Her hands battered and bruised, she plowed through the water. Her eyes watched the boat approach her. She made out the driver of the boat. "Rick, you crazy bastard." Her face felt warm again as he sped past her.

His attention was then drawn to the bloody parasail resting at the stern of the boat. He wrinkled his nose at the pungent scent of blood. "Get ready Ash! I'm bringing the gang with me!" Rick hollered as he kept his eyes on the three descending fins. He pelted the eroding stern with a blitz of bullets, sending Dylan's dead body sliding to the bay. He then jammed the Glock inside the steering wheel as the craft headed straight for Jason's emerging snout. Rick cracked a smile. "Enjoy your family reunion."

Ash tilted her head as the spray of water erupted behind her. Jason broke through the surface and obliterated Rick's boat with a grueling crunch of his mighty jaws.

"No!" Stephens had Jason locked in his scope and wasted no time. His finger released rounds in successive destruction, splattering the monster's blood across the bay.

Ash eyes swelled, unable to locate Rick. She felt her pack of sharks zoom by in a sea of red headed right for Jason. Gonzo and Kermit launched from the water and collided with Jason in mid-air.

"These sharks are the gods of this bay and justice is served," she hollered at the dying menace. "The whites tore Jason apart from all directions. Ash's ears welcomed Jason's throttled groans for mercy, before his throat ripped open from Gonzo's pinpoint attack. "Karma's a bitch, isn't it?" She began her painful swim back to the boat and reached her hand up in time to find Davenport's arms stretched out her.

He pulled her to safety from the water and draped a blanket around her wet body. "Rick?"

"No," sighed Davenport. "No sign of him yet."

"He saved my life. He saved all of our lives," she wept quietly.

"Hey! Down here!" Another voice echoed.

Ash leapt up and rushed to the starboard side. "Tom?" She was relieved to see her friend make it.

"Here, up you come." Ash and Stephens brought Tom safely on board.

"It's about time. I can only swim for so long before I'm shark food." Tom bounced on one ear releasing a stream of water. "You find your boyfriend?"

Ash sucked in a deep breath and gazed out across the water. Her pack of great whites soon disappeared off in the distance as silence returned to the bay. "No. He didn't make it."

"I'm sorry. I was praying he would be here for you."

"He was. He saved my life out there."

Tom stared out across the bay. His voice turned sullen and soft. "He saved the entire town. He's a hero."

"Well, I should hope so. I risked my life out there," Rick said.

Ash turned to see him limping across the bow of the boat drenched to the bone and wearing a sarcastic grin. She beamed with delight. "I saw you die out there."

"A friend once told me about this crazy myth," he began, as the two closed their distance until they stood face to face. "That sharks decide who lives and dies." His finger caressed her necklace. "You believe in that sort of stuff?" He reached inside his shorts and extracted a large shark tooth. "I brought you a new addition for your necklace."

Ash laughed before she pulled Rick in close for a kiss. "Yeah, I do believe in that sort of stuff."

"Good," he chatted through the kiss, "because I was on the fence about it."

The two laughed and enjoyed a tight embrace and passionate lip lock.

Tom watched the two engaged in a sweet kiss as the afternoon sun baked the bay. "Ah, isn't that nice?" He turned to Stephens. "You know, as a writer, I couldn't have written a better ending."

"I'm not hugging you." Stephens cradled his weapon.
"Yeah, I'm aware of that." Tom stared off in uncomfortable silence.

Whitebeard's Pub
38°19'10"N, 123°2'52"W
Two weeks later
Friday July 18
3:46 p.m.

"**I**'ve seen a lot of shit in my day, but this takes the cake," Davenport addressed the group. "First off, I've decided to take a leave of absence and regenerate these old bones with friends and family."

"It's about time!" Skip added with a laugh. His wife, Bunny shared in the laughter.

"In all seriousness, these sharks have taken their toll on me." Davenport reached for his beer. "Our city under siege for the entire week and we all managed to recover and rejoice in victory." He raised his beer to offer a toast.

Rick and Ash shared his favorite appetizer of cheese covered waffle fries and two colas. "Well, we've been through a lot." Rick rose from his chair. "I'd personally like to thank Felicia, Tina, and Tom for finding a way to defeat the shark. A solemn moment of silence for those we've lost - Patrick Ryan, Jonas Marsh, Rob Roy, and the countless others who sacrificed their lives."

The crowd raised their glasses in a toast for the fallen. "Rest in peace."

"If I may," Davenport continued, "I'd like to recognize Sergeant Stephens, Mr. Kenneth Black, and the Coast Guard for all their hard work and commitment to bringing survivors back from the bay."

Stephens and Black briefly stood for a short applause from the crowd.

"As the yacht and the remains of the sharks continue to be dragged from the bay, all of these weekend's festivities naturally are cancelled." Davenport had another beer as he made his way through the pub chatting with everyone. "But I hear there's a short film premiering later tonight called 'Heroes of the Bay'" Davenport motioned for the guest to walk in. "I have asked this young lady to join us here today in remembering those who have fallen in the fight."

She gingerly made her way to the front of the pub. Her hands bandaged in white gauze clutched the cane with tenderness. A walking boot held her right foot in a protective womb. Her eyes scanned the silent crowd. Her fears of everyone laughing at her swallowed her voice.

One by one hands began clapping for her. The thunderous sound of applause filled the quiet pub.

A weakened smile approached her face. "Thank you, very much for that."

The men raised their glasses to her in a toast. The women continued clapping for her and smiled in her direction.

"My name is Watson," she said adjusting her glasses. "I was on the yacht with my dear friend, Rob. He was a visionary, an innovative filmmaker with a keen eye for talent, the business and the craft itself." She choked back her tears. "When he died, my heart imploded a bit, my soul crashed and I felt a black hole swallow my life. And then, out there in the water, my God, how I hate the water," she paused as the crowd laughed at the last remark. "Yeah, the water sucks right?"

She enjoyed a laugh with her fellow friends. "I was dragged beneath the water, my right foot caught inside the jaws of that monster. But then something happened. A stroke of luck interrupted by death. Perhaps it was fate and not my time," mused Watson. "I mean, what are the odds of a shark that size choking on a piece of debris from the yacht? Its jaws released me with minor damage and I swam to The Rock and waited for someone to come."

"That's when we found her," Stephens added. "She's truly a hero."

"She saved my life," Felicia said.

"Yes, here's to Watson," Tom agreed raising his glass.

"I decided to make a film based on the heroes of the bay, not the monsters," Watson said. "It's a struggle between good and evil, but that's the key concept Rob taught me. Always deliver a conflict to your audience." Watson once again fought back tears. "We all survived. We all have scars, we all harbor some frightful nightmare that will never go away."

"Are you okay, Miss?" asked Davenport.

Watson nodded. "I used to embrace the darkness, the undeniable urge to soak myself in the darkest corners of the world. There wasn't anything that would deter me from that," she paused. "That was until I felt that monster invade my personal space and scrape away a piece of my soul. This film recognizes those who fought hard for the bay, fought hard against these sharks, and ultimately fought for the freedom of its citizens."

The crowd clapped once more.

"As I," she thought for a moment, "I mean, as we heal together

I ask each of you to embrace each other and rebuild this town together. Thank you." Watson made her way back to the rear of the pub and sat down. Stephens put his arm around her and let her weep on his shoulder.

"Wow, that was something else. That girl has guts."

"Yes she does."

"So what's the plan now?" Rick squeezed Ash's hand.

"We enjoy life," she replied with a grin. "These are so bad for you."

"The cheese fries?" Rick laughed it off as he piled in another wave. "That's the point."

"I'm very excited to enjoy a little reprieve from all of this." Ash wiped her mouth clean of cheese and mashed fries.

"Where do you want to go? Sea World?" mused Rick.

"Funny. No, I'm actually sick of sharks right now."

"Your job asks you to work with sharks and study them. You can't ignore your job forever."

"No, but we can find ourselves lost in Montana, Denver, or someplace away from an ocean and aquatic life." Ash leaned in for a kiss.

Rick kissed her back and pulled her chair closer to his. "I can certainly get into that."

"Me too," she said.

"But that kind of puts a damper on my present to you," he said taking out a picture from his pocket.

"Which is?"

"This." He slid the picture over to her. "I even named it after you."

"Rick, it's beautiful," she said. "Is this what you've been working on all this time with Skip?"

"Yeah. I mean, after our escape to the Midwest, maybe we can..." Rick was interrupted with a kiss from Ash.

"I would love to." Her smile widened as she looked over the picture of the boat Rick had finished and named "My Joy."

H is silver aquatic watch clicked closer to the expected arrival of his guest. The numbers were off a bit due to the cracked cover, but they were still legible. His shot of tequila nearly gone, he turned his attention to his half-eaten bleu cheese cheeseburger that now swarmed with several eager flies. A hasty flip of his fingers scattered them off.

The café had several customers enjoying their outdoor meals and engaged in random conversations. He found no sign of the man from the telephone call earlier in the day. The afternoon skies darkened with a surging cloud line and rainfall deluged the area.

The man ordered more tequila and shoved aside the burger. His bitten fingers, some severed above the knuckles, rapped against the table impatiently.

The rain continued to pelt the gulf forcing several customers to dash inside for comfort, but not him. He allowed the rainwater to cascade over him, soaking the table, and leaving the waterlogged cheeseburger in its wake. The red bill of his San Francisco 49er hat seeped water on the table.

"Ah, Mister Coyle?" the man's voice had a Spanish accent.

"Yes."

"I've heard about the sharks up north, is it true?" The man pulled out a chair at Coyle's table. The rain let up and both men settled in for the conversation.

"Yes." Coyle adjusted his wheelchair and backed up to show the man the wrath of the sharks. "I fought one right down to the bottom of the bay. I suffered many physical injuries. My fingers have been severed, my legs amputated below the knees, and I have a scar the size of the state of Texas running down my back where I had spinal cord surgery."

"I'm sorry Mr. Coyle," the man continued. "I've wouldn't have wasted your time if it wasn't an emergency." His hand retrieved a large yellow envelope from inside his shirt. "Many people, Senor, have died recently. This past week alone, many fisherman have gone missing, or have turned up missing body parts."

"How's that my concern?" Coyle became agitated.

"We believe this monster has certain qualities you may recognize." The man slid the photograph over to Coyle. "It's not from around here. Its length has been measured between thirty and thirty-five feet, Senor."

Coyle slid the picture closer. The photograph captured the monster the man had alluded to. On the lower right side of the picture, the shark's face appeared. It was clear as day. The nightmare came roaring back. His head pounded, his throat swelled. He stared at those eyes. They were black and soulless. The scars were the dead giveaway. It can't be.

"Where did you get this?" Coyle demanded. "Is this some kind of joke?" He felt the color drain from his face.

"Senor, you don't look so good."

"I'm fine," Coyle answered with a deep breath. "Continue, please."

"A survivor snapped this shot moments before their fishing crew went down in the Gulf."

Coyle stared at the shark once more. It was Freddy. "I killed him. I remember his gills bleeding out."

"It's the same shark from up north, Senor?" the man again prodded Coyle for an answer.

"Yes, yes. I need some time to think this over." Coyle rolled away in his wheelchair. A quick snap of the photo with his phone, he then loaded it and sent it off to San Francisco.

Coyle brought up his contacts list and found Ashleigh's number. A few rings later she answered.

"Hey Ash," his voice felt weird like he was calling her from beyond the grave. "Yes, I'm alive and well, and down here in the Gulf of California." His eyes scanned the café. "We have a big problem down here."

There was a short pause on the other end.

"What type of problem? Well, I could really use a crew down here for some shark hunting."

Another pause from Ashleigh allowed Coyle to polish off his tequila. "It's Freddy and he's down here terrorizing the local fishing community."

Coyle heard more silence before Rick entered the conversation.

"When? As soon as possible," urged Coyle. "You're bringing Davenport too? He's retired? Shit, it's like having the old team back together again. Yeah, you too," Coyle ended the call and returned to the man at the table.

"Senor?" the man welcomed him back.

Coyle cracked a smile. "When do we start?"

"Is he stabilized?" Doctor Morgan Gray hounded the nurse. "It's been close to a month since they found him in the bay."

"He's starting to come to," the nurse said.

"The coma's subsiding," Gray said shining his pen light in the patient's eyes. "The pupils are dilating."

"What do we do now?" she asked. "The patient has no family listed, no significant other to contact. He's a rogue."

"A rogue?" laughed Gray. "Yeah, he surely fits that description."

"The wounds have healed." She checked the machine for the patient's vitals. "Blood pressure returning back to normal, as is his heart rate."

"The deep cuts have survived infection," Gray paused. "But, I'm curious to see if the coma has left any lingering effects." He again pierced the man's eyes with the sharp light. "Sir, can you hear me?"

The man stirred in his bed. A short wisp escaped his lips, but no verbal sound penetrated the air.

"Sir, can you hear me. What's your name?" Gray begged for an answer. He already knew who the patient was, but wanted clarification for medical reasons.

The man twisted his head several times attempting to speak. His eyes widened with anger.

Again, no sound.

Snapping his fingers, Gray ordered the nurse to bring a pen and paper.

She soon returned with the items.

"Here, can you write your name?" Gray slid the paper beneath the man's right hand.

The man shook off the right hand.

"He's a leftie?" Gray switched sides and the man soon grasped the pen with his severed fingers. A chore for the man with the bandages, he scribbled his identity on the yellow pad.

"Just as I thought. The coma had adverse effects on his brain."

"A stroke?" she asked.

"It seems so." Gray read the paper and smirked. "Shit Tracy, would you look at that? Charlton Coulter, the reporter with the loudest voice, has not one word to say."

As Gray walked away he left the pen and pad near Charlton.

Charlton scribbled away, the same word over and over. First in small letters, then bigger with each line.

shark

Shark.

SHARK.

DEDICATION

Well, there's too many to mention here, so I'll keep it brief-
First and foremost, my truest love and best friend, Tammy for
everything you've done and the strength you've given me in our
marriage. Natalie, Delanie, and our newest 'chum', Cara, for all
the smiles and love you've added to my life. To Stephen "Bud"
Schultz, for being the kick ass uncle and the inspiration for his
character in this book, to Bruce and Suzie Wargo-Lockhart,
William Cook, Michele-Watson Baker, Gene O'Neill, Tim
Marquitz, and Joe McKinney for taking the time to beta read and
offer advice and blurbs for the book. To JWK Publishing for
making Red a gritty reality, and the fabulous artist Stephen
Cooney for his beastly and horrific cover [all compliments!], to
Black Bed Sheet Books for being the pendulum of my writing
career, and to the rest of my author friends and family for their
everlasting support.

Acknowledgement

After five long years of rewrites and character development, my shark novel 'Red Triangle' is finally here. It's been a lengthy process for my sixteenth novel which has become a fan favorite with my beta readers. In all honesty some publishers rejected this novel for reasons unknown, [except for the 'it didn't fit what we were looking for']. In any case, one man emerged from the bloody pack, a man with a vision, a clear, concise, definitive vision for his publishing house. Mr. James Ward Kirk made it known that I was his next project and we prepared to take the literary world by the throat. His independent strength, excellent cover artists and editors made this decision fairly simple. A publisher that will grind every last ounce of ink from the printer, a publisher that recognizes talent, and a publisher who has built a fierce creative realm of talent.

The process is now complete, the reviews have been strong and positive, and the debate over the two main characters ex-Sheriff and gruff surfer, Rick Chatham and the younger, energetic, passionate shark expert/researcher, Darin Coyle has exploded among the betas.

Enjoy the water. It's crisp, cool, refreshing.
Until it fills with red...

JG

Made in the USA
Lexington, KY
15 March 2014